WASCO

To David Aschbacher —
With best wishes,

Martel Gross —
December, 1987

Wasco

*An epic novel of early San Francisco
and the untamed Oregon frontier*

By Martel Scroggin

Binford & Mort Publishing
Portland, Oregon

WASCO

Printed in the United States of America

Library of Congress Catalog Card Number: 87-71308

ISBN: 0-8323-0457-3

First Edition 1987

To Gretchen and the gang:
Leslie, Wendy and Jeff

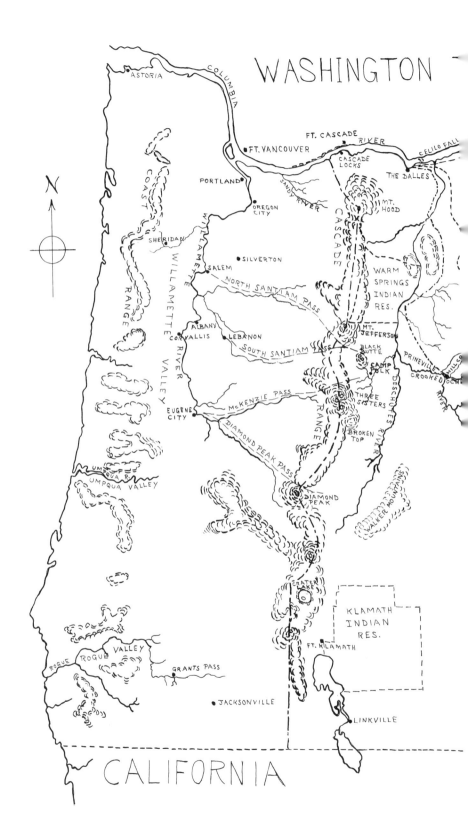

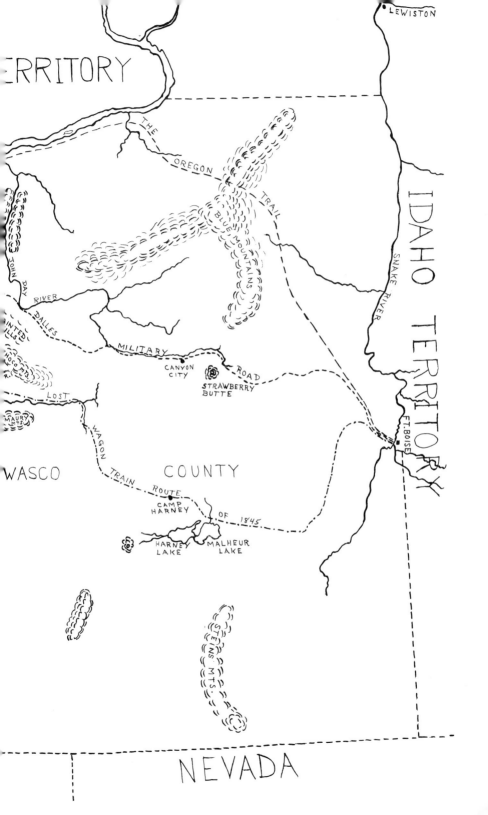

INTRODUCTION

The history of The Oregon Trail and The Oregon Territory has fascinated readers for well over a century, particularly the time frame 1856 through the mid-1870's. It was during this period that Oregon became a state, gold was discovered, the devastating Indian wars were brought to an end and the lands east of the Cascade Mountain range were opened to cattlemen and settlers.

Although this is a fictional story, it is based on fact, taken from historical records, newspapers and personal journals kept by the cattlemen, miners and early homesteaders who played a part in creating the state of Oregon. For the most part, current geographical names are used for the benefit of readers who like to follow the action of a story with a map by their side. For instance, there was a myriad of names used to identify the numerous trails crossing the Cascade Mountains. Names which have been lost in the course of time: Minton and Hogg Pass, Wiley Pass, Scott Trail, Elliot Cutoff and Blanding Pass. These were just a few of the early references to what are now the Santiam, McKenzie and Willamette passes.

The names of many major cities and locations changed, too. The author has tried to keep these identifiable. Such is the case for Yerba Buena ("good grass" in Spanish), an early designation for San Francisco. Or the Willamette Valley, which until the early 1900's was still called Columbia

Valley by the local residents. The more common name for Portland in its early stages of develoment was Stumptown. The city of Bend was not named until 1904, the date it was founded. Up to that time it was referred to by a host of titles: Deschutes, Staats Place, Pilot Butte, Bend of the River and Farewell Bend. Before Prineville was founded in 1868, the area was known as The Ochoco* or Ochoco Valley. In 1871 it became Prine City, then later Prineville. Madras and Redmond did not come into existence until after the turn of the century.

A few names have survived the test of time. One of these is Crooked River, which has been called Crooked River since it was first charted by a fur trader in 1824. Those who have seen this river that feeds the Deschutes will understand why it was so named.

With the exception of Barney Prine, the characters are fictitious and are not meant to represent any particular individuals, living or dead.

*Author's note: The word Ochoco is pronounced ō-chuh-kō.

PROLOGUE

Southern Oregon,
late September, 1849

The first traces of white powder had lightly dusted
the tops of the surrounding foothills and low, dark clouds gave
promise of more snow. As the lone rider approached the edge
of the rimrock he stopped to give his horse a brief moment's
rest. With each breath a cloud of fog swirled around their
faces, added proof that it would soon be winter.

The rider stood in his stirrups to ease his tired muscles,
then turned to check his back trail. He badly wanted to stop
and roll a smoke, but some inner sense of urgency pushed at
him to hurry on.

With a sigh of resignation he reigned left and began
the tortuous descent, threading his way cautiously through
what thousands of years ago had been hot molten magma,
but which was now a rough jumble of hardened lava.

Preoccupied with his progress and bone-tired from too
many days in the saddle, the exhausted traveler failed to notice
the brief, illuminating flash of sun reflecting on metal across
the canyon.

Suddenly the horse stumbled as the rider pitched sideways. The sound of a shot rolled flatly through the canyon,
causing a group of crows on the next ridge to flap frantically

into the sky, cawing their alarm. The roan stood, blowing nervously as it waited for some word of command from its master. The scent of blood made its eyes flare. The horse nickered expectantly, awaiting a reassuring word or pat. Receiving none, it turned and nudged the lifeless form beside it, not realizing that the gaping red hole in the man's chest meant they would never ride together again.

Across the canyon, concealed behind a fallen juniper, the Paiute Indian who had fired the shot lay motionless. When the chipmunks had resumed their chattering and scurrying, he was satisfied that his aim had been true. Rifle in hand, he slipped nimbly down the game trail he had been watching and carefully worked up the draw to a vantage point where he could again observe the sprawled figure.

Noting no change in the position of the body, he stealthily approached the skittish mare. Trained to be ground-reined, the horse backed up a few steps and stopped as the Indian stripped the cartridge belt and handgun from the man on the ground. After rifling his victim's pockets, the red man cast aside an unopened letter that carried the news of a birth and death in San Francisco, leaving it to the weather and the whims of scavenging wild animals.

Unsheathing his knife, the Indian cut the cinch and pulled the saddle from the horse's back. With a disappointed grunt, he saw there was no rifle — a prize he had anticipated.

Holding his Winchester in one hand and taking the reins in the other, he guided the saddleless animal down the canyon to a spot where a string of hills rose out of the ground to create the long, narrow valley that sheltered the hidden camp of this renegade.

The primitive being had no idea of the series of events that he had set in motion by his actions. Nor of the name of the man he had killed, which was Arnold Bland.

CHAPTER

1

San Francisco,
three weeks earlier

It was late evening and the thin figure that lay on the worn mattress was bathed in sweat. Her time was near and the sharp pains of childbirth racked her frail body.

The suffering that showed in her pale features belied her years. She looked middle-aged. She was seventeen.

Abandoned by her husband when she was six months pregnant, she had been making a living as a laundress at Washerwoman's Lagoon. Every day, from early morning until dark, she washed clothes for the men who had come to San Francisco to seek their fortunes in the gold fields.

She no longer resembled the attractive young woman who had left Oregon with her new husband just nine months before. She had not wanted to leave her family or the security of the ranch where she had been raised, but an argument with her father, who objected to her marriage, left her no choice. As a good wife she dutifully accompanied the man she married to California, where he had been lured by visions of instant wealth.

A burning spasm again cramped her body and she cried out in fright, "Tessie!"

"It's all right, Mary," said her bedside companion,

grasping her hand and sponging away the sweat from Mary Baca's fevered forehead. "I'm right here."

Mary had met Tess Shaunecy when she came to work at the laundry. They had become fast friends. Tess was Mary's age and had been making her own way since the loss of her parents, who died crossing the Sierras. They had drowned when their wagon overturned in the flood-swollen Truckee River. By some miracle of fate Tess had been thrown free, but her mother and father perished when the wagon pinned them beneath the freezing waters. Even after all these months, Tess would still wake in the middle of the night with a silent scream in her throat after dreaming about the swollen water and the shouting and cursing of the outriders as they desperately tried to save her parents.

Tess was seventeen at the time of the accident. As she had no living relatives, and as there was no work for a girl her age in Sacramento, she traveled to San Francisco with a couple and their five children who planned to settle in the Santa Clara Valley.

Lost in the bustle of a boom-town that was virtually doubling its population every other month, the only work open to Tess Shaunecy was that of a saloon girl, prostitute or washerwoman at the lagoon.

To Tess there had been no choice. She took the job of laundress. Even so, she had been approached on several occasions by those who saw the opportunity to make a profit on her good looks and well-developed figure. "Just sit with a man at the bar or a card table for an evening", she was told, "and you can make as much as $16.00 a night. That's all there is to it." But Tess knew that inevitably this would lead to the next logical step. A devout churchgoer, Tess had been shocked by the brightly dressed, heavily rouged prostitutes who blatantly circled the block of the First Presbyterian Church at Portsmouth Square on Sunday mornings to solicit single — and even married — men as they were leaving services.

She also learned from the gossip at Washerwoman's Lagoon that although some of the highly paid "saloon girls"

4

on the Barbary Coast were making as much as $400.00 a night there were others in the area known as Sydney Town who were forced by age or the ravages of their profession to display themselves in casement windows, much as wares were displayed in the shops on Montgomery Street. These women were selling themselves for twenty-five to fifty cents, and to make a living were forced to take in as many as eighty customers a night.

Again Mary cried out and tightly clutched one of Tess's red, rough hands in her own. "My darling Tessie, I don't know what I would have done without you these past months."

Patting her hand reassuringly, Tess said, "Don't worry, Mary. Everything will be all right. I've sent for Mrs. Schwartz. She should be here any minute." Rearranging the covers in an effort to make her dearest friend more comfortable, she leaned forward and asked, "Does it hurt very much?"

Biting her lip, Mary could only nod.

At that moment the tent flap burst open and Mrs. Schwartz arrived with an armful of clean sheets. Putting these down, she rolled up her sleeves and immediately took charge.

"Hot water we must have. And fill up with warm water and soap a basin for washing the hands." Looking at the feverish face before her, Mrs. Schwartz placed a broad, calloused hand on Mary's brow. After a few moments she muttered, "Lieber Gott" under her breath and turning to Tess said sharply, "Hurry to do these things I have told you. Then run and fetch Dr. Meyer. Tell him at once that he must come."

The urgency in Mrs. Schwartz's voice and the look in her eyes made Tess's heart rise in her throat. Tess knew that despite her brusque and gutteral manner, Mrs. Schwartz was the best and most compassionate midwife in the camp. Tess also realized that in the dozens of babies Mrs. Schwartz had delivered, this was the first time she had sent for a doctor.

Holding Mary's two small, delicate hands in one huge hand and patting Mary's cheek with the other, Mrs. Schwartz leaned over and whispered in Mary's ear, "Not to worry darling. Here is Mrs. Schwartz, and everything all right will be."

Yet Mrs. Schwartz was not sure everything would be all right. It was as she had feared when she looked in on Mary earlier that afternoon. The baby was due but it was not in position for an easy delivery. Knowing how weak and frail Mary was, she feared that neither Mary nor the baby would make it through a difficult birth.

With what seemed to be a burst of new-found strength, Mary reached up and grabbed Mrs. Schwartz's worn wool shawl in both hands. Pulling her closer she whispered, "I must tell you something. I must tell you who my parents are and where I came from." With her last reserve of strength she told Mrs. Schwartz about the past ten months of her life, ending with the plea that her parents be notified. Mary also told Mrs. Schwartz that if she had a daughter she wanted it named Eleanor after her mother. If a son, she wanted him named Todd which was her father's middle name. "Please, Mrs. Schwartz, I want my baby's last name to be Howard. I don't want it to carry its father's name, Baca."

In a flurry of wind and driving rain the doctor and Tess entered the tent, both soaked to the skin, their shoes caked with mud. "I've never seen anything like this," Dr. Meyer said. "Fifty inches of rain already this winter and it doesn't look like it's going to stop."

The doctor paused briefly to warm his hands over the pot-bellied stove in the center of the tent. A short, slight man, his face was clean-shaven with the exception of a neatly-trimmed Van Dyke. Sharp, penetrating brown eyes were set squarely in a face permanently lined by the sight of suffering that he saw every day. He was not dressed in the frock and longcoat that most of his profession preferred, but wore the traditional miner's garb: a heavy woolen shirt, canvas trousers held up by a wide belt and pants tucked into knee-high boots. When he removed his slouch hat to shake off the water, he displayed a full head of silver-flecked black hair — hair somewhat unkempt but neatly trimmed and short, not like the shaggy, collar-length style preferred by most of the local residents.

Although his clothes were muddy, they were clean. Dr. Meyer had a fetish about his appearance and kept himself as neat as conditions would allow. Rumor had it that he sent his shirts to China to be laundered, but Mrs. Schwartz knew he had them done weekly at Washerwoman's Lagoon.

"Good!" he exclaimed, turning from the stove. "Hot water to wash with. Mrs. Schwartz, you are a rare jewel." After soaping his hands and rinsing them thoroughly, he bent to examine Mary.

Seconds later he exchanged a meaningful glance with Mrs.Schwartz and muttered wearily, "I'll do the best I can." Then he opened his cracked leather medical bag and removed the instruments he needed.

With a brief look at Mrs. Schwartz he spoke quietly. "I have no opium or anesthetic, so you will have to hold her." Nodding soberly, Mrs. Schwartz moved her huge bulk behind Mary and placed her hands firmly but gently on Mary's shoulders.

As Mary's screams filled the tent, then echoed and re-echoed down the ragged line of squalid huts and makeshift shanties, Tess fled from the leaky shelter into the downpour, holding her hands over her ears to shut out the cries. Her first thought was that she would never get married and have babies.

Her next thoughts were more bitter. Looking up into the sky with the rain streaming down her face she called out, "Why, Lord. Why do you hurt Mary, who is so kind and good?" In her own innocent beliefs she could not understand why her friend should suffer so when those who openly lived a life of debauchery, violence and crime were going unpunished.

A single, shrill scream jolted Tess back to reality. Following this sharp cry came complete silence. Silence broken only by the splash of raindrops on the camp tents, the gurgle of water as it ran down the V-shaped wooden gutters to the lagoon, and some undecipherable, mumbled conversation between Dr. Meyer and Mrs. Schwartz.

Clasping her hands and closing her eyes in prayer, Tess said aloud, "Please God, be merciful. I have never asked for anything before, but please, please let Mary live."

In the next instant she heard a wet slap and the piercing cry of a baby. Thinking her prayers had been answered Tess joyfully rushed back inside. Mrs. Schwartz was tenderly wrapping the newborn child in swaddling clothes. Her moment of happiness was short-lived, however, when she saw Dr.Meyer gently close Mary's eyes with his thumb and index finger and heard him say, "God bless you, child. May you rest in peace," as he pulled a blood-splattered sheet over Mary's face.

"No!" Tess screamed. "It's not fair. It's not right."

Turning to Tess, Dr. Meyer put both of his hands on her shoulders and in a tired, resigned voice said, "It doesn't seem fair. Or right. And maybe it's not. But who are we to judge? Last week over one hundred people died from cholera. In just one week! Babies, mothers, fathers, the elderly, beautiful young men and women in the prime their life. I continually ask myself, 'Why,' and I have no answer. But I do know that somehow there has to be a reason for it all."

After patting Tess paternally he walked across the room, poured some water in the basin and began scrubbing his arms.

Mrs. Schwartz, tears coursing down her swollen face, rocked the baby gently in her massive arms. "May the good Lord grow you up to be the kind, wonderful person that your mother was, Todd Howard."

As he wiped his hands the doctor posed the inevitable questions. Did Mary have any family? Who would make arrangements for burying the body, and who would take care of the baby?

It was left unsaid, but they all knew how bodies of the poor were disposed of. Only the wealthy could afford having the remains of their loved ones interred at Mission Dolores, the only cemetery in town. Otherwise people buried the dead wherever it was most convenient — often by their tents or in the nearby sand dunes. Many times bodies were thrown into the bay in the hope they would float out to sea. So haphazard was the burial process that on a still day the odor of putrefaction hung over the city like a persistent cloud.

Taking the burden of the decision from the two distraught women the compassionate medical man said, "I will send someone for the corpse tonight. But who will take care of the baby?"

Knowing the alternatives, Tess heard herself saying, "I will." Then in a whisper more to herself than the others in the room, "I don't know how, but I will."

Mrs. Schwartz then replied, "Her parents I will write. Mary told me of their names, and in Oregon where they live. I know of a man who is riding that way and this letter I will ask him to take. His name is Arnold Bland."

CHAPTER

2

Clay Howard woke with a start. He was sweating heavily, even though it was cold in the small cabin. Reaching out he felt the warm, reassuring bulk of his wife beside him. She was sleeping soundly, lost in a mound of blankets. If Ellie had not interrupted his sleep, then what had?

Now wide awake, he settled into the warm hollow of the bed and listened for any noise that might give hint of a problem. Imitated owl hoots or trills of night birds that could mean Indians were after his stock. Or the restless nervousness of their domestic animals, alerted to some form of danger from wild animals.

He heard nothing but the normal night sounds: the dying embers of pine firewood cracking in the hearth; the wind stirring through the pines, their branches scraping softly against the roof; the rustle of kitchen window curtains, stirred by the gentle night breeze. Thinking again of his wife, he turned to watch her steady breathing by the pale moonlight that cast its dim rays through the open window. "Clay Todd Howard," he thought to himself, "you are one lucky man." The hardships of pioneer life had not taken their toll on her. The pretty girl he married had turned into a handsome,

10

mature woman, still vibrant and full of life.

Things were just starting to look up for them. Their herd was growing, and this year for the first time he was able to set aside some savings for a rainy day.

Suddenly the feeling of foreboding struck again. There was something wrong. What was it? Then it came to him. Mary. Something had happened to Mary.

Several years before he had experienced this same sensation. It was the night his father had died. At that time, too, he had awakened from a deep and untroubled sleep. The feeling was the same. As if a cold wind had passed over his own open grave, leaving him in a cold sweat with an unshakeable foreboding.

When it had happened before, he told Ellie at breakfast. She had laughed and said he had just eaten too much of her dried apple pie for supper. Days later, when they got the news, Ellie had turned to him gently and said, "I guess it wasn't the pie after all."

"Yes, it must be Mary," he thought to himself as he recalled their bitter parting.

He would say nothing to his wife in the morning. She had grieved enough over the matter already. Although she made every effort not to show it, he knew Mary's leaving still troubled her. After twenty years of marriage it was impossible for them to keep secrets from each other.

Realizing that sleep would not come easily now, Clay Howard's thoughts churned back to his own private hell: that day when his daughter stormed out of the house to run off with a drifter named Luis Baca.

Thinking of how his daughter met and fell in love with Baca filled him with anguish. Mary was their only child and had been the center of their life. When she left it was as if some vital part of his being had gone with her, creating a void that could not be filled and a wound that would not heal.

Instead of creating a barrier in their own feelings toward each other, it had brought Clay and Ellie closer together. But Clay still suffered. He and Mary had shared

11

a special father-daughter relationship, and even Ellie didn't realize how heartbroken he truly was. Not because she had gotten married — she was getting to that age when a young woman should be thinking of marriage — but because Clay felt her choice of a husband was the worst she could have made.

Luis Baca was not from the area. He had drifted into town from Portland.

Baca claimed to have Spanish nobility in his blood, but Clay suspected differently. However, it was not Baca's bloodline that bothered Clay, because Clay looked on all men as equals until they proved otherwise. It was Baca's manner. For one thing he was not a man's man. His dress was much too fancy. He wore shirts with lacy fronts and cuffs, a black preacher's suit and a flat, black Stetson. On his gun belt hung an ornate holster, adorned with a highly-polished silver "B".

Baca also spent all of his time in the town's only saloon. He never joined the neighborly group of ranchers and farmers who gathered at the blacksmith shop or livery stable, the social meeting places where the latest news was passed on and a genuine feeling of camaraderie prevailed.

Baca also felt it was necessary to tell everyone how important he was, which didn't go over too well in a community where a man proved his worth by his deeds, not his mouth.

But two things bothered Clay the most: Baca would not look you in the eye when he talked to you, and there was no firmness to his handshake.

Pete the hosteler had commented, "That man is slick as bear grease with the women. He could charm a female rattlesnake out of her rattles and a she-bear out of one of her cubs." Clay had to admit that Pete had a point. Baca was overly courteous to the ladies. As he passed them on the street he would take his hat off with a grand sweep of his arm. This gesture was usually accompanied by such flowery remarks as, "My that's a pretty bonnet, is it new?" or "You look mighty nice today, Ma'am." Even if the bonnet was years old, or they were dusty and tired from a long ride into town, such comments were rare and flattered them. They were not used to receiving this type of attention. Baca knew it and played on it. Clay had noticed that even Ellie reacted to such gallantries with a pleased blush.

It was just such charm and guile that had smitten their daughter Mary. The first day she met Baca, on the boardwalk in front of Grant Wither's General Store, he had bowed and kissed her hand, saying, "What a thing of beauty you are in this desolate land." Ellie was so shocked by the boldness of this gesture that she hurried Mary away. But at that exact moment Mary became hopelessly and romantically stricken.

Ellie had never mentioned this incident to Clay, who became aware of Baca's interest in his daughter only when Baca came to call late one afternoon. He called again the next Sunday to ask Mary to the Grange dance the following Saturday night.

It was at this dance that Luis Baca proposed. And it was to Mary's credit that she answered, "before I say yes I must get my father's permission."

It was in the character of Luis Baca to avoid the responsibility of asking Clay Howard for his daughter's hand. He left this task to Mary, who came to her father and said simply and straightforwardly, "Daddy, Luis Baca has asked me to marry him, and I want to be his wife."

At that moment Clay Howard made one of the biggest mistakes of his life. Raised in a hard land where each day's problems were faced square on, he spoke his mind openly and honestly. He told Mary exactly how felt about Luis Baca.

Heated words were exchanged and they both said things that should never have been said. Had Ellie been there, she could have salved over this bitter argument between a father and daughter whose deep love for each other was lost in a confrontation of emotional irrationality. But she wasn't. Ellie had left that morning to stay overnight with a sick neighbor, so the die was cast. Tears streaming down her face, Mary challenged her father: "If you don't give me your blessing, Luis and I are going to be married anyway. I love him and I intend to become his wife."

Her father snapped back, "You'll never have my blessing if you do." Mary stood as if she had been struck. In a barely audible whisper she replied, "Then so be it," turned and hurried out of the house.

Clay knew in his heart that he should stop her. That he should hold her and tell her he loved her, and that if this was what she really wanted then he was happy for her. But foolish pride kept him from calling out, and as the hoofbeats of her horse faded into the distance he realized it was too late.

The next morning, Ellie returned home. She came through the door bursting with gossip, then stopped when she saw Clay slumped over the kitchen table holding a cold cup of coffee in both hands. "Clay, what is it?" she asked anxiously, looking around. "Where's Mary? Has something happened to Mary?"

"She's gone, Ellie. She's gone to marry Luis Baca," Clay said, his words barely distinguishable. "And it's my fault. I drove her to it."

Ellie, dizzy from the shock of this news, sat in a chair facing Clay. Holding his hands in her own she quietly asked, "What happened?"

Clay told her, leaving nothing out.

"Ellie, I just didn't know what to do. All night long I've wondered if I should go get you, or if I should go find Mary. Every time I started to do one or the other, I..."

Rising and going to her husband, Ellie leaned over his back, hugged him and put a wet cheek to his. "There's nothing we can do now except pray that she will come to her senses and return home. Or that it will be a good marriage and she will forget the harsh words."

Seeing that he had not eaten either last night or this morning, she patted him gently and in a more cheerful voice than she felt said, "Now go unhook the team while I fix breakfast."

CHAPTER

3

San Francisco,
six months later

The best thing that could have happened to Tess Shaunecy was to become surrogate mother to Todd.

She literally blossomed with the challenge of taking care of him. She no longer wallowed in an existence of self-pity. She had something to live for. With Mrs. Schwartz's advice, and with the help of a wet nurse who had lost her own baby at childbirth, Todd flourished.

He was a happy baby and was delighted to see Tess at the end of each working day. They would chatter at each other incessantly, and as she spoke he would gurgle happily, as if overjoyed to hear the latest news. "They say that soon we will be having board sidewalks. Can you imagine! Now maybe we can walk to church in style instead of following that muddy old path of planks, broken boxes and barrels."

At this news, Todd waved his arms, kicked his feet and babbled with pure glee.

Laughing gaily at his antics, Tess continued, "The only problem is the church better stay put or they will have to build sidewalks all over town." This statement referred to the fact that the location of the Presbyterian Church was constantly changing. First, service was held at the schoolhouse on Portsmouth Square, then the courthouse on Grant Avenue. Next, in a room on the second story of a commercial building. After that, in a tent that leaked so badly the congregation was forced to gather in a storeroom in the Custom House. Sunday's meeting was to be held in the chambers of the Superior Court.

"Mrs. Miller, who was washing clothes with me today, said she had to go to church every Sunday or she wouldn't know where to go the next Sunday."

On hearing this Todd shrieked happily.

Picking him up and holding him at eye level, Tess wiggled him gently from side to side. "How would you like a pretty new outfit for church this week? Mrs. Caldwell's baby grew out of his. It's practically new and she'll let us have it for a little embroidery work."

The following Sunday, Todd dressed in his new finery, they attended worship. It somehow seemed appropriate to be hearing the damnation of sin and evil in a Superior Court room. The pulpit was the judge's bench, and the Reverend Andrews, possibly inspired by the surroundings, was in rare form. When the congregation rose to sing the hymn "Rock of Ages," Tess noticed the man in the second row behind them, to their left. She had seen him at the last two services and recalled he had been seated near them both times.

When the song ended she turned slightly and caught him looking at her. Visibly blushing, he closed his hymn book and sat down.

As they were leaving, the man was waiting at the courthouse steps. Doffing his hat, he said, "I hope you won't think me bold. I apologize for staring, but I couldn't help but admire what a lovely picture you and your baby make."

Looking at him directly, Tess saw that his face was flushed with embarrassment. She guessed he was ten years older than she. His clothes were of better material than most, and fit a frame that was neither broad-shouldered and narrow-waisted, nor slight. He was solidly built, with a square, open face to match. Unruly brown hair fell over a lineless forehead that sheltered earnest brown eyes. He was clean-

16

shaven and his ready quick smile denoted a man at peace with himself and with the world.

He introduced himself. "My name is Jamie Fields. I have a small clothing and dry goods shop. On Battery Street." Fearing that she might turn and walk off, he quickly added, "Originally I'm from Pennsylvania. Williamsport. All my family are back there. I mean my parents and two sisters. There wasn't much opportunity back home so I came West. Most came for the gold, but I figure there's not enough gold to go around and I can do better selling to those who find the gold."

When he paused to catch his breath he saw the twinkle in her eye.

"I guess I did ramble on, didn't I?"

"Yes, Jamie Fields, you did. But I didn't mind. My name is Tess Shaunecy, and this is Todd."

As she opened the blanket to better show Todd's sleepy face, she noticed Jamie Fields steal a quick glance at the ringless finger of her left hand.

Giving Jamie a big grin, Todd made some wordless noises and waved both of his arms.

"I think he likes you, Mr. Fields. Now we must be going."

"Will you be at church again next Sunday?"

"Yes. We come every Sunday."

She turned to leave, following a footpath of discarded redwood lumber. At the corner she glanced back. He raised one arm and waved. "Todd," she said to the bundle she was carrying. "I don't think the likes of a washerwoman are for him. Particularly one with a ready-made son!"

But already she was looking forward to seeing him again next Sunday.

Tess thought of Jamie Fields all week. She was flattered that he considered her attractive and had mustered the courage to tell her so. The fact that he had been so nervous made her chuckle. As his image kept reappearing in her mind, she scolded herself, "Don't jump to conclusions, Tess my girl.

17

You'll probably never see him again. Or he might even be married!" At this thought her heart noticeably skipped a beat.

That night she talked it over with Todd, who responded in his usual positive manner.

It was Sunday morning, and the drizzle that had been falling all week stopped. The cloudless sky turned a bright, crisp blue, outlining the buildings in sharp clarity against the silken haze of the hills across the bay.

Tess chose her best dress and spent an hour dusting and pressing it. Next she dressed Todd. Then they left for church. Arriving a little earlier than usual, she chose a seat on one of the benches halfway down the aisle, leaving a vacant place to her left and several vacant spots to her right.

Not wanting to be so obvious as to blatantly look for Jamie Fields, she held Todd a little closer to contain her nervousness. Should she have left him at home with one of the women? "No," she thought, "I have no reason to be ashamed. Besides, Sunday is the only full day I get to spend with Todd and I'll not give that up because of a few minutes' conversation last Sunday."

The services were about to start. She held her breath as the seats around her began to fill. Those to her right were taken by a portly man, his wife and two young daughters. The one on her left remained empty.

Well into the sermon someone slipped quietly into the seat beside her. Glancing timidly out of the corner of her eye she saw it was an elderly gentleman. Her mouth went dry.

When it came time for the hymns, she surreptitiously glanced behind as she rose. Jamie Fields was nowhere to be seen.

As the service ended she waited, fussing with Todd's blanket, so that when she stood she might better see the people in the crowd as they filed out. Up until this moment she had not realized how much she was looking forward to seeing Jamie Fields again. As she walked out into the clear, bright sunlight tears misted her eyes. You should have known better,

18

she told herself, almost stamping her foot in disappointment.

When she reached the bottom step she felt a gentle, almost unnoticeable touch on her elbow. Turning, she instinctively drew back. Facing her was a dirty, disheveled figure, covered from head to foot with the residue of ashes and soot.

"I'm terribly sorry to have missed the worship this morning, but a building in our block caught fire and I tried to help save it. My store wasn't damaged but. . ." he continued with a trace of humor in his voice, "I guess I am. Somewhat."

Impetuously she leaned over and kissed him on his grimy cheek. They both exploded with relieved laughter. He could easily have stayed at his old fire with good excuse, and have come next Sunday. But he did come. Even if it must have been embarrassing to wait outside the church in his bedraggled condition. She could not remember ever being so happy.

He asked her to dinner the next Sunday, and the following Sunday he asked her to marry him. Her answer was, "Yes."

CHAPTER

4

August, 1868

It was nineteen years later. Todd Howard was sitting on a hill overlooking San Francisco Bay. His arms tightly hugged his legs and his chin rested on his knees.

He was thinking about his foster parents Tess and Jamie Fields, and his mother Mary, who had died when he was born.

Tess often talked about his mother, but the only thing she knew about Todd's father was that his name was Luis Baca. Tess had not told Todd that after he was born a letter had been sent to his maternal grandparents. When they never replied she assumed they did not want to accept Todd as their grandson. Had Tess known that the rider who was delivering the message had been killed and the letter he was carrying lost, she would have done everything possible to find them. But Tess didn't know, so she never mentioned them.

As Todd's mind wandered to his real father and what he might have been like, a voice shattered his reverie.

"Todd. Todd Fields Howard. I knew I would find you here!"

Todd glanced up with a mixture of pleasure and irritation at the rider on the chestnut gelding that stood a few yards away.

"Ann, what are you doing here?"

"Don't be upset with me, Todd. It is such a beautiful day that I wanted to share it with someone," she said. Then she added impishly, "And my foster brother happened to be my first choice. Besides, you shouldn't be up here all alone. It's just downright selfish to spend so much time by yourself."

Todd had to smile. There was no way he could ever stay mad at Ann. They had a special relationship. It was as if they could read each other's thoughts. It wasn't like this with Katy, the Fields' older daughter. Katy, a year older than Ann, was more like her father: quiet, reserved and shy, with feelings that ran deeper and did not show as readily.

Ann on the other hand was vivacious and full of high spirits. More like her mother. At sixteen she had not yet reached full womanhood, but her fair complexion, honey-blond hair and developing figure gave every indication that she would break a few hearts before she made a final decision on the man she was going to marry. She wasn't a bit shy either, about showing her trim ankles as she rode her chestnut, Bob, which elicited considerable comment from the older ladies in their neighborhood.

"Well, as long as you're here I guess you might as well light and tell me the latest gossip. If you don't do it now, you'll just pester me later."

He reached up to help her down and she dropped easily from the saddle. Giving him a peck on the cheek she held his left arm, looked up, for he was a good six inches taller than her own five foot four inches, and gave a mock sigh.

"You know, you truly are handsome." Standing back and giving him a critical appraisal she teasingly continued. "One of the most available young men in San Francisco. Well-built, gorgeous brown eyes, no pock marks and . . .," she said, turning to skitter away, "clean shaven."

This last remark was a reference to his efforts to show his manhood by trying to grow a mustache at the age of seventeen. It had been a dismal failure at the time and a source of amusement to the family ever since.

21

Running after her, he easily caught up in two strides. Locked arm-in-arm they walked together, between fits of laughter, as Ann told him somewhat embellished versions of the local scandals. They stopped at his favorite viewpoint at the top of the hill.

It was late September, the month that displayed San Francisco at its best, and from this vantage point they could see the entire city, sitting like a jewel in its surroundings. In front of them, over Clark Point, was the burgeoning community of Oakland. On their left was Fort Point, where the waters of the Bay combined with the Sacramento River to join the turbulent Pacific Ocean. To their extreme right was Twin Peaks and beyond them the blue horizon of the Peninsula, just now becoming fashionable as an area where wealthy San Franciscans went in summer to avoid the damp city fog.

The hundreds of abandoned sailing vessels that only a few years back had dotted Yerba Buena Cove were gone. Those that had not been broken apart for their lumber had been sunk and used as a base for landfill to extend San Francisco's shoreline beyond Montgomery Street. "Like Phoenix risen from the ashes," Todd often thought as he watched the teeming waterfront with its forest of masts and furled sails, backed by steamers that belched clouds of black smoke as they splashed their way out to sea.

"Daddy says that someday this is going to be one of the most expensive places to live in the whole city."

"I know," replied Todd. "It's hard to believe, isn't it? The only way to get here is either by foot or horseback, and when it rains it's a quagmire. The soil is so sandy even lupine can't survive, and oak won't grow because there isn't enough nourishment for it to get beyond the scrub brush stage."

On impulse Todd jumped up. Grabbing a nearby stick, he planted it in the ground and said, "I declare this hill and all surrounding sand dunes, here and henceforth to be the exclusive domain of Queen Ann."

Ann rose to her feet. Curtsying daintly she responded, "And you, Sir Todd, shall be the official keeper of the Royal

22

Domain and shall reside here with me and our Royal Family forever and ever." Then, in a more practical voice, she added, "Let's start for home or we'll miss supper."

Turning to her horse, she missed the look that crossed Todd's face. "It's going to be hard but I must tell them tonight," he said to himself.

They rode back in silence. The high point of fun and companionship had passed. Both were comfortable with this change of mood, knowing that when the time was right it would swing back again. Not forced, but naturally.

Todd was thinking about how Jamie Fields had wanted to adopt him. When Todd was still a baby, Jamie felt his name should be changed to Fields. Tess, too, would have liked this but knew it would be a betrayal of the dying wish of Todd's mother Mary that he bear the name of her parents. As Mary had not stipulated a middle name for Todd, they arrived at a compromise. He was christened Todd Fields Howard. The christening took place at the new Presbyterian Church, which had finally settled for good at a permanent location on Stockton Street near Clay.

Todd thought, too, of Ann's remark about Jamie Fields' feeling that the desolate knoll on which they had spent the better part of the afternoon would one day be sought-after property. Jamie Fields had an uncanny knack for business, and real estate in particular. He had expanded his holdings from his small dry goods store on just such feelings of observation and intuition. He was fond of saying, "The good Lord is making more people, but He's not making more land." This was a philosophy that he lived by, and whenever he saw an opportunity, put into practice. After San Francisco's second big fire, one that devastated most of the buildings from Portsmouth Square to the waterfront, Jamie Fields made the decision to sell his store and move his family out of the area. "Too many old wood and canvas buildings and too many people," he had said. "What isn't being burned by accident is being burned on purpose." His vision proved to be correct when the next major fire, set by an arsonist, destroyed three-quarters of the town — more than 18 square blocks — just fourteen months after they moved.

Jamie Fields bought land a mile south of the center of town. People at first said he was foolish. Even Tess had been privately concerned. Then industry started moving in that direction as property downtown became scarce and expensive. Realizing that industrial growth would bring in more people, Jamie acquired residential lots in an undeveloped area called Rincon Hill. San Francisco's wealthier citizens, who were becoming more and more concerned about the health and safety of their families in frame homes along the streets of Stockton, Clay and Powell, began moving there. At Rincon they could build better houses, with room for yards where their children could play, free from the undesirable element that frequented the downtown saloons or openly solicited customers on the now boardwalked streets. Rincon had excellent weather and provided an unobstructed view of the bay. Only a few months after Jamie Fields purchased the land it became the most exclusive place to live in San Francisco. It was to their home in this section of town that Todd and Ann were riding now.

"Todd," Ann spoke out suddenly. "Why do you spend all of your summers working on ranches in the valley when you could be helping Daddy?"

"I don't really know, Ann," Todd replied, turning his horse to miss a sizeable chuck hole. "I guess I feel the need to be out in the open where a man can be on his own. I don't dislike San Francisco, but I don't seem to be cut out for desk work. Besides," he added with a twinkle in his eyes, "the jack rabbits and cattle don't ask a lot of questions."

"Oh, you're despicable," she said, lashing her horse and leaving him behind in a trail of dust.

This was a good stretch of road, so Todd spurred his mount and raced after her. As they approached their house he gallantly held back so she could finish first.

Knowing that he had done this she could not resist

saying, "Here you are, a tough old range-rider of nineteen, yet you can't beat a defenseless, refined young girl riding sidesaddle."

Not wanting to let her have the last word, he answered, "Young and refined you may be, but defenseless you are definitely not!"

In high spirits, they dismounted and led their ponies to the stable behind the blue-trimmed, white Victorian house.

As they entered the back door they were greeted with a stern admonition. "There you are. We were about to send the vigilantes out to find you."

Anyone who had seen Tess Shaunecy nineteen years ago would never have recognized her now as she greeted Todd and Ann with kisses on their cheeks. Although pretty at nineteen, she had been underweight, exhausted and in a frame of mind that could only be described as desperate. At thirty-eight she was poised and self-confident, with an inner beauty that radiated about her, attracting friends wherever she went. In fact, she had no enemies. Everyone who met Tess liked her. This was the woman that Jamie Fields had foresight enough to see in his mind's eye that day after church when he had impulsively blurted out his feelings for her.

Tess Fields was a caring mother and a loving wife, and the qualities that she possessed reflected in the being and manners of her children.

"Hurry up now. Get washed," she said. "Your father has some exciting news and he won't tell anyone until we're all together. Frankly, I'm afraid he's going to burst, so don't dawdle." Turning to her daughter she said, "Ann, you simply must not race Bob down the street. It's not ladylike."

Taking the stairs two steps at a time, Todd arrived at the second floor and was making his way to his room when Katy stuck her head out of her bedroom.

"Todd, you must see my new party dress. It just arrived, and I could hardly wait for you to get back so I could show it to you."

Humoring her, he entered her room, expecting to see

25

the dress in the packing box or lying on her bed. Instead she was wearing it. "It's beautiful, Katy," he told her, sincerely meaning it.

Hearing his reaction, she blushed with pleasure. "I knew you would like it. I just knew it. Daddy said it was too revealing, but you don't think so, do you?"

In truth the dress did show a great deal of her shoulders, but it was very becoming. The dark green taffeta matched her hazel eyes, and the lighter satin bow in front set off her dark hair. "No," he answered, "but if you're going to the Fireman's Ball in that dress with Jim Weatherspoon, he's going to have to fight off the competition with a ten-foot pike pole." Having paid this compliment, Todd hastily added, "Now I must hurry and wash. Orders from Mother."

As he left, he realized the announcement he was going to make at supper would be even more difficult.

Talk ceased as they took their seats around the table and bowed their heads to receive the blessing. After a resounding "Amen," Jamie Fields looked up. "Now. Before we are served there are two important pieces of news I must tell you all. First, I have accepted an offer on this house and next year we will be moving to Pacific Avenue, west of Van Ness."

This wasn't really news as they were all aware of the city's plans to make Van Ness Avenue comparable to Park Avenue in New York or the Champs Élysées in Paris. Made aware, in fact, by the enthusiasm of Jamie Fields over this project and his many dinner conversations about it. What with his real estate investments in that area as well as the recent decision by City Hall to cut a 75-foot gap through the heart of Rincon Hill, the future of the area they now lived in was becoming less and less attractive. But official pronouncement of a move to a more fashionable area was truly exciting and started them all talking at the same time.

Jamie raised both hands. "The second bit of news. It is quite certain that the transcontinental railroad will be completed next year, and I have made advance reservations for all of us on the first run from San Francisco to New York."

With that statement came happy squeals from the girls and an expression of delight from Tess. Everyone was thrilled. Everyone, that is, except Todd, who tried desperately to mask his true feelings. He knew this was not the appropriate time to tell them he was planning to leave the following week to seek his own fortune in Oregon.

Dinner at the Fields' household the next day was not the spirited one of the evening before.

Todd had sought out his foster parents, who were enjoying their quiet period in the sitting room before supper, to tell them of his intentions.

The news came as a complete shock to Tess but not to Jamie. He recognized the same restless spirit in Todd that had brought him to California from a much farther distance.

"But why Oregon?" Tess asked. "You know how much your father wants you to join him in business."

"Mother, I can't explain. It's just something that I have to do. I need to prove to myself that I can make it on my own."

Dabbing at the tears forming in her eyes with a lace handkerchief, Tess turned to the only logic she could think of. "But all of the opportunity is here. Oregon has been a state only a few years. It's just one large Indian reservation."

Somehow the irrationality of this last statement broke the ice. Jamie affectionately put an arm around her shoulder and said, "Come, Mother. Oregon's not that far away. Certainly not as far as Pennsylvania or Ohio, where we came from. And despite what most San Franciscans think it's not occupied solely by Indians." He paused to chuckle, "I guess California wasn't developed much at one time, either. Besides, it's not as if Todd were leaving home forever. We'll have a place for him when he comes back to us."

Todd knew at that instant the Fields would support his decision. Overcome with emotion and gratitude, he hugged them both tightly.

"Now, how are we going to tell the girls?" Jamie asked, blowing his nose heartily into his pocket handkerchief. He had looked forward to having Todd work with him but understood, as every father does, the need for a son to feel independent and want to cut his own niche in life.

The announcement was made at suppertime. Only this time instead of cries of joy, the news that Todd would be leaving caused Ann and Katy to sit in stunned disbelief.

Katy barely managed a whisper. "When will you be leaving, Todd? Surely not until after next year when we all get back from New York?" She waited, hoping that his answer would be "yes," which would give them all a little more time to adjust to the situation.

"No, it will have to be next week. Father said he would help me arrange passage on Captain Geyer's ship, and it leaves for Portland Wednesday. Besides, I want to get there before winter."

Unexpectedly, Ann pushed her chair back and jumped to her feet with such violence that the dishes rattled and water spilled from her crystal water glass. "Todd Fields Howard, I hate you!" she cried in a voice filled with emotion. Gathering her skirts, she bolted from the room. Her sobs could be heard as she ran up the stairs.

Excusing himself from the table, Todd went to Ann's room and gently knocked. Hearing no response he knocked again, calling out, "Ann, it's me, Todd. May I come in?"

"No," was the shouted response. "I never want to see you again!"

Opening the door, Todd slipped into the room. Ann was sitting on the edge of her bed, her satin slippers not quite touching the floor, tears streaming down her face.

Sitting beside her, Todd took her hand in his own. For a long time nothing was said. Finally, in a flood of tears Ann threw her arms around him and resting her cheek on his shoulder, sobbed uncontrollably. "Tell me you were joking. Tell me it isn't true." Raising her head and looking into his eyes, she said, "I just couldn't bear it. How can you leave me? I love you."

Kissing her gently on the lips he said, "Ann, I love you,

too." But the type of love he was expressing and the love Ann felt for him were entirely different. Even though her heart was at the breaking point, she was wise enough to say no more.

On the day of his departure the Fields all gathered at the wharf to say goodbye. Jamie had seen to it that Todd had sufficient funds and a substantial letter of credit, "for emergency use or if a good opportunity turns up." Tess had helped prepare his wardrobe, taking particular care to see that he had ample clean shirts and socks. Particularly socks, as she was aware of the tendency of most working men not to wear them. Katy had baked some of his favorite cookies, boxed and tied with a satin bow. At the last minute Ann slipped a small package into his pocket, asking that he not look at it until the ship *Lucille*, on which he was sailing, was out of sight of land. Todd was thankful that he and Ann had made their peace before he left. The day after her outburst she had acted as if nothing had happened, and joined the family in seeing that he had everything he needed for his journey.

"Time to heave to, lad," hailed Captain Geyer, the vessel's master, from the ship's bow. "We're to be off shortly."

Coming down the gangplank, Geyer paid his respects to the family. "Don't you be worrying none. *Lucille* and I will see that he gets to Portland safely, and that he's well taken care of." With this parting reassurance he gripped Jamie's hand in a bid of farewell, then slapped Todd heartily on the back. "Quickly now, or we'll be missing the tide."

Orders were shouted to the crew, the gangplank was lifted into place and the ship shuddered as the anchor was hoisted. After two blasts of her steam-whistle, the *Lucille* shook herself loose from the pier.

Todd stood at the stern rail and waved until the small group that was his family disappeared into the distance. His feelings of guilt about leaving faded and were soon replaced by the excitement of this new venture and the anticipation of being on his own for the first time.

The spirit of high adventure vanished once they

29

reached the Farallon Islands, just out of San Francisco Bay. The rise and swell of the ocean, combined with the pitch and roll of the ship, made Todd violently ill. Even the gift Ann had slipped to him, a gold locket containing her picture and the inscription "All my love, Ann," failed to cheer him up. He knew one thing for certain: he would never try to earn his living at sea.

CHAPTER

5

"Well lad, you made it," exclaimed the jovial captain to his forlorn passenger, who was slumped against the ship's railing.

Although weakened by his siege of seasickness, Todd had managed to climb the stairs from his cabin to the main deck and was now surveying the docks that ran the length of Front Street, Portland's center of commercial activity.

The busy waterfront, with its hastily erected sheds and haphazard piles of freight, was a beehive of activity. As far as he could see, dozens of vessels were being loaded and unloaded. Some were trying to do both at the same time. Todd watched the confusion in amazement. A hodgepodge of freighters, drawn by teams of mules or horses, and in one case a pair of yoked oxen, fought for space. Shouts and oaths filled the damp morning air. Occasional fights broke out between those impatient to unload their goods and those who broke into line ahead of them to load and be gone before nightfall.

Captain Geyer spoke again. "I made my first trip to Portland over twenty years ago. It was called Stumptown then. And for good reason. They were selling timber as fast as they could cut it. All you could see were acres and acres of stumps sticking up out of the ground. When I took out my first load of lumber there were only six houses here. I remember them well. Five frame ones and a new brick one. Plus a half-dozen

31

or so log shelters. There wasn't much in the way of roads either, and you wouldn't dare leave the ship unless you were armed because of the wild animals. Now the four-legged critters aren't the problem, the two-legged ones are."

Pausing only long enough to spit into the murky, refuse-littered waters of the Willamette, he continued. "Four years later there were 700 people here and a whole town had sprung up. Three dozen shops, two steam sawmills, a flour mill and at least twenty places a man could buy a drink. The most ships I ever saw then numbered no more than what you could count on the fingers of both hands. Now look at them. Waiting to load, waiting to unload, waiting in line and coming and going." Shaking his head, and at the same time scratching his greying beard, he reflectively pondered, "The last count put the population of Portland at over 8,000 people. It's getting to the point where it's hard to turn around without bumping someone. Yessiree, Portland has come a long way. But there's one big improvement. There's a sight more than twenty bars here now. More like half a hundred."

He stood back from the rail and squinted at the dark, low-lying clouds. "Gather up your gear, lad, and we'll get you settled in before it rains. Then I'll buy you a drink. That'll help calm the butterflies in your stomach."

His canvas ditty bag slung over his left shoulder and his smaller carpet bag gripped firmly in his right hand, Todd followed Captain Geyer through the shoving, milling crowd. On several occasions Todd was jostled violently and just managed to keep his footing. The days at sea had not steadied his step, and he stumbled often as if he was still trying to maintain his balance on the rocking stern-wheeler.

"Steady as she goes, son," said the captain, noticing his difficulty. "We're about there. Just across the street. Careful now, don't get run over by one of these damn fool landlubbers." As if to lend credence to this remark a buckboard came careening around the corner, its driver and passenger bouncing from side to side on the wagon's quivering spring seat.

They were yelling for the pure joy of the moment, scattering pedestrians in all directions.

"Well, we're here," the captain said, shouldering aside a set of swinging doors and putting down his own sea bag.

Shouting in his most dictatorial manner and pounding on a counter that served as the registration desk, he called out, "Marie! Where are you, woman? Confound it, you're keeping us waiting!"

Shortly after this outburst, the oilcloth curtain that separated the back room from the front hall was pushed aside by two massive arms. A woman whom Todd guessed to be somewhere in her late forties appeared. She was short, about five foot two and solidly built. Wisps of brown hair streaked with grey hung over her forehead. Smudges of flour spotted her apron and covered her forearms. There was even a touch of white powder on her face.

"Phil Geyer, you floating horsethief," she said in a low-pitched, cracked voice. "They're still not particular who they let dock, I see." After wiping the flour off her hands onto her apron, she gave the captain a hearty handshake.

"Who's the good-lookin' young feller you brought with you?" she asked.

"His name is Todd Fields Howard. He needs a place to stay until he decides what he wants to do with himself." Turning to Todd he said, "This is Marie Blevins, Todd. At least that was her name the last time I was in Portland. She's been married so many times, I can't keep track."

At that remark, Marie cracked Geyer in the ribs with one of her elbows hard enough to make the stout captain wince.

"Pleased to meetcha, Todd Howard," she said extending her hand. Crushing his fingers in a strong grip she added, "Don't listen to him. I've only been married twice. Widowed both times. My last husband was Tom Blevins, God rest his soul. And that's the name I intend to keep. For a while anyway," she cackled, slapping a hand against her sizeable hip in good humor.

33

"Well, sign in or not, as you wish. Here are two keys. They're numbered, so you can find your own way." Turning to re-enter the back room, she said over her shoulder, "Supper starts at five and lasts 'till seven, Todd. Dining room's the door on the left coming down the stairs. You can't miss it."

"Let's drop our gear, wash off the sea salt, then we'll go wet our whistles," said the captain, leading the way upstairs. Handing Todd one of the keys Mrs. Blevins had given him, he said, "You're number ten. I usually get eleven, which is across the hall."

On entering the room, Todd saw that it was clean and well-kept. The mattress and springs on the iron bed sagged in the middle from too much use, but Todd guessed it was as good as any that might be available. Freshly starched chintz curtains covered a window that overlooked a back alley filled with boxes, bottles, assorted broken machinery and some old spring mattresses that had been dumped there. He also guessed the captain's room probably had the more scenic view of the harbor and surrounding mountains.

In addition to the bed, the room contained a board attached to the wall with pegs for his clothes, a wooden storage chest, and a nightstand with a tin basin and a china pitcher full of water. Near the basin was a small hand towel, clean but heavily stained from much previous use. Over the washstand was a mirror that showed the backing.

Stooping to fill the basin, Todd remembered how Mrs. Blevins had addressed him when they met. "This is the first time I have been thought of as just Todd Howard," he mused. Before, everyone had thought of him as the "Fields boy" or "Todd Fields Howard," with the emphasis on "Fields." Jamie had always added "our son" when he made the introductions.

"Well, Todd Howard," he said, looking at his wavy reflection in the mirror, "you wanted your own start in life and you got it. I hope you're up to it."

He had just finished storing his possessions in the footlocker when Captain Geyer pounded on the door. "Let's hit the deck, Todd. My throat's dry as a bone, and if I don't have a drink soon I'm going to be as mean as a one-legged seaman with a case of the scabies.

"The Buckhorn is the place for us," said the captain. "It's one of the few bars in town that serves a decent drink. Most of the rotgut they sell around here comes from the local spirit manufactory, and it's not fit to swallow. Some local Tennessee boys have a still farther back in the hills, but their 'shine is kind of chancy. Sometimes it's pretty good but most of the time it tastes like kerosene. Them as don't go blind from it usually catch fire when they light their cigars," he joked.

A blast of sour tobacco smoke and heat from a dozen milling bodies, combined with smoke from an iron wood stove and music from an upright player piano, greeted them as they entered the noisy saloon. Todd noted the door had been repaired with overlapping cross beams so that it was several layers thick. The wooden floor was built of rough planks, worn smooth by shuffling feet. Facing them was a bar that stretched a good thirty feet along one length of wall. Behind the bar, two bartenders were busy filling orders. In front of the bar were several cheaply-constructed tables and chairs, a few of which were occupied. Most of the crowd preferred to stand at the bar exchanging news and opinions. Old cigar butts and flattened cigarette stubs littered the tobacco-juice stained floor.

Taking a seat at one of the tables, Captain Geyer signaled a bartender. "What's your poison, lad?"

Todd, whose stomach had not yet completely settled, replied, "A beer would be fine."

"A beer it is, then," said the captain, turning to the red-faced Irish bartender who was waiting nearby. "And I'll have a bottle of your best rye whiskey."

After their order had arrived and they both had a chance to sit back and relax, the captain asked, "What are your plans, Todd? Knowing your father, I'm sure he'll look me up on my trip back to ask what you're up to." Not waiting for Todd to answer, the captain continued, "Seems to me if you want to make your mark in Oregon, you have four choices: farming, getting into the logging business, the gold fields, cattle, or," he added with a twinkle in his eye, "marry Mrs. Blevins and become an innkeeper. A thought I have considered once or twice myself on cold, rainy nights. Besides being a good cook, there's enough of her to keep a man nice and warm when it's freezing outside. There's also shipping," he joked, "but I don't think you're cut out for a life at sea."

Todd, now on his second beer, was feeling lightheaded and found himself slurring his words. This had not gone unnoticed by the captain, who had consumed half of the contents of his bottle with no apparent effect at all. "Finish up, my boy. It's been a long day. A hearty meal and a good night's sleep is what we need if we're to get an early start tomorrow on your future."

Mrs. Blevins had outdone herself for supper, expecting them both to be starved for a good home-cooked meal after so many days at sea. But Todd, feeling the effects of his trip and visit to the saloon, barely touched his food. Captain Geyer, on the other hand, more than made up for Todd's lack of appetite.

Excusing himself, Todd went to his room, undressed and fell into bed.

The next morning Todd felt considerably better. After a breakfast of eggs, potatoes, venison, bacon, homemade biscuits and flapjacks, and while lingering over a third cup of black, scalding coffee — "the way coffee should be served," Mrs. Blevins had told Todd — he posed a question to Captain Geyer. "Tell me more about the cattle market, Captain. I know nothing of logging, and farming doesn't appeal to me. I have watched those who went searching for gold and I think my father was right when he said, 'There's more money to be made from those fools who find gold than there is in finding fool's gold.' I've worked summers on ranches in California and I understand what it takes to turn a profit. I like the work and the type of people who are in it." Then with a suppressed smile he added, "I'm not ready for marriage yet, and I guess you're right: the life of a seafaring man doesn't have much appeal to me."

Captain Geyer studied Todd. A keen judge of people, he thought to himself, "The boy should do well. He listens to advice, evaluates it and acts decisively. Plus he has a sense of humor." His choice impressed Geyer, who occasionally thought of investing in that line of business himself.

Realizing Todd's question required more than a superficial answer, the captain put his cup down, belched, and let his belt out another notch. Then he told Todd all he knew about the history of cattle in Oregon and what had been the Oregon Territory.

"The first effort at bringing in livestock was made by the Hudson's Bay Company, but they wouldn't sell any of their animals. You could borrow them, but you had to agree to give them back if they wanted you to. They were fair, though. If any of their stock died, they suffered the loss themselves."

"Why would they do that?" Todd interrupted.

"I guess this was as good a way as any to have some-one else take care of their inventory. They could increase the size of their holdings but didn't have to feed their own critters. Cattle to them meant anything on four legs that bawled. Milk cows, oxen or steers like you worked with in the Sacramento Valley." Going on, the captain said, "Of course some of the settlers had a few head of their own, but these were usually for milking, eating or working purposes — not for breeding.

"The first beef brought to Oregon about 25 years ago were pretty miserable. Scrawny Spanish stuff from California, half-wild, mean as sin, and so skinny you could play a tune on their ribs with a stick. About the time you were born, two large drives came up from Northern California. One by a seagoing man as a matter of fact. His name was Joseph Gale." He paused, contemplating whether to elaborate on this story, then deciding he would, went on.

"Gale built a boat here and sailed it to 'Frisco, where he traded it for 350 head. The boat was called the *Star of*

37

Oregon. Wasn't much of a vessel but it got him started. On his way back, by the time he reached the Rogue River, he had acquired more than 1,200 head of beef and 3,000 sheep."

Getting up, Geyer went through the open door that joined the dining room to the kitchen and came back with a hot pot of coffee. Filling Todd's cup, then his own, he sat the pot on the table. "Now it seems to be working the other way around. What with so many people in California, we're sending beef to them. I read in the *Morning Oregonian* last month that by June over 20,000 head had been sent south out of the Willamette and Rogue Valleys alone."

"Yep," he paused to stare across the room, "it seems to me that with the demand in California and the Sandwich Islands — which also take a lot of Oregon meat — there's a fortune to be made if a man were lucky and played his cards right."

Seeing that Todd had taken in every word, and had not interrupted with a lot of premature questions, Captain Geyer narrowed his eyes and in a statement rather than a question, said, "I know a fella that knows a darned sight more than I do. If you're interested we can look him up."

"Yes sir. I am interested. Very much so," said Todd.

As they rose to leave, the captain paused momentarily, pulled a coin from the pocket of his embroidered waistcoat, and left it on the table. "She'll fuss about that," he said. "But she works hard and charges a fair price. Besides, she can use the extra money."

The sky sparkled with freshness. A light, night rain had settled yesterday's dust. Todd breathed deeply, filling his lungs with the pine and pitch scented air. Even the fragrant wood smoke was invigorating. Not at all like the choking oil and coal fumes that filled the streets of San Francisco.

"Gettin' nippy," said the captain. "Pretty soon you'll be digging out your long-handles and wool Mackinaw and glad you have 'em." Pointing down the street he added, "There's one thing about Portland. It's still small enough that you don't have to walk far to see the man you want to do business with."

Todd took a moment to look around. Somehow Portland seemed more attractive than it had yesterday. Probably the result of a good night's sleep, he surmised. Wisps of smoke and fog hung in the trees, emphasizing the hills and craggy peaks that swept down to the valley in which Portland was located. The rhythmic "chunk, chunk, chunk" of pile drivers that split the air in San Francisco was replaced by the searing noise of steam-driven saws as they cut through giant logs that had been hauled down from the adjoining mountains. The sound of axes against wood rang through the hills as more trees were felled to create boards for new homes, buildings, streets and sidewalks.

The main thoroughfare in town was somewhat quieter than it had been late yesterday afternoon, but Oregonians were early risers and the stir of activity had already started. The road, barely wide enough for two wagons to pass, was built straight as an arrow and ran parallel to the Willamette River.

As if reading his mind, Captain Geyer said, "An accommodating street now, but when it really starts to rain, you'll wonder why they ever built a town on this spot."

Todd and Captain Geyer stopped before a door on which the words "Columbia Cattle Company, Tom Pickett, Prop. Pls. knock" were lettered on the windowpane. They entered without knocking.

The office was small, about eight by nine feet. There was one worn armchair facing a roll-top desk. Both looked as if they had been retrieved from the junk pile. Or maybe a back alley, Todd thought, remembering the view from his room. A cuspidor stood within spitting distance of the chair. Trails of tobacco juice showed that sometimes the mark had been hit, other times missed. There were coat pegs in the rough plank walls, but no coat rack, as would befit most respectably furnished offices in San Francisco. The only light came from the door window. Beside the door was a wooden bench.

The man who was seated in a straight-backed chair with his boots on the desk jumped up quickly when they came in. He was thin, wiry and mustached. About twenty-four or twenty-five, Todd guessed. Coppery red sideburns and a full head of unruly red hair topped a deep-set pair of piercing blue eyes. He wore a broad leather belt as well as bright red braces.

"Well, Captain Bligh," the owner of the Columbia Cattle Company said, greeting them. "You gave me quite a start. I thought you might be one of those highway robbers from the Oregon Steamship Company come to talk business with me again."

Stepping out from the shadows to shake hands with Geyer, Todd noticed for the first time the bruised and swollen left eye and the recent cut on the bridge of the nose of the man facing them.

So did Captain Geyer, who shook his head and frowned. "Tom, if you keep pulling the tiger's tail, you're bound to get clawed."

"Guess so," said Tom Pickett. "But when he's in the way and you want to move him, the handiest thing to grab hold of is his tail."

Giving Captain Geyer a deep, searching look Pickett added, "I wish you would reconsider and make your runs up and down the Columbia River instead of all the way to 'Frisco and back. We both know there's more money in it."

"Yes, and more risk, too," the captain replied. "And I don't mean just from the elements. You and I don't have enough fingers and toes to count the number of people who have tried to buck the OSC and failed. Most ending up broke. No thanks, Tom. The tail pullin' is all yours."

Geyer turned to introduce Todd. "Tom, this is Todd. . ."

"Howard," interrupted Todd, holding out his hand. "Todd Howard. It's a pleasure to meet you."

Grasping hands firmly, they sized each other up, both

40

liking what they saw in the other.

"Todd is from California. He's interested in the cattle business, and as you're the only expert I know. . . ." Here the captain good-naturedly emphasized the word "expert" and continued. "I thought as a favor you might be willing to answer some of his questions."

"Sure, Cap'n. Have a seat, Todd. What can I tell you?"

"I guess I don't know enough to even know what questions to ask," Todd answered as they all sat down. "Captain Geyer told me how beef cattle started in the Willamette Valley and about the markets in California and the Sandwich Islands."

"Those are the current big markets," Pickett answered, leaning forward intently. "But with the gold strikes in Eastern Oregon at Canyonville, and in Idaho and Montana, there are even bigger markets that are a lot closer. The only problem is getting to them. You can drive cattle to California, or ship them there, or to the Pacific Islands by honest men like Captain Geyer, but the Oregon Steamship Company has a chokehold on the Columbia River from here to The Dalles. And the Columbia is the best way to move cattle East from the Willamette Valley. That's what my 'discussion' with the OSC coyotes was about last night. I refuse to pay their thieving prices, and am holding near to a thousand head in Lebanon that I won't move an inch unless they give me a better shipping price." Going on, he added, "My gut feeling is that too much beef is being moved into California, and in a year or two the bottom is going to fall out of that market. Right now the Oregon Steamship Company — most people refer to them as the OSC — has me between a rock and a hard place."

"Why not drive your herd?" asked Todd.

"Land east of the Cascades is still unsettled for the main part. Although the Indians have supposedly been put on reservations by the government, they're not staying there and are causing a lot of trouble. What animals they don't steal they kill just out of plain cussedness. A few folks have tried to push their cows on through, but those who make it usually

41

end up with nothing left to sell. It's as dangerous as sin. Going up the Columbia is faster and safer. If it weren't for the Indian problem more cattlemen would be going through the passes.

"God-damned steamship bandits!" he exploded unexpectedly, "They'll sink or shoot anyone who competes with them, and they're big enough to get away with it." Catching his temper, he nodded to Captain Geyer. "I've been trying to talk Captain Bligh into throwing in with me. I could supply the stock, he could supply the transportation, and we'd split 50-50. Of course," he reflected, "we'd also need a little financial backing to protect our assets."

Rising to his feet, Captain Geyer said, "Tom, I never figured on being a rich man. And I certainly see no sense in being a dead rich man. All this talk about beef has made me hungry. How about us all going to the Red Dog for a drink and something to eat? Besides, today is the day the packet *Jeremiah* brings in the latest news from Fort Boise and The Dalles. And if I know Captain Rielly, that will be his first stop."

The Red Dog looked like the Buckhorn Saloon they had visited the night before. The main difference being there was no player piano. A large table was set up in the center of the room on which sandwich fixings had been put out. The bar was almost an exact duplicate of the one in the Buckhorn. Built of unfinished planks, it was designed for rough usage, not appearance.

After last night's supper and this morning's breakfast, Todd wondered if the main occupation in Portland was eating. Surprisingly enough, after his first bite, he found he was famished.

"How about a beer, boys?" the captain said. When his companions both nodded yes, unable to talk because their mouths were full, Geyer rose and pushed his way to the bar. The crowd had increased considerably since their arrival, and it was with some difficulty that he was able to catch the bartender's eye. As Geyer picked up three foaming glasses, his right elbow was jolted hard.

"Well looky-here, if it ain't the Captain of the washtub Lulu-Belle," a voice snickered. "It looks like you spilled your beer, Cap'n."

Whirling around angrily, Geyer saw that it was Jack Bartels, an employee of the Oregon Steamship Company. At one time Bartels had competed with Geyer on the run to San Francisco. He had been captain of the packet *Henry Johnson*. Having lost his vessel in the rough mouth of the Columbia, Bartels was now first mate on an OSC steamer that shuttled between Portland and the Cascades, the portage stop below The Dalles. He still used the title of "Captain," however, and liked to be referred to as such.

"You got the name of the ship wrong," Geyer said, fighting to control his temper. "But then I suppose you never had the chance to see it much, as her name's on the bow and she always passed you so fast you would have missed it if you blinked. I should have painted 'Lucille' in big letters on the the stern, but then it probably wouldn't have made much difference as I doubt if you can read anyway." Here he paused, glared at Bartels, and slowly and deliberately added the word "mate."

For a moment it looked as if Bartels would press the issue. Geyer warily eyed his opponent, ready to drop the three mugs on the floor and defend himself. Knowing this, Bartels snorted derisively and turned back to the bar.

Returning to their table and putting down the half-full glasses he said, "Sorry, gents. Seems I spilled a little on the way back."

As neither Todd nor Tom had noticed the incident — they had been deep in conversation — Tom was astute enough to catch the inflection of anger in Geyer's voice. Looking up, he saw something in the captain's eyes that made him search the room. Seeing Jack Bartels at the bar and knowing of the enmity between the two, he drawled, "Guess you must have bumped into your old friend Jack Bartels."

Turning back to Todd, who was already on his second sandwich, Tom continued their talk about the potential for selling cattle to the beef-starved miners, ending with the premise that if he could find some way to get the animals to these markets, the price of a cow would be worth three to four times more than its current price in the Willamette Valley.

At this precise moment, a great shout went up from outside and a wild-eyed teamster burst into the bar. "God-a-mighty, he done it! Crook done it. He made the murderin' redskins beg for mercy." Talk stopped as everyone turned toward the speaker. "Cap'n Rielly done brung the news hisself and is posting it outside. The Injun country's been opened up."

All else was forgotten as everyone stampeded for the door. Crowding out, they gathered on the sidewalk and the street in front of the Red Dog. Captain Rielly was standing on a wooden box preparing to nail a notice to the front of the building where most of the town's announcements were posted.

His face flushed with excitement, Rielly raised both of his arms for silence. The notice was held in one hand, hammer in the other, and two tacks were sticking out of his mouth.

As the crowd quieted down he put the hammer handle in his belt and the tacks in a shirt pocket. Holding the message over his head he said, "To save time, I might as well tell you what it says. I guess you're all interested." A roar of approval followed, then all conversation died. Even the jaws of the heartiest tobacco chewers stopped as they waited to hear what Rielly was going to say.

Clearing his throat, the captain of the mail packet *Jeremiah* began. "General George Crook moved against the Malheurs and Shoshones and whipped them so badly they sued for peace. Those that aren't going back to the reservations have been made the responsibility of Chief Wewawewa."

Pausing to control the rising voices of the crowd, he raised his hands again to get their attention. When he got it, he went on. "This means an end to Indian unrest east of the Cascades! It's all here," he shouted, waving the document as the crowd roared its approval. Some joined the line to read the report for themselves, but most headed back into the saloon to celebrate.

Exuberantly Tom slapped the captain on the back, then danced a little jig. "Do you know what this means?" he asked. "Now we can drive our cattle over the pass without interference from Mr.High-and-Mighty Oregon Steamship Company. Or being slaughtered by the Indians. This is the best news I've heard since Oregon voted to become a state. The drinks are on me!"

Tom explained the situation to Todd as they pressed through the crowd. "Two years ago a rancher shot Chief Paulina near Maupin Station for stealing his cattle. Paulina had been stirring up the Paiutes and Snakes. When he was killed everyone thought the Indian raids in central Oregon might be over, but then the Malheur and Shoshones started acting up. The government brought General Crook up from the Shasta area in California to calm them down. He did such a good job they made him commanding general of Fort Boise, with jurisdiction over all of Oregon and Idaho. Chief Wewawewa, whom Reilly mentioned, is friendly to the whites and will keep a tight rein on those redskins put in his charge."

The saloon was at fever pitch. Seated back at their table, Tom Pickett started talking about how he would move his herd. "There are two good routes: one directly east of Lebanon over the Santiam Pass; the second a little farther south over the McKenzie Pass, out of Eugene City. Should take no more than two or three weeks at the most to get them over the mountains."

"Hold on, Tom," said Captain Geyer. "Don't get yourself in an uproar. First off, they haven't penned up the Indians yet, and they might not take too kindly to being swooped down on all of a sudden. Second, it's getting late in the year, and in another week or two there's going to be snow in the pass, if it hasn't started already. Seems to me you need to think things out a bit." From the corner of his eye he noticed that

45

those in the bar who worked for the Oregon Steamship Company were gathering at a table in the corner. Jerking his head in their direction he said, "Besides, I doubt if that bunch is too happy about the news. It just might be a good idea for us to wait and see what they're up to."

Tom's ears picked up. "Us? Did I hear you say us?"

Stung by the remarks of Jack Bartels, the OSC's first mate, and caught up in the passion of the moment, Geyer sighed hard and said, "Yep, I guess I'll have to throw in with you. If the OSC sinks *Lucy,* I'll just have to learn to ride a horse and we'll go over the mountains." His eyes flashing at the thought of this new enterprise, Geyer cautioned Tom. "Don't say a word about my decision until we have everything worked out and are ready to move. I don't want *Lucy* burned at the docks before she has a chance to show her stuff. I also need time to shape her up a bit. Maybe make a few changes." As he said this, a tight smile appeared on his face.

Todd, who had been left out of the discussion, interrupted. "Don't forget you're going to need some financing."

Tom snapped his fingers. "We certainly are. Cap'n, let's get to Ladd & Tilton this afternoon before everyone else does."

To Todd he said, "They were the first bank in town. Most banks are asking five percent for loans, but because I did a lot of business with them when they were just getting started, I'll bet I can talk them into a loan at two-and-a-half or three percent."

"Maybe that won't be necessary," said Todd, pulling out his wallet and taking a slip of paper from it. "Here's a draft on a San Francisco bank from my father for $6,000. Would that be enough?"

"Enough!" shouted Tom, jumping from his chair and yelling, "Yippee" so loudly the chattering of excited voices in the saloon paused momentarily. Most of the patrons looked his way then turned back to their own conversations, figuring the news of General Crook's victory had just sunk in to some slow-witted soul.

Dropping back into his seat Tom said with a wide grin, "Guess it would." Then, exchanging a look with Captain Geyer, who nodded his head, Tom stuck out his hand and added, "Partner."

CHAPTER

6

Early the next morning Tom, Todd and Captain Geyer met in Tom's small office to make plans for spring. For this was when they decided to make their move.

The herd would be split into two groups. One would go through the Cascades. The other would be driven to Portland for the steamer trip up the Columbia.

They agreed to keep the name Tom had already established — the Columbia Cattle Company. However, each of them would have his own brand. The profits were to be split by the total number of cattle sold, not by brand. The reason was that any gain or loss would be shared by them equally.

The brands they selected had a personal meaning. Todd chose the Circle F, in honor of the Fields. Geyer picked the Flying L after his ship *Lucille*, and Tom kept his mark, the 3C.

While the three partners of the Columbia Cattle Company were finalizing what needed to be done before spring, the directors of the Oregon Steamship Company were holding an emergency meeting. It had been called by the president, Homer Siebold, of Siebold and Hanson, Portland's largest mercantile store. A methodical man, Siebold was taking roll, even though he knew everyone was present.

"Cecil Hershey."

"Here," replied Hershey, owner of the largest farming operation in the Willamette Valley.

"Frank Allen."

"Here," answered Allen, a rancher who had started with two cows and a bull, and was now the largest cattle rancher in Oregon. His holdings extended from the Rogue River, where he made his headquarters, throughout Western Oregon. Everyone there knew if you had killed and skinned one of Allen's cows ten years ago, more likely than not you would find another brand showing under the hide.

"Jim Nikol."

"Yup," said Nikol raising his hand. "I hope this special meeting is necessary, because the salmon are running and this is our busy season." Nikol controlled fishing along the coasts of Oregon and the Washington Territory, as well as up the Columbia River to Celilo Falls.

"Dennis Mitchell."

"Present." A taciturn man, Mitchell held the position of Secretary to the Governor of the State of Oregon. This job made him one of the most influential members of the group. It was common knowledge among those present that Mitchell would keep information from the governor for weeks if it suited his purpose. It was Mitchell who had first alerted the directors of the Oregon Steamship Company to the fact that land east of the Cascades would be opened as a result of Crook's victories, providing them with the time needed to call a meeting so quickly.

"Robert O'Conner."

"Present, Mr. Chairman," said O'Conner, one of The Dalles' leading merchants and the OSC's authorized shipping and receiving agent at The Dalles landing.

"Henry Tabor."

Raising his hand, Tabor indicated his presence. A large man with fists to match, he owned most of the sawmills and lumber operations in the area.

"Arnold Boden."

"Here," responded Boden, who held the position of

teller with Ladd and Tilton, Tom Pickett's bank. A short, sallow accountant, Boden was tolerated by the directors but not accepted by them as an equal. He was chosen only because of his access to information about who needed money and who was doing well. Boden was not even an officer of the bank in which he worked: such was the esteem in which he was held by his employers, who were unaware of his relationship with the OSC.

Satisfied that he had followed the proper procedures in conducting the meeting, Siebold turned to Boden, who was acting as secretary. "Please note that all are present." Continuing, he faced the group from his position at the head of the table. "Gentlemen, I guess you know why we are here. This special meeting is extremely important, both to the OSC and to us individually. The sudden resolution of the Indian problem puts us in a compromising position. Although we had anticipated successful action by the military against the warring tribes, I think you will all remember that we felt it would be at least another year or two before this happened — giving us time to further consolidate our strength and allow us to expand our control of commerce throughout the State of Oregon."

Unbeknownst to anyone but those at the table and the few men they had selected to negotiate for them, the OSC had been in active contact with the Yakima, Flatheads, Cayuse, Paiute, Walla Walla and other tribes to the east and southeast. The purpose being to purchase the thousands of head of cattle the Indians had stolen in exchange for guns, ammunition and trading goods.

Siebold went on. "Those very cattle that we were planning to acquire have now been confiscated by General Crook on behalf of the United States government. I regret to say that most of the chiefs we were dealing with have been hanged, in spite of the efforts of those 'volunteers' we placed at the service of the General to advise moderation."

Leaning over the table and placing the fingers of both hands on its highly polished surface, he looked slowly and deliberately at each member of the group. "The big question is, what do we do now?"

Siebold's statements hit a responsive chord. If there was one thing the group had in common, it was greed. Greed and a need to stoke their own feelings of importance. The fact that selfless, God-fearing men and women had blazed the trail to Oregon, many dying for the ideals of honesty and integrity they believed in, meant nothing to the directors of the OSC. They were like all the parasites and opportunists before them that brought the great civilizations of the world to their knees. The only decisions they would ever make would be those that were of direct advantage to themselves. The idea of contributing constructively to the benefit of their fellow man never entered their minds, and never would.

O'Connor spoke first. "I say we make damn sure nothing that floats reaches Celilo Falls, or beyond The Dalles. Unless we own it."

At this remark Allen snorted. "Seems we've been doing that already. The real problem is, how do we stop the overland movement of livestock? There's not enough cattle coming up from California to worry about. It's beef that will be going east from the Willamette, Rogue and Umpqua Valleys that should concern us."

At this point Mitchell interjected, "I think Bob and Frank are both right. We have to make sure we continue to control shipping on the Columbia, and we have to do whatever is necessary to keep cattle out of Eastern Oregon."

The group around the table responded to this statement by nodding their heads affirmatively.

"Seems to me we're pretty much in agreement then," said Tabor. "It's twofold. We keep up the pressure on the Columbia and stop any cattle trying to get through the passes. Sounds simple enough, but how do we do it?"

"Frank," Nikol said, addressing Allen. "You own the largest herd in Oregon. What would stop you from crossing the Cascades?"

Pausing to think out his answer, Allen looked up. "Only

51

four ways. Having my stock rustled, not being able to get my cattle to water, or Indians. The surest way, though, would be to have me killed."

This last suggestion shocked no one. They were all hard men, and killing was frequently used as a means of solving their problems and eliminating competition.

Howard Siebold summed up. "Looks like Frank has the answers. Any disagreement?" There being none, he continued, "My suggestion would be to name two men we can trust — men who have proven themselves to us — to head up two groups. One for the Columbia and the second to oversee our. . ." and here he cleared his throat, "shall we refer to it as 'land operation'?"

"Seems to me we already have our man for the Columbia," Nikol spoke out. "Jack Bartels."

O'Conner said, "I agree," and the other members indicated their approval.

"Now we need our second man," Siebold said. "Any thoughts?"

Mitchell, the governor's secretary, spoke up. "I imagine Frank might be able to answer that one, too. Whoever it is must be wise to the ways of cattle and cattlemen. He's got to be controlled, though. If our actions get too obvious or," he coughed nervously, "too crude, we'll have the military and state government on our backs and our efforts will be wasted."

"I've got just the man for you," Allen said as he leaned forward on his bony elbows. "His name's Luis Baca. He's one mean customer, but he'll take orders."

"That settles it then. Gentlemen, if there is no further business, I suggest we adjourn."

Bartels was notified that day and accepted the job with a wolfish grin, knowing this would enhance his stature as an important man in the waterfront community.

Baca would be informed by the end of the week when Allen returned to his ranch.

Later that afternoon Captain Geyer was making special arrangements of his own. He had no delusions about what he was getting into, and his remark that he needed time to "shape *Lucy* up a bit by adding a few things" had gone unnoticed by both Todd and Tom. But Geyer was dead serious when he said it. Until the time was right, it was best that no one found out what he had in mind.

After spreading the original construction plans for the *Lucille* on his chart table, he went to the door and locked it. Then he leaned over the drawings and began making notes.

Two hours later, satisfied with his efforts, he rolled up the plans and stored them away. Shortly afterwards he was discussing these notes with Henry Tines, who ran the foundry and blacksmith shop that served the needs of the vessels berthing in Portland's harbor.

Geyer trusted Tines. But equally important, he respected Tines' ability to do the job he had in mind.

After reviewing Geyer's rough sketches, the Scottish foundryman looked at the Captain, his face wrinkled in a frown. "It will be no easy task, laddie. I suspect you will want me to work on this myself. I can't get to it, however, for another three or four weeks."

"That will be fine, Henry. I need that much time to pick up the necessary supplies anyway."

Straightening his back from the long period of time they had spent laboring over the details of the work to be done, the testy Scot said simply, "I guess you have thought this out." Some spark of inner amusement flickered in his eyes, "And I guess we'll both be out of business if anyone ever finds out what you're up to and who helped you." Sticking out his hand he said, "It's time someone did something about that bunch of scoundrels."

Across town in the Red Dog, Todd and Tom were relaxing over a pitcher of beer, having spent the day talking about cattle. Tom was a patient teacher and enjoyed sharing his knowledge. Todd on the other hand was a receptive pupil, learning quickly and retaining the information that Tom was passing along.

53

Tom had just taken his first swallow when Jack Bartels swaggered into the saloon with his second mate, Sid Bacon.

Full of self-importance as the result of his new position with the Oregon Steamship Company, Bartels started to pass the table at which Todd and Tom were seated, but turned back and arrogantly commented, "Been bumping into doors, Pickett, or did you cut yourself shaving?"

Putting down his sandwich and planting his feet firmly for support, Tom replied, "Neither. Tell me, Bartels, are you sleeping with a she-bear or haven't you taken a bath this year? You stink."

With a curse, Bartels charged. Quickly slipping up and out of his chair, Tom grasped it by the back, and sidestepping neatly stuck it between Bartels' legs, sending the first mate crashing headlong to the floor.

Bartels got to his feet. His pupils were dilated and his nostrils flared. "That will cost you, Pickett," he said, swinging a roundhouse right that caught Tom on the side of the jaw.

Seeing that he now had the advantage, Bartels closed in to get his massive arms around Pickett in a bear hug that would break his back.

Sensing what was coming, Pickett stepped forward. As he did he sent a powerful left to Bartels' midsection, then thrust the palm of his right hand hard under Bartels' chin.

After this exchange they separated and faced each other, both panting heavily.

Bartels outweighed Pickett by a good forty pounds, but Tom was quicker. And he could take punishment.

Lashing out, he hit Bartels in the windpipe. This was followed by a right jab to Bartels' eye and a punch that landed squarely on the bridge of Bartels' nose.

Blood spurted over Bartels' shirtfront and ran down the back of his throat, enraging him even more. His only thought now was to kill Tom Pickett.

Pickett moved in again, hitting Bartels twice in the midsection. Then he hit him squarely on the temple with a knuckled fist that dropped Bartels to the floor with a resounding crash.

Getting groggily to his feet, Bartels shuffled forward flat-footedly.

Seeing his condition, Pickett backed up to put the finishing touch on Bartels with a wide sweeping right.

Reading his intention, Bartels' companion stuck out his foot, catching Pickett off balance. Tom stumbled backwards and fell.

"Hey, wait a minute!" shouted Todd, rising to his feet. "Keep the fight fair."

"Stay out of this, sonny, if you know what's good for you. We've got a little score to settle with this loudmouth," Sid Bacon growled.

Fear gripped Todd. He knew these two bullies intended to cripple or kill Tom, just as he knew he was no match for either one of them. Despite Tom's pleading glance for help, Todd took a step back.

Noticing Todd's reaction, Bartels sneered. "Don't worry about him, Sid. Momma's boy doesn't want to get hurt."

Both Bartels and Bacon turned their backs on Todd and moved toward Tom. Bartels feinted with a right and Tom reacted with a punch of his own, which threw him off balance. Immediately Bacon moved in and grabbed Tom's arms, pinioning him tightly. With a grin that bared his rotten teeth, Bartels moved forward. Methodically he began to hit Pickett, first in the stomach and then in the face.

Todd stood watching. He realized he had to fight or be branded a coward. Even now he was getting glances of contempt from the crowd who had gathered to watch. The words "Momma's boy" and "sonny" rang in his ears, and a rage swept over him. Swallowing the bile that had risen in his throat he grabbed at Bacon, who reacted with a wild swing that caught Todd on the chest. The punch knocked the wind out of Todd. And it did something else: it ended the fear that had momentarily paralyzed him.

Kicking aside the fallen chair, Todd began to circle the husky sailor. Twice he jabbed at Bacon's head with his left. As Bacon made no effort to protect his face, Todd swung hard with his right, catching Bacon on the nose and cheekbone. Although Bacon was heavier by about twenty pounds and stronger, Todd could see his two advantages. The man was slow and his arms were short.

Suddenly Bacon lashed out. Misjudging the distance of his adversary, he threw himself off balance. Todd struck with his left, over Bacon's extended arm, then threw a hard right to his exposed rib cage.

Grunting, Bacon turned, both arms at his side, fists clenched.

Seeing that Bacon had his guard down, Todd swung with all of the strength he could muster.

Bacon ducked and sent two punishing blows to Todd's ribs. When Todd's arms dropped, Bacon rammed into him with a throaty growl. Bacon's momentum knocked them both off their feet. As they fell Bacon's head slammed hard against the edge of a table, and he sprawled on top of Todd.

Todd braced himself, too dazed to stop the blow he knew was coming. When Bacon didn't stir, Todd opened his eyes. Bacon was out cold! Todd rested for a moment, then struggled free of the hulk that held him down.

Barely able to stand, and thankful for Bacon's clumsiness, Todd looked around to see how Tom was faring.

Pickett and Bartels had fought to a standstill. Their labored breathing filled the room. Tom, knowing he had energy enough for one final swing, reached deep down within himself and threw a windmill punch that landed solidly under his opponent's chin.

From the loud crack that followed Todd knew, as Bartels fell, that Tom had broken his jaw.

Tom gripped the back of a chair to keep from falling himself. He looked as though he had been kicked in the face by a wild steer. The knuckles of his two hands were bleeding and already beginning to swell. So was his upper lip, which was three times its normal size.

Tom and Todd stood looking at each other. Tom, laboriously trying to get air into his oxygen-starved lungs, his feet spread for support, studied Todd who could imagine what Tom was thinking: is this someone I can trust when the chips are down, or will he cut and run when the going gets tough? Todd waited for Tom to say something.

Lisping as a result of his swollen lip and several loose teeth, Tom grinned and gasped, "Thanks, pardner. You'll do to cross the river with."

CHAPTER

7

It took several days for the news of General Crook's victory to work its way down the Willamette Valley. Clay Howard heard about it at the blacksmith shop in Sheridan when he and Ellie went to town to do their Saturday shopping.

The smithy, George Yancey, had given him a full report between blows of his hammer as he forged a rod of red-hot steel. With each stroke sparks flew in all directions, as if giving emphasis to his words.

"Seems like. . .the government's done. . .opened up the whole. . .eastern shebang." As he uttered the last two words, the brawny blacksmith gave the glowing rod an extra hard swing of the hammer. Eyeing the newly-formed wagon tongue bar critically, Yancey nodded in approval, then thrust it into a nearby barrel of water. The steam rose as the water hissed and bubbled.

Wiping his brow with the back of a huge, sweat-streaked hand, the smith turned to dip a cupful of fresh water for himself from a nearby bucket. Then he gave all of the details to Clay as he had heard them. "I expect business will pick up considerable. Those intending to move out to Eastern Oregon will want some shoeing done, and a lot of wagon wheels that have been rusting away in the rain will need repair." Casting a sideways glance at Clay he said, "Imagine you might even be giving it some thought yourself."

"It's something to think about all right," Clay answered. "See you around, Yance."

The last twenty years had been good to Clay. His herd had grown from a few head to over 500. He was well-respected, and his reputation for honesty was known from Portland to Grants Pass. People who dealt with Clay Howard never needed a piece of paper, or ever asked for one. His handshake was considered as good as gold. Unlike the directors of the Oregon Steamship Company, Clay Howard lived by his word. The set of principles and morality that Clay Howard and others like him lived by were the bedrock on which the foundation of Oregon, and the country, was built.

No man, red or white, ever passed the Howard's place hungry, either. Those too proud to ask for help were often surprised to see Clay's wagon drive up loaded with beans, potatoes, flour and a side of bacon or beef. On these occasions Clay's approach was usually, "Sure would appreciate it if you could help us out. Seems we have more than we can keep. Ellie's cold cellar is bursting at the seams, and the only place left to store this stuff is in the barn where it will either spoil or the rats will get it." Thus he made it seem as if the recipient would be doing them a favor by taking it off their hands.

In winter, when the Indians needed food, usually two or three braves would make an appearance by the river behind the house. They would build a fire in the early morning hours and squat around it until noon. Then they would disappear. Later in the afternoon they would return, usually to find dried corn or beans, half a beef, and occasionally some tobacco.

As Clay walked to the Mercantile Store to meet Ellie, he began to daydream. He was in his mid-fifties and so was his wife. "Are we too old to start all over?" he said to himself half-aloud. Startled by his own voice, he quietly laughed. "They say a sure sign of age is when you talk to yourself."

Reaching the plank walk that ran along the front of the four shops in town, he stopped. "I must be crazy. Ellie and I have worked for years for what we've got. Why risk it all? We have everything we need, and no one to pass it along to."

They had not heard from Mary in twenty years. Although there were rare moments when he felt he should not give up hope, he knew in his heart that he would never see his daughter again.

Clay stepped onto the boardwalk and turned into the store.

Ellie was at the counter, checking off her list. With the exception of some curtain material which was being measured, everything had been loaded on the wagon. Seeing Clay she said, "I'll be through in about two or three minutes, Clay, if you're ready to leave."

"Any time, El," he answered. "I'll be waiting outside." He waved a greeting to the proprietor Hal Enemark, then left. Their buckboard was parked in front of the store. After checking the harness and scratching the horse behind the ears, Clay climbed onto the seat. A short time later Ellie arrived. Reaching over, Clay helped her up, and when she was settled he clicked his tongue and flicked the reins.

Sitting primly at his side, Ellie told him the local gossip. Halfway home she ran out of news, and they rode on in silence. Words were not necessary in their relationship. They enjoyed just sitting together, rocking along with the sway of the wagon, taking pleasure in each other's company.

After awhile, Clay spoke. "Heard from George Yancey that the Indians are under control east of the Cascades. That should open up that part of the state."

"Guess keeping tight rein on some of those tribes won't be as easy as it sounds," Ellie replied.

"No, guess it won't. Those Snakes can be mighty mean. But General Crook claims he can tame them."

They rode another quarter mile in silence.

"Remember Art Buckley telling us about the train he was on in '45?" Clay spoke out again, referring to the story of the lost wagon train that carried the first band of settlers

60

to pass through Eastern and Central Oregon. Organized in Missouri, the wagons left the Oregon Trail. Instead of going north after leaving Fort Boise, they headed directly west through Oregon's high desert country. There they lost their way. But for the efforts of two volunteers who reached The Dalles and returned with a rescue party, they would all have perished.

The most exciting aspect of the lost wagon train of '45 was the discovery of gold — the famous "Blue Bucket" find. So named because some children had picked up a number of pretty rocks which they kept in a battered blue bucket. These later turned out to be pure nuggets. Because the settlers were so hopelessly lost, they could not tell their rescuers where the gold had been found. Consequently, miners turned out by the hundreds to look for the site, but were never able to locate it.

"It isn't the gold that interests me, El. It's what Art said about the land. Lush valleys fed by mountain streams and vast meadows sheltered by high rims of sedentary rock. 'Perfect cattle country.' Those were his very words. 'Rye grass stirrup tall, and meadow grass so thick you could hardly walk through it.'"

Before hearing the news at the blacksmith shop, Clay had not given more than a passing thought to the country Art Buckley had described. It was in the middle of Indian territory, and everyone agreed only a miracle kept the members of the lost wagon train from being slaughtered. The standing but somewhat macabre joke was that the train was so lost even the Indians couldn't find it. Somehow though, Buckley's description of the land had lodged in the back of Clay's mind, and he followed the accounts of army expeditions through The Ochochos where the train had been found.

The military was searching for a better route to the Salt Lakes — one that would bypass the rugged and treacherous Blue Mountain Road that ran farther to the north. Just last June, Clay read in the *Morning Oregonian* that they had discovered and mapped a new trail. The paper said it might even have been the same one taken by the lost wagons of '45 and later by the lost train of '53. The one that confused the larger of the Three Sisters with Diamond Peak and wandered south to find an accessible way from the upper Deschutes to Eugene City.

These explorations eventually led to the four passageways that now existed over the Cascades: two from Eugene City, one from Salem and one through Lebanon.

Thinking of these crossing points Clay said, "Suppose most of the people who will be leaving from here will be taking the Santiam Pass through Lebanon."

"Guess they probably will," Ellie replied as they turned into the narrow lane leading to their house.

The next morning Clay was up earlier than usual, fussing with some repairs that needed to be done on the plow team's harness. After hearing Ellie's call that breakfast was ready, he went to the pump at the back of the house and washed his hands. Then he opened the back door and entered the kitchen. Avoiding Ellie's eyes he said, "Thought I might ride over to Horace Singleton's place after breakfast to see how he's fixed for hay this winter."

Holding the hot oven door open with her apron to avoid burning her hands, Ellie pulled a tray of fresh, steaming biscuits from the stove and set them on the table. "Don't forget your slicker. It looks like rain."

Later that afternoon Clay returned home, stopping at the steps to scrape the mud off his boots and shake the water from his hat and poncho. Going directly to the stove, he held out his hands to warm them. Steam soon began to rise from his wet clothing and formed on the windows.

"Everything all right at the Singletons'?" asked Ellie as she lifted the stove lid and slipped in another piece of firewood.

"Yep." Clay then turned to his wife. He didn't have to say what was on his mind. She read it in his face and said it for him.

Reaching out, she touched his arm and asked, "When do we leave?"

Holding her two hands in his own, he replied, "This spring, if you're willing. Horace is thinking of going, too. And Archie Ridley."

"I'm willing," she said, glad the decision was made. Clay was always at his best when he faced a challenge. Besides, this place is so full of memories of Mary that a change will do us both good, she thought, as she began setting the table for supper.

CHAPTER

8

Four days after Clay Howard had made his decision to leave Sheridan, Frank Allen was nearing his ranch in the Rogue River Valley.

As Allen passed through the Umpqua Valley and rode over the mountain range that connected these two Southwestern Oregon valleys, he thought back to when it would have been dangerous to ride the trail he was now taking.

No more than a dozen years ago this area rang with sounds of gunfire as settlers, miners and the military skirmished with bloodthirsty Rogue Indians. At one point — when the Rogues, Shastas and Umatillas had joined forces — it looked as though everything he had worked for would be lost. Indian raids had decimated his herd and despite many treaties with the warring tribes, no isolated ranch or farmhouse was safe. Even small communities had been attacked.

These were the times when Frank Allen was almost finished as a rancher. But Allen was a tenacious fighter. His philosophy was that you accepted the hand fate dealt and went on from there. The only time you were beaten was when you thought you were beaten. The word "lose" was just not part of Allen's vocabulary.

That's why he felt no guilt, when treaties with the Indians were being enforced by government troops, about raiding their reservations, stealing their cattle, or even killing when necessary.

Because of his "dog eat dog" credo, it didn't bother him, either, to change a brand on one of his neighbor's steers. And wild cattle he considered his own, no matter whose land they were on.

Standing down from the saddle to stretch his legs, Allen hitched up his pants and made himself a promise. He had fought hard to become the biggest rancher in Oregon, and he intended to stay the biggest. Not only in the valley, but east of the Cascades, too.

Remounting and spurring his horse, he took the shortcut over the ridge that lay due west of his spread.

As he cantered toward the hitching rack, Allen noticed his crew had not been idle in his absence. The hay shelter was filled, and the stock had been gathered and were grazing peacefully in the foothills.

He was greeted by the cook, Swede Osterman.

"Have a good trip, Mr. Allen?"

"I did, Swede. Take care of my horse, will you? And see that he gets some grain. Is Luis around?"

"Reckon you'll find him at the corral. They're shoeing today."

Getting stiffly to the ground, Allen walked toward the large barn that housed the blacksmith shop. Rounding the corner of the barn, he stopped short. Luis Baca stood over a sprawled figure writhing in the dirt. Baca was kicking him methodically and unmercifully with his heavy, pointed range boots. A small group of cowhands looked on in disgust.

With one last vicious kick Baca said, "Now get up. And the next time I ask you to do something I want to see you hop like a jack rabbit. When Frank's gone, I give the orders around here."

"Frank's back," Allen spoke up dryly. "Baca, I'd like to see you in my office. Right now." With these words he turned and headed for the main building.

On entering his combination office and living room,

Allen removed his hat and hung it on a rack of deer horns near the door. Then, walking to a corner oak cabinet, he pulled open its two doors, reached for a bottle of bourbon that was specially imported from San Francisco, and poured a stiff drink into one of the barrel glasses from the cupboard. Seating himself comfortably in the deep leather chair he had brought down from Portland, he put his boots on a scarred hassock and waited for Baca. Before long his lean, dark-complexioned foreman knocked at the open door. Allen set his drink down. With a grunt he motioned Baca in.

Baca entered, braced for a reprimand. Deferentially he removed his hat and started talking the moment he stepped inside. "Just trying to maintain a little discipline, Mr. Allen. Things got pretty lax while you were away."

Eyeing him sharply, Allen recalled the shape the ranch was in and knew the men hadn't been idle at all. Threats and beatings don't result in the well-cared-for stock and the maintained grounds he had seen.

You're natural-born mean, Baca, he thought. Discipline is one thing. Bullying is something else. He knew Baca was villainous enough to do the job the OSC wanted done, but he would have to earn enough respect from his crew to get it done properly.

"We'll get to the bottom of that later," Allen said aloud. "If you were right in what you did, I'll have to let the man go. . . ." He trailed off so Baca would know he would look into the matter, but probably do nothing about it. "Right now we've got something else to discuss. Sit down."

Baca took the chair facing Allen which was specially built to Allen's specifications. It was three inches lower than the one in which Allen was seated. Baca knew this and resented it. He also disliked being ordered to sit. By anyone. And that included Allen.

This resentment clearly showed on his face and in his oval, black eyes, giving Frank Allen a certain amount of satisfaction. Because he knew Baca was now properly put in his place, Allen deliberately changed his tone and said in a conciliatory manner, "Luis, we've got a big job to do." Going to his desk, he opened the top drawer and pulled out a box of Havanas. Carefully selecting two, he handed one to Baca and bit the end off the other. Striking a match in one hand with his thumbnail, he lit his cigar. Waving the match out, he threw it toward a nearby spittoon.

"Been talking to the directors of the Oregon Steamship Company. There's news from Fort Boise that involves us all." Then he filled Baca in on what had transpired. He also told him about the two groups the OSC was forming.

Leaning back in his chair, his eyes met Baca's. "I made my recommendation for the cattleman and they all agreed." Pausing for effect, he thought he could discern a flicker of interest in Baca's face. "The man I recommended is you, Luis. There's one thing, though. You'll still be taking your orders from me. When I say squat, you squat. When I say jump, you jump. Like a jack rabbit. Take it or leave it."

This time he couldn't miss the reaction in Baca's face. It was a look of pure hate. Standing, Baca put on his hat and did not extend his hand to seal the bargain. Instead he said, "I'll take the job," put the unlit cigar in his pocket, and left.

He bears watching, Allen told himself, contemplating his foreman's reaction. I hope I made the right decision.

By the time Baca reached the veranda, plans were beginning to formulate in his mind. Here was the opportunity he had been waiting for. He was doing all the work but getting only an occasional bone in return. It was comeuppance time for Mr. Frank Allen. The logical successor to the FA spread would be Luis Baca. He would see to that.

Baca had joined Frank Allen's outfit twenty years earlier in Red Bluff when the FA crew was returning from a drive to Sacramento. Allen hadn't intended to do any hiring, but when he saw Baca cold-bloodedly gun down two men who had accused him of cheating at cards, he offered him a job.

Baca wasn't hired to be a cowhand, but he did know

a little about cattle. His father had eked out a living by stealing from the herds that passed through Monterey. As a young boy Luis helped. His job was to change their mark with a running iron which the senior Baca carried in his saddlebag.

When Luis was fourteen his father told him to make his own way in life. Luis had no memory of his mother, who had left with another man when he was three.

For the next ten years Luis Baca survived by doing odd jobs and cheating at cards. He spent another three years being supported by a prostitute who thought he would marry her. Instead, he took the money she had been saving and left for the gold fields of Northeastern Oregon. A year later, when this money ran out, he was in Portland. Three months later he decided to return to California.

On his way south he stopped at Sheridan to pick up a few dollars gambling. It was there he met Mary Howard. He had proposed to Mary for the simple reason that he wanted her, and knew the only way he could ever have her was to marry her.

The night of Mary's argument with her father, they left. Two days later they said their vows in the small mining town of Jacksonville. In two weeks they reached San Francisco.

Baca spent most of his time playing cards in the saloons along the Barbary Coast. To make ends meet, Mary took in washing. One day a swamper knocked on the door of their tar-paper shanty and handed her a note. It was cruelly short:

I don't want to be tied down. Don't
look for me. I am leaving for good.

It was signed "Luis."

Baca had known his wife was pregnant, but this didn't bother him. That was her problem. He traveled to Sacramento, then joined the gamblers who worked the Sierra mining camps.

In Georgetown he tried to waylay a drunken miner and steal his gold. The miner's cries brought help, and although it was too dark to see Baca's face, he was recognized by the reflection of light from their lanterns on the silver B

68

attached to his holster. Baca ran to collect his meager belongings and hurried to the stable. He left town minutes ahead of a lynch mob.

Two weeks later, Baca met Frank Allen and accepted his offer of a job.

CHAPTER

9

Rain swept over Portland in relentless sheets, turning streets into quagmires of mud through which horses, men and wagons struggled. It was a cold rain that saturated heavy clothing, penetrated woolen long johns, and soaked boots and shoes until they became as pliable as raw bacon. Sudden squalls drenched pedestrians as misshapen black clouds sent forth rumbles of thunder that tumbled across the heavens and down the flood-driven Willamette River.

Todd was awakened by a loud crack of lightning. It was the morning following the fight, and he was stiff and sore. After breakfast he shrugged on his coat and headed for the bank to deposit his draft. Then he returned to his room and sat down to write to his family in San Francisco. He told them how he planned to use the money Jamie Fields had given him and that he had structured his end of the deal to include them as co-partners. He also mentioned Tom Pickett's experience with cattle and covered their reasons for entering Eastern Oregon by two routes: the Columbia River and one of the Cascade Range passes. Todd was careful to omit any reference to the dangers they faced.Not wanting to worry his family, he avoided any mention of the incident at the Red Dog Saloon.

As he finished, a wave of homesickness engulfed him. The only tangible reminders he had of his family were a few

70

letters and the locket Ann had given him. In a postscript he added: "Dear Ann. The locket you gave me is open as I write. I do miss you. Todd."

Mrs. Blevins had been extraordinarily kind to Todd all morning. She sensed his loneliness and it touched her maternal instincts. When Todd had returned from his scrap with Sid Bacon, she insisted he soak his swollen knuckles in some warm salts. News travels fast in Portland, and she knew of the brawl within minutes of its finish. She also heard that, for awhile, it looked like Todd might turn tail and run.

Proud that he hadn't, she still voiced her concern. "That Jack Bartels and Sid Bacon are bad ones, and the company they work for is no better. Their kind ain't likely to forget a beating and won't fight fair next time."

As for Tom Pickett, he had barely been able to make it back to his cabin. Todd had offered his help, but Tom was far too proud to be seen leaving on Todd's shoulder. Each step had been a painful ordeal. He knew he had some busted ribs and that his mouth had been damaged.

When Tom got home he was so exhausted he fell into bed, boots and all. "I'm going to sleep a week straight," he mumbled to himself, and immediately dropped off. He didn't sleep a week, but he slept the clock around. When he awoke, he found he could work his jaw, so decided to fix coffee and fry some bacon. By dipping day-old biscuits in the bacon grease and sipping the hot coffee, he managed to get a little food down.

An hour later he was back in bed. One of his last conscious thoughts brought a mental chuckle. At least he could eat. That was more than Jack Bartels would be able to do for a while. Thinking of this, he started to grin, but the movement hurt his facial muscles so badly he shuddered at the thought of looking in the mirror to assess the damage.

Across town, near the waterfront, Jack Bartels was nursing his broken jaw. The doctor had wired it shut and warned Bartels to keep his mouth immobile so that it would mend properly.

The pain was all-consuming, as was his hate for Tom Pickett. He growled his feelings to Sid Bacon between clenched teeth: "I'll kill that son-of-a-bitch. You wait and see. He's a dead man." The mortification of having to stay out of sight until his face healed fueled his anger. Spring wasn't far off. He would settle the score with Pickett then.

Bacon, who shared the room with Bartels, was getting tired of hearing him complain. He knew they both had been beaten and didn't want to be reminded of the fact. It rankled Bacon to lose. The next tangle he had with Todd Howard would be one he would win.

The rain had soaked Arnold Boden to the skin, even though he was outside for only a few minutes — the time it took to leave his desk at Ladd & Tilton and report to Homer Siebold.

He carried important news. Todd Howard had been in the bank to deposit a $6,000 draft to Pickett's Columbia Cattle Company acount. Boden would not have ventured out in the storm for this bit of information alone; it was what Todd Howard had asked for at the bank that sent him scurrying into action. He was now telling Siebold.

"He wanted a form that would enable three people to co-sign on the account."

"Did he say who the third person was?"

"No, sir."

"Why didn't you ask him in some way? It could have been an offhand remark and he might have told you."

"I didn't think of it, Mr. Siebold. He rather caught me by surprise."

Homer Siebold paced the room, lost in thought. Obviously something was up if Pickett was taking in partners. Perhaps the $6,000 was merely a down payment and more money was coming. It might somehow signify a direct threat to the OSC itself. His mind raced: Who is this man

Howard? He's from San Francisco, and there was some gossip about big money coming into Portland from the California gold fields. If they're teaming up with Pickett, it's not land they're after. How long has Pickett been involved with Howard?

"Arnold," Siebold said, "It's vital that we learn more. Let me know the minute you hear anything."

With this statement he dismissed Boden. Going to his desk, Siebold picked up a pen and resumed the letter he had been writing to Dennis Mitchell, the governor's secretary. He would add what Boden had told him in the hope that Mitchell might know something himself.

Boden, who had remained standing through their exchange, did not realize for a few seconds that he had been forgotten. Twirling his hat nervously, he waited for some sign from Siebold. When none came, he turned and tiptoed quietly out of the room.

At the FA ranch in the Rogue River Valley, Frank Allen and Luis Baca had just finished going over Allen's plan of action.

"Luis, I want you to take Rivera and ten men of your choosing out of here as soon as the snow starts to melt. This should give you three or four weeks head start on even the earliest cattle drives. Locate your base of operations on the Deschutes. At this point," he said, stabbing his finger at a spot on the crude map he had drawn. "East of the base of the broken-topped mountain that is near the Three Sisters. Some people still call these mountains Faith, Hope and Charity, so don't get confused."

Luis nodded his understanding and Allen continued. "After you take care of Howard and Pickett, leave Rivera and a few men at the base of Diamond Peak, south of your camp. This should cover all of the major passes. Is my plan clear?"

"Very clear," Baca responded in a flat voice, bitter that Allen had not once asked his advice. "Just be sure the trade goods are ready. We'll need plenty of rifles and ammunition

73

if we're going to talk the Indians into leaving their reservations and helping us." He couldn't resist adding, "As long as I'm in charge, the only cattle getting into Central Oregon will be those bearing our brand."

Luis was secretly pleased that Allen had given him Jose Rivera. Had Allen not suggested Rivera, Baca would have asked for him. Rivera was as quick as a rattler with his guns, and just as vicious. Besides, when Baca made his move he wanted Rivera on his side, not Allen's.

"That's it," Allen said, signifying their meeting was at an end. "Any instructions you get from me will be by messenger, either from The Dalles or the Diamond Peak trail. Should you need to get in touch with me for any reason, send a rider."

Captain Geyer had been mysteriously absent from Portland for three weeks. When he returned, his ship was loaded with a number of boxed crates. He left several of these with Henry Tines at Tines' foundry. The balance he stored in his dockside warehouse, under heavy lock.

By this time, Tom Pickett was back to normal. Other than a few sore ribs, some bruises that had turned yellow, and a front tooth that was loose, he was his usual self.

Todd, weary of the rain that had not stopped since the fight, was in much better spirits now that the three of them were together again.

They met at the 3C office. Both Tom and Todd were curious as to the reason for Captain Geyer's sudden leave-taking. When pressed by their questions he answered, "Just needed a few things to make *Lucy* shipshape and ready. She's going to be hauling cattle now, not people." This explanation seemed to satisfy the two younger partners' curiosity.

Tom had not been idle during his convalescence and presented his ideas: "Since the cattle are at Lebanon, it makes sense to take them through the Santiam Pass. The McKenzie River Pass is too far south. If we crossed there, we would have to double back. There is another way, a northern route, that

74

starts east of Salem, but I hear it's fit only for mules. What do you think, Cap'n?"

"Sounds good to me," said Geyer. "I'll coordinate my departure up the Columbia River with your drive overland. I suggest the herds join up near the Deschutes, due east of the northernmost Sister."

"Good idea," rejoined Tom. "The cattle will need to rest up from the trip, and it will give whoever gets there first a chance to scout out the country."

"Well, Todd, what's your opinion?" asked Tom.

"Frankly, I'm a little embarrassed. Here I've been moping around these last few weeks while you two have been doing all the thinking. Both plans sound good to me. What can I do?"

"Two things," said Geyer. "The second best thing is to pick the first day it stops raining and get in some target practice."

"What's the best thing?" Todd asked.

"Oil your holster and practice your draw," responded the Captain.

Satisfied that the basic details had been worked out they said goodnight, aware that the coming spring would spell success or failure for their venture.

After the three partners disappeared into the swirling mists of fog that blanketed the rain-soaked street, a small ferret-like shape arose from behind some barrels by the office and splashed hurriedly through the puddles. It was Arnold Boden, going to tell Homer Siebold who the third partner was and what the three were planning.

That same evening Siebold wrote to Frank Allen, informing him of the 3C's plans to use the Santiam Pass. Siebold intended to personally notify Jack Bartels about what part the steamer *Lucille* would play in getting cattle up the Columbia River.

CHAPTER

10

It was one of those rare days in Portland. The sky was crisp and clear, with no trace of cloud cover to mar its pale blue surface. The very essence of the day gave every indication that winter had blown its last icy breath. Small birds chirped happily as they darted about gathering materials to build their nests. Their melodic tunes hung in the morning stillness, then mixed with the saucy chattering of squirrels who were also expressing their pleasure at being free from the isolated confinement of winter.

Todd was up early. As he listened to these magic sounds of spring, he took a deep breath of fresh air. It was going to be a beautiful day. He had seen it rain before, but the rain he had experienced in San Francisco was nothing like what he had been through these past few months. It had taken awhile, but he gradually became accustomed to the constant drizzle and, like most of the permanent residents who lived in Western Oregon, gave up worrying about wet clothes, which became a way of life.

Later that morning Todd met with Tom and Captain Geyer. Satisfied that everything was in order, and encouraged by the early break in the weather, they decided that next week they would send for the cattle that were to make the trip up the Columbia River.

Both Todd and Tom noticed Geyer was not his usual cheerful self. Besides being jumpy and nervous, he seemed abnormally preoccupied. They knew the work Henry Tines had been doing on the *Lucille* was nearing completion, but neither of them had been invited aboard to see what had been done to turn her into a cattle-carrying vessel. When pressed for an invitation the captain had responded, "Soon. When the herd arrives and is ready for loading, then I'll give you the grand tour."

Tom had worked hard the past three years to improve the quality of his beef. He was proud of the fact that over half the stock of the Columbia Cattle Company were Durham Shorthorns. Thus his response had been, "The quarters better be first-rate, Captain. Our cows are among the best to be found in Oregon. They're not like those Spanish breeds, scrawny and full of Texas fever."

At noon they went to Mrs. Blevins' boarding house for dinner.

"This weather may be deceptive," said Tom, spooning some hot soup into his mouth, "but my guess is it's the start of an early spring."

Geyer picked up a fresh buttermilk biscuit and answered, "I agree. I think we should be ready to pull out within the next three weeks. A lot of folks are going to wait until they're one hundred percent sure the heavy rains are over, but by then the early birds will have a jump on 'em."

Tom nodded his agreement. "Not only that, the first drive over the pass may hit a little snow. After a thousand head have been on the trail, it will be a muddy bitch kitty."

"I don't like what I'm seeing from the Oregon Steamship Company," Geyer spoke out, abruptly changing the tone of the conversation. "They're up to something. For some reason they've been watching me and *Lucy* like a hawk. I've spread the word around that I'm going to take cattle to San Francisco by ship. Even looked at the bark *Nellie Gray* that has been taking stock to 'Frisco, just to throw them off the track." Stirring some sugar in his coffee he paused, then

77

continued, "But they're not falling for it. It's like they know what we're doing."

"They're a nervous bunch," said Tom. "It's been a long winter, and they're probably just getting geared up for spring. They'll have their hands full getting their own passengers and freight to The Dalles."

"I hope you're right," said Geyer.

Rather than meet again for supper, the three partners elected to double-check their areas of responsibility so they would be ready to leave as soon as the opportunity presented itself.

As Todd had little to do, he decided to purchase some heavier riding boots, organize his belongings, write to his family and turn in early. At eight o'clock he turned down the lamp, and after a brief mental check on what he had to do the next day, immediately fell into a sound sleep.

In the middle of the night he was awakened by frantic shouts and a series of loud explosions. Jumping out of bed, he put on his shirt and pants and was just pulling on his boots when Tom burst into the room.

"Something's going on at the wharf. I think it's where *Lucy* is docked. Grab your iron and let's go! If it's the Cap'n, he'll need help."

Todd reached for his gunbelt and followed Tom. They raced down the stairs two at a time and ran out into the street.

It looked as if half of Portland was up. As they joined the stream of people heading toward the docks, the clear night was momentarily illuminated by a bright flash which was followed by a deep boom. The boom was punctuated with a series of sharp cracking reports.

"Rifle and pistol shots," Tom told Todd. "I don't know what the loud noise is. Doesn't sound like dynamite, but it's an explosion of some sort."

By the time they reached the waterfront, the action was over.

The center of attention was the *Lucille*. On the aft deck was Captain Geyer, a lighted punk in his left hand and a Navy Colt in his right. Smoke was emerging in wisps from the barrel of a four-pound cannon that had recently been installed on the forecastle.

Todd and Tom could barely believe their eyes. "So that's what he was up to," whispered Todd.

"Come aboard, lads. You missed the fireworks," the captain shouted down at them. The crowd, buzzing with questions, hung around waiting to get the details on what had happened. Meanwhile, Geyer spoke privately with Todd and Tom. "Seems like we had visitors. See that dinghy over there?" He pointed to a splintered, capsized oar boat being carried downstream in the moonlight. "Guess it must have been carrying powder, as old Betsy's second round hit something that blew." As he spoke, the captain gave the still-warm cannon an affectionate pat.

"By morning the tide should bring in the brigands who were in her — if there's anything left of them to wash ashore." Turning to the two armed members of his crew, he shouted, "Good eyes, men. If it hadn't been for your warning, it might have been us feeding the fish. Keep your wits about you. They may not be through playing their games yet."

In an aside to Todd and Tom, he said, "I doubt if we'll see any more action tonight, but we'll keep our guard up just the same. Let's go below. This calls for a drink."

After pouring each of them a generous measure of whiskey, the captain turned grim.

"One of the men aboard the dinghy worked for the OSC. I recognized him. Whatever they were carrying was meant for the *Lucille*." He took a hefty swallow from his glass. "They must be on to us. They haven't bothered me in the past, and there's no other reason for them to try and blow us up. If they do know what we're up to, they'll try again. The sooner *Lucy* is moving up the Columbia, the better. Tom, can we speed up getting those cattle here?"

"I'll leave tonight. If the herd is where it should be, I can be back in a week. Or less. Better yet," he said, grasping Todd's arm, "come with me, Todd. You can drive the cattle

79

back while I go on to Lebanon and pull the rest of the herd together. After you and Cap'n Geyer get *Lucy* loaded, leave all but three of your crew to go with the Captain, and meet me there."

In his room several blocks away, Jack Bartels was in a rage. Now that the wires had been removed from his jaw, he was able to talk. Pounding on the table, the veins in his forehead prominent and pulsating, he shouted at Sid Bacon. "God damn you, Bacon. I give you a simple job to do and you foul it up. Not only that, but you lose two men in the process." Spittle coming from his mouth, he ranted on. "I want Geyer's ship sunk where she berths. If he moves her into the Columbia with a load of cattle, you'll have me to answer to."

"Don't worry, Jack. Who would have thought Geyer had a cannon aboard? He got off a lucky shot, that's all. We'll get him for sure next time."

"You'd better," threatened Bartels, more worried about the reaction he knew he would get from Siebold than he was about Bacon's failure on a second try.

Todd and Tom picked out four horses at the stable. "Two day's provisions are plenty," Tom said as they hastily packed. "And with spare mounts we can make better time."

An hour later the lights of Portland had faded in the distance. Todd had been brooding since they left. Tom knew something was bothering him, and guessed what it was.

It came out when they made their first stop to change horses.

"Tom, I've been wanting to talk to you about our fight with Bacon and Bartels. The way I acted has been chewing on me."

"Wait a minute," Tom interrupted. "Before you go any further let me say something. You gave me a hand when I needed it. No man could ask for more. Far as I'm concerned the matter's closed."

Visible relief washed over Todd's face. "Thanks, Tom. I guess I've still got a lot to learn and some growing up to do yet."

"We all have, Todd," Tom replied. Then he changed the subject. "There's a ferry to catch at Oregon City. We'd best move on."

As they mounted, false dawn crept into the sky and the stars began to fade. On their left the heavens turned a lighter shade of blue-black, then a shadow-filled grey as the sun inched over the horizon.

By mid-morning they were waiting for the rope-pulled ferry. "This is not the way we'll bring the herd back, but it's faster for us," Tom said. Gesturing toward a group of buildings on the other side of the Willamette he commented, "That's Oregon City. Used to be the territorial capital of the state. The legislature doesn't meet there anymore, though. For a while they met in Corvallis, then in Albany. Now all branches of state government are at Salem, about forty miles south."

Shaking his head at the indecisiveness of politicians, he looked at the sky and immediately put them out of his mind. "Looks like the weather is going to hold. That's good. In this country you never know from one day to the next whether it's going to rain or not."

Kicking damp leaves and dirt over the fire he had built for morning coffee, Tom added, "Not necessary to worry about leaving hot coals this time of year. Too wet. But it's a good habit to get into." Nodding toward the approaching raft, he concluded, "Time to get going."

After they had boarded the log float, Todd asked about the majestic mountain that crowned a range of snow-capped peaks in front of them, and the hills behind them that were bare of snow and shrouded in mist.

Tom replied, "Coastal range behind us. Other side of them is the Pacific Ocean. Those deceptive-looking devils ahead form the Cascade Range, the one we'll be crossing. I guarantee they look a sight prettier from here than they will when we're in the middle of them. The big one is Mount Hood."

After paying their toll they headed east, then veered south. Their route took them through valleys lush with grass, fields sprouting shoots of green wheat and, in more settled areas, cultivated land and acres of fruit trees.

"Mark my words, Todd, one of these days the big money here is going to come from farming. It's ideal for cattle now, but soon they're going to be crowded out for want of pasture land. The opportunity for ranching lies over the mountains."

That night they made camp. Bone-weary from their long ride, they ate a cold supper and fell asleep.

The next morning they awoke to a chilly, penetrating fog. Shaking the dampness from his slicker, Tom shrugged it on with the comment, "Should burn off by noon. When it does, keep your eyes open for the herd. 'Till then, keep your ears tuned for their bawling. I'd hate to pass 'em by and lose time having to back-track."

Around midday Todd and Tom climbed a small butte to get their bearings.

"There they are," said Tom, spurring his horse and starting down. Todd followed. In the distance, six riders appeared and formed a defensive line. As they drew closer, a lone rider rode out to meet them.

"That's Darrel Vaughn, the trail boss. A better man you won't find." Standing in his stirrups, Tom waved his hat and yelled, "Halloo, Darrel!"

Reaching them, the rider leaned over his saddle to shake hands. "Howdy, Tom. I shore am glad to see you. Someone's been dogging our trail for the past week."

"Do you know who it is?" Tom asked.

"Yep," Vaughn replied. "Shorty snuck up on 'em one night as they were bedding down. It's Frank Allen's bunch. I don't understand why they're this far north without cows, or why they're tagging along behind us."

Pulling a tobacco sack out of his shirt pocket, Vaughn carefully rolled a smoke. Before lighting it, he looked up. "It smells like trouble." Scratching a match on the butt of his six-gun, he cupped it in his hand, lit his cigarette, and inhaled deeply before adding, "My guess is they're after the herd."

CHAPTER

11

"Well," said Tom, "they're not wasting any time. Let's join the others, Darrel, and we'll fill you in."

They pulled up before the group of waiting cowhands. Tom dismounted and walked from rider to rider, shaking hands and calling each by name. Then Tom introduced Todd, going on to explain the partnership they had formed with Captain Geyer. He also brought the crew up to date on their encounter with the OSC, ending with the combine's attempt to blow up the *Lucille*. "The main thing right now is to keep moving. We'll stop at the forks tonight. They won't bother us there."

Just before dusk, when the cattle were settled in for the night and the herd guard was in position, they gathered to discuss their situation. Smoothing out a patch of bare ground, Tom picked up a nearby stick and started making marks in the dirt.

"Here's where we are now," he said jabbing a hole. "This is the direction we'll be taking, and here's Silverton." Pausing he looked up. "If I was going to steal this herd, this is where I'd do it." Tom marked an "X" on the spot he had just indicated. "If I'm right we should expect company about mid-afternoon tomorrow."

Looking at Vaughn he asked, "What do you think, Darrel?"

84

"I think you've guessed right, Tom. If we go much farther than that, we'll be too close to Oregon City and there are too many farms around. They'd want to move the cattle through Barlow Pass, south of Mount Hood. If they just mean to scatter the herd, they know it will only take us a day — maybe two at the most — to round them up again. My vote is for the place you indicated. And my feeling is they intend to take the herd, not just slow us down for awhile." Vaughn rubbed the back of his neck. "We're outnumbered, but the one thing we've got going for us is the fact we know they're there."

"Todd?" asked Tom.

"I don't know the country at all, so I'd go along with whatever you and Darrel say."

Tom rose and dusted off the seat of his pants. "If the FA spread is making a play for our herd, I'd better get on to Lebanon fast. They may try for the cattle there at the same time.

"If you're agreeable, Todd, here's what I'd like to do. Leave you in charge and hightail it on alone. Assuming you get to Portland," he grinned wryly, "and with this bunch I have no doubt you will, help Cap'n Geyer load up. Bring Darrel, Shorty and Reub on back with you and meet me at Mount Washington." For Todd's benefit, he explained, "There's another Mount Washington near Lebanon, not the big daddy Mount Washington we'll be heading for near the Sisters."

Tom added a further word of caution. "Obviously the Oregon Steamship Company is on to us, so don't hang around Portland any longer than you have to. And don't get into any fights.

"Any questions?" Tom glanced at each man in turn. His gaze stopped at Todd.

"Sounds good to me, Tom," Todd said, trying not to show his nervousness at being put in charge of a group of men who knew nothing about him. After supper, as Tom was preparing to leave, Todd sought him out. "Thanks for the vote of confidence. I'll try not to let you down."

Tom's reply kept him awake most of the night. "Trying's not good enough, Todd. This is for keeps."

Next morning they moved out slowly. The cattle were reluctant to leave the lush bottomland grass. After fording the stream near camp, the herd increased its momentum, urged along by the yipping of the cowhands and the lead brindle steer who set the pace.

Todd had met with Darrel earlier. They decided to post outriders around the perimeter, a half-mile from the cattle, and double the guard on the left flank where they expected the attack. When trouble was sighted, a smoke fire was to be lit if there was time. If not, the group was to be alerted by any means possible.

"I don't want the men turning their backs on gunfire to hold the cows," Todd told him. "The first priority is to look out for themselves. The whole lot isn't worth one life. If we have to let them run, then let them run."

Darrel leveled his gaze at Todd, a blossoming respect showing in his eyes. Nodding his head in agreement, he said, "Fair enough, Mr. Howard."

Twisting in the saddle, Todd replied, "Todd. If we're to get along, the name is Todd. To you and all the hands."

Vaughn took the lead, with Reub Hassler riding drag. Todd rode ahead.

Clarence Whippet, one of their outriders, came racing in from the northwest shortly before noon. Vaughn and Todd rode out to meet him.

Out of breath, Whippet pointed over the rise and gasped, "There's a big drove coming our way. At the rate we're both going, they'll cross behind us in an hour or so."

Reacting to the news, Darrel Vaughn said, "Clarence, you take my place in the lead. I'll ride out and see who it is." Then, remembering his position, he turned and said apologetically, "Sorry, Todd. I keep forgetting I'm not the trail boss now."

"As far as I'm concerned, on this drive you still are," Todd replied. "Whenever a decision needs to be made, you make it. If I don't agree we'll discuss it privately. Ride on over and find out all you can. Meanwhile I'll circle our back trail in case it's a trick of some kind."

An hour later Darrel joined Todd, who was still watching the rear of the herd.

"Nothing to worry about. Just a bunch of cattlemen from Sheridan getting an early start over the mountains. They're going to settle somewhere in Wasco, but haven't decided where yet.

"The man who did the talking went by the name of Howard. His cattle carry the Bar H brand. Any relation to you, Todd?"

"Not that I know of. Guess there must be a lot of Howards in the world."

Shifting in his saddle to get more comfortable, Vaughn went on. "Told him about the bunch following us. Said he'd keep his eyes open for trouble, and that if we needed help and they were close by we could count on them. Seemed like a right nice fella."

Around two o'clock they bunched the cattle. Signs of strain began to show in the riders' movements. Bursts of energy and nervous glances from the herd to the surrounding hills punctuated their regular routine.

In constant motion, Todd rode from lead to drag. Darrel Vaughn had resumed his position at point.

They were now at the location Tom Pickett had predicted the ambush would take place. Todd was crossing a ridge to the front and left of the herd when he spotted a group of riders working their way down a draw that would put them at a distance of only two hundred yards from the lead steer. An ideal spot. They could let the herd pass, then attack on the side, front and rear simultaneously.

Slipping quickly off his horse, Todd gathered as many dry branches and twigs as he could find, using the paper receipt he hadn't bothered to remove from the pocket of his new shirt to start a small blaze. When the flames caught he added some wet leaves. A thin tendril of smoke rose straight up in the windless sky.

Darrel Vaughn was standing in his saddle to look around for what seemed like the hundredth time when he spotted the smoke. Signaling the others, he drew his revolver and was turning the cattle when thirteen FA riders broke out of the draw at full gallop, guns firing.

The shots startled the animals and started them running.

Vaughn realized it was too late to stop the herd, and knew he was in trouble. If he veered right or left, he would be caught and trampled. His only recourse was to stay in front of them.

Vaughn had seen the remains of a cowboy that had fallen in a stampede, and he shuddered at the thought. There had been nothing left but a few remnants of clothing, some unidentifiable bones and a mangled set of store-bought teeth.

Spurring his horse, Vaughn turned sideways to see two riders moving on him from the left. He snapped off three shots in their direction, then lost sight of them. His horse, a sure-footed bay, slowly pulled ahead of the hard-running steers. Carefully Vaughn worked him to the left, praying the horse would not hit a gopher hole and stumble. Vaughn was too preoccupied with his own plight and the sound of pounding hooves behind him to hear a new burst of gunfire far to his rear.

Todd, after seeing the fire take, quickly mounted and raced down the slope. From his vantage point he saw the herd break and Vaughn's futile effort to turn them. He also saw his men whip around to face the charging riders. Then his blood ran cold. Another bunch, about forty in number, emerged from a cut-bank and were heading toward the rear of the herd at full gallop.

This was something they had not expected. When Shorty had scouted their backtrail he had estimated that no more than a dozen or so men were following them. They had not anticipated their opposition would be in two groups, with the second being the size it was.

"Well, horse, if we're going down, we might as well go down fighting," Todd told his dun as he charged forward.

Within moments he was in the fray. Two riders turned toward him, their guns blazing. Caught up in the flow of frightened cattle, he swept by them. But not before he had gotten off two shots of his own. He gave his horse its head and was soon free of the panicked beef.

Again in the open, he found himself facing another FA rider. They fired simultaneously and the rustler slumped over the neck of his sorrel. Reining hard to the left, Todd saw that Clarence Whippet was in trouble. Caught between the herd and three FA hands, Clarence was frantically wheeling his horse, first left, then right, in an effort to find a means of escape. The attackers had fanned out and were stalking the trapped cowhand, ready to make their kill.

Todd gave full spur to his horse, firing as he went. He wondered about the high-pitched yell until he realized it came from his own throat.

Two of the riders that had boxed Clarence whirled. Todd crashed into the horse of one and squeezed off a round. His shot threw the man from his saddle. Turning, he took dead aim on the second. In the surrounding noise and confusion, he could not hear the dull click. Nor was he aware he was out of ammunition, such was the affect of the adrenalin pumping through his body. He continued to pull the trigger, the hammer hitting expended percussion caps.

As if in slow motion, he saw the arm of his opponent rise and point at him. At the same time he saw an orange flash. Suddenly Todd felt as light as a feather. It was as if a puff of some gentle wind came from the muzzle of the other's gun, lifting him up and carrying him gently to the ground. His mind was at peace. If this is death it's not at all like I imagined, he thought euphorically. A gentle wave of black velvet obscured his thoughts as he lost consciousness.

In actuality the bullet, hitting its mark, had lifted Todd violently from the saddle and slammed him hard to the ground.

"Looks like he's beginning to stir."

"'Bout time. He's been out quite a spell. If his neck wasn't straight, I'd swear it should be broken, the way he landed on it."

"He's a tough young feller. I'll say that for him."

Bits of conversation wormed their way into Todd's brain. Opening his eyes, he saw a flurry of white and yellow spots skimming over his vision, like waterbugs in the eddy of a slow stream. Through this blur swam a group of faces looking down at him. Not knowing who they were, and momentarily confused, he reached for his holster.

"Steady there," a voice said. He felt a hand on his shoulder holding him back. "Lie back awhile and give your eyes a chance to get uncrossed."

Taking this advice he drew his lids shut, both to stop the spinning images and to give himself time to collect his wits. As his head began to clear his muscles tensed, sensing they would soon be receiving instructions from the brain to act.

"Looks worse than it is. He's lost a lot of blood. I reckon he'll be pretty weak for awhile."

Todd didn't recognize the voice. That meant it wasn't one of his crew. Realizing this, he felt the smart thing to do would be to pretend he had lost consciousness until he knew what his odds were.

"Looks like he's dropped off again. Sure hope he ain't busted up inside."

That voice brought Todd's eyes open immediately. It was Darrel Vaughn. He tried to sit up but a searing white light exploded in his head. As he fell backwards, two arms kept him from hitting the ground.

Another voice said, "Try it a little more slowly and get your bearings. The fight's over and you're among friends."

Todd followed these instructions, feeling a fresh surge of pain throughout his entire body.

Soon the ringing left his ears and he could hear the bawling of cattle and the whinny of an impatient horse nearby. As his balance returned, the images around him came into sharper focus. Looking up, Todd saw Darrel's serious, wide-jawed face. Vaughn was almost shirtless. The cloth of his right sleeve was still attached to his collar and one shoulder, but the rest was missing.

To Vaughn's left was Clarence Whippet, whose hat was pushed back on his head. A forelock of damp hair was plastered to his brow and congealed blood left its crusty trail on an open scar that ran from the corner of Whippet's left lip to a point about an inch from his ear.

The man holding him up was in an army uniform. Blond mutton-chop whiskers partially covered his face and accented his sunburned cheeks and expressive hazel eyes. The soldier's coat was muddy and dirty, and long brown hair hung below his campaign cap.

"What happened, Darrel?" Todd croaked.

Relief in his voice, Vaughn replied, "Seems like you slept right through the best part, Todd. About the time you went down, we were beginning to think we were on the losing side. Then the lieutenant here showed up with his men and turned things around for us."

Waiting to see if his words were sinking in, and satisfied that they were, Darrel Vaughn continued. "We killed six of their men. Four or five more won't be making trouble for anyone for awhile, either. They'll be too busy lickin' their wounds."

"You got two of them," Clarence Whippet broke in. "Shot one clean through the gizzard and gutshot the other. That one rode away, but I doubt he'll go far. I guess if it wasn't for you, I'd be pushin' up daisies. I sure was in a jam and appreciate your helpin' me out of it."

By now Todd had recovered enough to ask, "Did we lose anyone?"

"Nobody killed. At least not now that you're sitting up. Clarence collected a graze on his cheek and Hugh James got knocked off his horse and broke his arm. That's it. We were lucky, thanks to Lieutenant Springer here."

"My thanks too, Lieutenant. When that large bunch jumped us from the rear of the herd, I thought we were goners for sure," Todd said.

Chuckling, the officer answered, "That large bunch you saw was us. We've been traveling from Fort Hall to show our presence in the area since a small band of Indians stole some cattle near New Albany. We were tracking them when we met a group of cattlemen headed for the Santiam Pass. They told us you were worried about some riders that had been following your tracks. Since we were only a couple of miles away, we decided to take a look. Good thing we did, too. When we heard the shooting we came at a gallop. Fortunately we had our medical officer Captain Bynum with us," Lieutenant Springer added, nodding toward an elderly officer in a frock coat who was wrapping a splint on the arm of Hugh James. "He's the one that patched you up."

Todd realized for the first time that part of the reason he was having trouble getting a full breath was because his rib cage was tightly encased in bandages.

"You can count your blessings and this," said Springer, holding up a heavy gold locket, one side of which looked as if it had been hit with the round side of a ball-peen hammer. "Evidently the bullet didn't hit you full on. You must have been sideways when it was fired. In any case, this deflected the slug just enough. Other than two inches of hide, a little bone from one of your ribs and a lot of blood, you're in one piece. You can thank your ramrod here," he said, pointing to Vaughn. "He saw you fall and fought his way to your side. He's the one who got the doctor to you quick when he found out we had one. That's why he's missing half his shirt. He used it to patch your bullet hole."

"Thanks, Darrel. I owe you one."

Embarrassed at being the center of attention, Vaughn mumbled, "It wasn't anything. Guess you'd have done the same for me."

"Lucky you were carrying this in your pocket," said Lieutenant Springer, handing Ann's locket to Todd. "And lucky you bought one as substantial as it is. Sure is a pretty young lady inside. You're double lucky. The shot hit the inscription and not the picture."

"I didn't buy it. It was given to me by my...by a young lady I was raised with," Todd said.

"The next time you see her you'll certainly have a story to tell," said the lieutenant, straightening up and rising to his feet. "I doubt if that bunch of sidewinders will attack again, but we'll ride along with you tomorrow until we reach Silver Creek. Just in case. From there, you'll be safe the rest of the way to Portland."

"Lieutenant?"

"Yes?"

"Thanks again."

"Goes with the territory," said the young military man, giving Todd a cursory salute and walking away.

As Todd got unsteadily to his feet, a wave of nausea engulfed him. "How many head did we lose?" he asked Vaughn when the dizziness passed.

"Very few if any," Darrel replied. "The hills kept them in the valley where they plumb ran themselves out. The boys are out now gathering 'em up, but I reckon they won't get the job done tonight." Gazing west at the fading light, he continued, "Shouldn't take more than an hour or two to finish the job in the morning. Now, how about some grub? Then I suggest we call it a day."

"Just coffee for me," said Todd, limping toward a blazing campfire. "A scalding cup of coffee, black enough to chew."

That night as he lay in his bedroll, Todd's mind was a blur of activity. It was rare for him to lie awake for long. He was a man who usually fell asleep in a matter of minutes.

And he normally slept hard, without the disturbance of dreams. But tonight was different.

He tried to recall each step of the fight until he realized he was incapable of cataloging it and playing it back in sensible order. Next his thoughts turned to Ann and the locket she had given him, which saved his life. What made him put the locket in his shirt pocket, and why hadn't he left it with the rest of his things back at Mrs. Blevins' boarding house? Had fate guided his hand? His head spinning, he dropped into a fitful sleep. As he slept Ann elusively entered his dreams, only to disappear as he reached out to touch her and to talk to her.

At the half light which precedes dawn, Todd awoke with a start. He had been disturbed by a nightmare about the fight. Then he relaxed as he heard the reassuring sounds and smells of a cow camp coming to life: someone's hacking cough, the shaking out of a bedroll, the sizzle and scent of bacon frying in a hot pan, and a grunted response to a question asked too early in the morning. A good life he thought, one in which each day is faced for what it will bring, and is not used up planning a schedule of events weeks and months away. Plans that probably would change anyway, so weren't worth worrying about in the first place.

Todd started to get up in his usual waste-no-time manner, but his body rebelled. Pain pierced the center of both eyes, and at the same time it felt as if a red-hot branding iron had been rammed into his left side. "This isn't going to be as easy as I figured," he muttered. Half rolling to his right elbow, he was able to make it first to one knee, then the other. He stopped all movement of his body until the heavy throbbing in his head subsided. Then he rose unsteadily.

He was up. That's what counted. Picking up his bedroll and gunbelt would be another matter. He would worry about that after breakfast. The smell of coffee made his stomach growl. He was hungry, a good sign. Squatting to eat, he wolfed a plate of bacon and pan biscuits. These were washed down with several cups of tar-black coffee.

Darrel Vaughn had risen before daylight to check the stock and get the Columbia crew moving. Spotting Todd he stopped by the fire. "I'm leaving with a couple of hands to round up the strays. Everything's quiet and peaceful. The Army's astir so I imagine they'll be ready to go as soon as we are. Feeling okay?"

"Yep. A little cranky, but I'll make it. Join you at the herd as soon as all these bees settle in their hive."

Todd threw the dregs of his coffee on the fire and told himself he would be feeling better once he was up and about. At least he hoped so.

By mid-morning the cattle were in place and ready to move. True to his word, Lieutenant Springer — Lieutenant Dennis Springer is how he had reintroduced himself when he stopped by to say hello and have the doctor check Todd's condition — stayed with them as far as Silver Creek. He watched them cross, then gave a farewell salute as his patrol turned south to resume the search for the renegades he was chasing.

The warming rays of the afternoon sun had a healing effect on Todd, as did that morning's breakfast. Subconsciously he reached up to feel the damaged locket, which had saved his life.

The remainder of the trip was uneventful. They reached Portland the morning of the following day.

The first thing Todd wanted was a bath; the second, one of Mrs. Blevins' meals. The thought of these pleasures was replaced, however, by the need to know if Captain Geyer had had any more trouble, and if the *Lucille* was still afloat.

CHAPTER

12

Leaving Darrel Vaughn and the crew to watch the cattle, Todd rode into the main business district of Portland and cantered slowly down Alder Street.

The rain had started again: gentle, moisture-laden drops that made large splashes in the puddles and created swollen rivulets that sought out the wagon-size lakes of water that never seemed to dry up. Knowing that a horse or man could sink to their knees in these mud holes, Todd skirted each one carefully, letting his horse make its own way.

At Front Street Todd swung left, toward where the *Lucille* was berthed. As he turned the corner at De Pue's warehouse he breathed a sigh of relief. There she was, floating peacefully at anchor. The reason soon became apparent. Two armed guards were patrolling dockside, and another could be seen on her stern deck.

Not wanting to alarm the watch, Todd hailed them. "Ahoy. Is the captain about? If so would you tell him Todd Howard would like to see him?"

Captain Phillip Geyer, who must have been watching the approach of this mud-caked, unshaven rider, immediately stepped into view on the foredeck, a shotgun cradled in his arms.

"Todd lad?" Geyer shouted down. "You look a mite worse for wear than the last time I saw you." Springing down the gangplank, Geyer hurried to meet his partner, who was now trotting past the posted sentries.

"You're a sight for sore. . ." the captain stopped as Todd stiffly dismounted, his alert gaze spotting Todd's bloody clothing and bandages. ". . .eyes," he finished lamely.

Todd was still weak from loss of blood and this showed in the pallor of his face, the drawn, tight lines around his mouth and the heavy dark half-circles under his eyes.

Squinting slightly Geyer said, "I gather the trip wasn't exactly an easy one?"

"Yes, you could say that."

"Come aboard. I have some remedy in my cabin that might put some color back in your cheeks." Turning to the nearest guard he said, "Bert, keep an eye on Todd's horse. But not both eyes."

As if in explanation he said, "They tried again. This time by causing a diversion at the Crow's Nest." He indicated a seaman's saloon a half block down the street. "Started a fight, during which a lantern was knocked off the post into a barrel of saloon sweepings. Made a lot of smoke but nothing that couldn't be put out easily. You know how people feel about fire around here. Guess they figured in all the excitement we wouldn't be watching our backside. Two swabs tried to climb aboard. When their heads poked over the rail, we busted them with a couple of belaying pins. We belayed them, all right," he said, chortling over his own joke. "One's wearing a roll of bandages big as a turban. The other still can't remember his name."

Sitting at the table in the captain's cabin, Todd finished the drink which had been had poured for him. Feeling its effect, he waved aside the bottle as the captain started to refill his glass. "One's enough for me. Another and I'd sleep for a week."

"Tell me about it, Todd. From the beginning."

Todd related the journey in detail: where they met the drive, Vaughn's discovery they were being followed, the attempt to take the cattle, Lieutenant Springer's intervention

97

and the uneventful last two days en route to Portland.

Geyer had been leaning forward, arms on the table, fingers interlocked, as Todd reviewed these events. He had not moved. Now he leaned back. "Can we load today, or will they need to graze a day or two?"

"Darrel seems to think they're in good shape. Plenty of grass on the way up. They weren't pushed too hard and winter pasturage was good. As long as there's hay for them on board there should be no problem."

Geyer slapped his hand on the table, palm down. "Then let's get to it. We've nothing to gain by waiting any longer. The water's high and fast, but if *Lucy* can make it from here to San Francisco, getting to the Cascades should be no problem. I'll leave before dark."

Eyeing Todd, who had visibly slumped due to the effects of the whiskey and his physical condition, he said, "We'll take care of the cattle. Get Mrs. Blevins to fix you a hot bath and soak out some of those aches. She's also got her own brand of liniment that could turn a lame horse into a trotter."

Todd didn't argue, but nodded his head weakly in agreement. He knew the best remedy would be what the captain had suggested.

Mrs. Blevins knew Todd was in town; one of her boarders had seen him and had told her. Knowing that he would be by soon and how much he liked sweets, she had set about fixing one of his favorites and her specialty — mince pie. Going to the wood stove, she opened the oven door, stepped back a moment to get out of the way of the escaping heat and placed the rich pie inside.

As the front door slammed and Todd's voice called out, "Mrs. Blevins!" she wiped her hands on her apron and hurried to greet him, intending to give him one of her bone-crushing, motherly hugs. She had missed him more than she realized.

When she parted the alcove curtains and stepped into the hall, she stood in shocked silence, looking at the figure before her.

"What in the world?" she finally managed to say. Then she grabbed his arm and marched him upstairs to his room. "You get those filthy clothes off, what's left of them, and I'll fix you a hot tub."

Seeing that he was having difficulty removing his shirt, she moved in to help. Spotting the bloody bandages for the first time, she gasped aloud. "Now you sit still. I'll get the water heated, then I'll send for Doctor Atkinson. This compress has to be changed and whatever is under it looked at." She hurried out of the room.

Todd let out a long sigh as he sat on the edge of the squeaky, coil-spring bed. Although he was pleased with the attention he was getting from Mrs. Blevins, and happy to have her take charge, he resented the fact that he was being treated like a youngster.

What Todd didn't realize was that he was going through the stage every young man reaches as he approaches manhood: the conflict between boyhood's need for family dependency and the desire for independence that is the prerogative of being an adult. A line that is never definitely drawn, but a separation that occurs gradually — sometimes too slowly for the impatience of youth.

In Todd's case the feeling of irritation passed as he realized how grateful he was to have someone care enough to worry about him.

The hot water arrived as Todd finished undressing. He gingerly seated himself in the galvanized tub and began to relax as the near scalding water sought out and released the aches in his tired muscles. Mrs. Blevins made periodic trips to dump a fresh kettle of boiling water in the tub, causing momentary discomfort for Todd until the hot water circulated with the water that had already cooled.

As he scrubbed himself with strong homemade lye soap, he could feel the tension drain away. Then, hearing the doctor at the door, he rose from the tub and toweled himself dry. At a knock, he wrapped the towel around his waist and called out, "Come in."

Dr. Atkinson entered and gave a brusque nod, appraising his patient as he did: a well-developed boy who would be even broader of shoulder and larger in build in a few years. Six feet give or take an inch, with an open, trusting face. Medium-boned, he would hold his age well. A natural smile, which means an easy disposition. Concluding his analysis, he guessed whatever happened was not of Todd's own choosing. Putting out his hand he introduced himself, reassured in his judgement by Todd's firm handshake and level gaze.

As Dr. Atkinson put his bag on the nearby table and opened it, Todd made his own analysis of the doctor. Near sixty. Frail but not fragile. Slightly stooped, probably due to his line of work. And a manner that immediately put him at ease. Dr. Atkinson's grey hair and mustache were neatly trimmed and his hands were clean — as was the back of his neck, Todd noticed, as the physician bent over his bag.

After removing Todd's bandage, the medical man cleaned around the area of the wound with some disinfectant that made Todd gasp and his eyes water.

"Strong stuff," said the doctor. "Made by a local moonshiner. Some people even have the courage to drink it."

Peering closely at the wound and probing gently with his fingers, he added, "Whoever dressed this did a first-class job. Couldn't have done better myself." Half talking to Todd and half to himself, the doctor made another observation. "Can't take any stitches as too much hide has been scraped off. The skin is healing nicely, but you'll have a scar. Can't see any infection." Looking questioningly at Todd he asked, "Any fever? Do you ramble in your sleep?"

"Hurts pretty bad every once in a while, but that's all."

"Numbness in your arm, or pain in your fingers?"

"None."

"Good. It's natural for a wound like this to hurt. As a matter of fact that's a good sign. Pretty soon it will start itching. That's another good sign. But don't scratch it or you'll start an infection. Best I can do is put a clean bandage on. Then see me in two or three days."

"I can't do that," Todd replied. "I'll be leaving first thing in the morning."

"In that case have it looked at by another doctor as soon as you can. The main thing is to keep it clean. If the bandage works off, pour a little whiskey on it every day or so. If you don't have whiskey, horse liniment will do.

"You've also obviously lost a good bit of blood. Try to get as much rest as possible and don't overdo."

Seeing the answer in Todd's eyes, he turned to put his instruments back in his case. "Seems everybody wants a doctor's advice when they're hurting, but as soon as they get to feeling better they don't take it." Pausing at the door, he looked back. "My charge is two dollars. You can leave it with Mrs. Blevins."

While the doctor had been attending Todd, Mrs. Blevins had been seeing to dinner. Sticking her head inside the door she said, "I've fixed a special place for you at the kitchen table. It's ready when you are."

Todd dressed quickly and hurried downstairs. Mrs. Blevins had outdone herself: Three meat courses — venison, pork and mutton; mashed potatoes and flour gravy; creamed corn; fresh-baked bread; turnips; spiced peaches, and two jars of preserves — gooseberry and apple — were spread out before his plate. "Save some room for dessert," she said, placing the aromatic mince pie on a hot mat near the center of the table.

Todd was famished and ate ravenously. Mrs. Blevins stood by, her large, plump arms folded together, a wide, satisfied smile on her face. His appetite was her reward.

Pushing himself back from the table, Todd looked up. "I couldn't eat another bite. That was magnificent, Mrs. Blevins. I don't know how to thank you for your kindness."

"Just take care of yourself, that's how," Mrs. Blevins responded. Then putting the fingers of her right right hand to her cheek, she looked momentarily shocked. "Mercy," she exclaimed. "I completely forgot. Two letters came while you were gone."

The mail was from home. One from Tess and the other from Ann. He opened the letter from Tess first. Reading through it quickly he found that everyone was well so he re-read it a second time, more slowly.

They had received his note and were thrilled he had found, and taken advantage of, an opportunity so soon. Mr. Fields was in full agreement with what he had done and offered the opinion that Todd might want to look into the logging industry as prices for lumber were rocketing sky-high in California.

The family was now in their Pacific Avenue house. Two pages were devoted to it and their new neighbors. Heavy construction work was underway in their old neighborhood, and industry was moving in. Once more Jamie's instincts and foresight had proven right.

Katy was still seeing Jim Weatherspoon, who now had "quite a substantial job with Wells Fargo," as Tess put it. The rest of the letter was filled with news about the growth of San Francisco and about friends he knew. Tess ended by pleading with him to write more often. They all wanted to know what he was doing, what Portland was like, and how the new company was coming along. They missed him and sent their love.

Slipping the engraved stationery back into its envelope, he excused himself from the table. He wanted to read Ann's letter in the privacy of his room.

"Dearest Todd," it began.

I know you will think this foolish of me, but I have had the strangest premonitions about you lately. I have not mentioned this to mother or father as I did not want them to worry. As soon as you get this note, please write and tell me that you are all right. I know you may think me silly, but please humor me. *Please!*

I also realize how juvenile my behavior was before you left, and I would like to apologize for it. What I told you then is still true, however. My feelings have not changed. It is important to me that you know this. I miss you terribly and wish you were here with us.

It ended, "All of my love," and was signed, "Ann."

Todd replied immediately to both letters. He assured Ann that he was fine and her worries had been groundless. In neither letter did he mention the incidents involving the *Lucille*, the attack on the herd or his being wounded. He also told Ann that he carried her locket, but he did not tell her what had happened to it or that it had saved his life; only that it had brought him good luck and that he would continue to carry it.

He explained that he would be entering newly-explored areas of Oregon in a few weeks and they might not be hearing from him for awhile, but not to worry. He would be getting word to them as soon as he could. All mail should still come to Mrs. Blevins until he sent them his new address.

Realizing he would be gone for some time, he bought a number of presents for them that afternoon. With the packages, he added a joking note that they would have to celebrate their birthdays, Christmas and the Fields' anniversary all at the same time as the post offices in Eastern Oregon would be few and far between.

For Ann he selected a special cameo necklace. The ivory profile on its mauve background even looked like her, he thought.

It was dusk before Todd returned to the *Lucille*. The cattle had been loaded and Captain Geyer was anxious to be off.

"Thought I might have to leave without saying goodbye to you, lad. The sooner I have these pitiful creatures in the middle of the Columbia River, the happier I'll be. I must say," he said, looking Todd up and down, "you look a sight better."

"Captain Geyer," Todd said seriously, "getting from here to the Columbia is one thing, getting through to The Dalles is another. You know the Oregon Steamship Company will be waiting for you. We both know they have their men stationed along the river to turn back any competition."

"Lad, you underestimate your seafaring partner. We'll get through. The cattle will meet you where we agreed. I've a few tricks up my sleeve, and if it's necessary to play them, I will."

Looking at his pocket watch, Geyer ended the conversation. "Unless you're planning to go upriver with us, I suggest you abandon ship. We'll be casting off in exactly one minute."

Todd, Darrel Vaughn, Shorty Hansen and Reub Hassler stood on the dock watching the departing steamer.

"Sure hope he makes it," said Reub.

"If anyone can, he can," replied Todd.

Knowing these three men had been on the trail for weeks without the opportunity to clean up or relax, Todd slapped Darrel on the back.

"Let's stay over for the night. It will give you a chance to get sheared, have a bath and eat a square meal. Just be ready to leave at first light. I don't care what condition you're in, as long as you can ride. And don't forget Tom's advice. We want no one crippled up or killed by the OSC bunch. I'm not saying don't unwind, but do your drinking in a place that has a front and back door. If they come in one, you go out the other."

"Don't worry, boss," said Darrel. "I'm not much for taking on a load of firewater. I'll keep an eye on these two mavericks. We'll see you at the corral first thing in the morning."

True to his word, Darrel and the two riders arrived as Todd was adjusting the cinch on his saddle. His horse, hoping to spend another day eating grain and loafing at the livery stable, wasn't cooperating. He had sucked in enough air to bloat his stomach, making it impossible for Todd to tighten the strap. Irritated that the horse thought him enough of a tenderfoot to get away with this trick, Todd kicked him sharply in the ribs with his boot. As the horse expelled air, Todd jerked the latigo and secured the cinch tightly.

"Looks like old Jerry," Darrel commented, indicating Todd's horse, "is ten minutes short of work this morning."

"Can't say as I blame him. Felt the same way when I got up," Todd answered. Looking at Darrel's companions he said, "Looks like that goes for Shorty and Reub, too."

A broad grin split Darrel's face. "Told them they couldn't drink the town dry, but they wouldn't listen." Raising his voice he said, "We may have to tie 'em to their saddles. Otherwise they might slip upside down and not know the rocks were hitting their heads." Getting no response, he added a little louder, "They sure missed a good breakfast. Greasy bacon, just the way I like it. Eggs fried in lots of lard and a juicy steak rimmed with a thick slab of fat."

Turning a shade whiter, Shorty and Reub silently saddled their horses, mounted, and started out of the stable. Darrel, laughing out loud, trailed behind.

Pausing just long enough to put a bottle of liniment Mrs. Blevins had given him into his saddlebag, Todd settled on his own horse, now resigned to its fate, and joined them.

Their return route retraced the one he had taken before with Tom Pickett. Talk ceased as they worked along the banks of the Willamette River, its roaring waters drowning out all other sound.

Swollen by hundreds of rain-fed tributaries, the great river of the Willamette Valley frothed and tumbled as it raced north to its destiny with the Columbia.

Full-grown trees, logs and other forest debris swept by. Todd thought of the problems these obstacles must present to the navigators of the steamships that carried passengers upstream to New Albany and other ports farther south.

As they rode west out of the dense undergrowth and brush that crowded the trail, they entered a flat, green meadow carpeted with buttercups and field daisies. Todd stopped to better see the country on his left. The brief morning shower had cleared, and only a few scattered cloud puffs remained in the sky. There was nothing to obscure the magnificent sight before him. Giant, snow-laden Mount Hood, its grandeur illuminated by a pastel blue background, loomed over the horizon. Its base was a foundation of vivid blue-green and deep black forests.

"Like a picture, ain't it?" commented Darrel Vaughn, who had ridden up.

"Even prettier," answered Todd.

"Named after a commander of the British Navy who fought us in the American Revolution. Kind of ironic when you stop and think about it. It was named for an Englishman who fought us. Yet the road at its base — Barlow Pass, that runs from The Dalles to the Willamette Valley — opened up this territory, which was English, and let in enough Americans to take this country away from the British, peaceful-like, without a fight."

Chortling at the thought, Darrel Vaughn offered one more comment. "Some Indian tribes call the mountain Wy'east. Other tribes call it Tum Tum. Both roughly translated mean 'sacred place of falling waters.'"

Leaving the meadow, they cut sharply into the foothills. At midday they stopped to eat the cold lunch Mrs. Blevins had prepared for them.

As they ate, a camp robber flew down and arrogantly strutted before them. Reub Hassler threw out a piece of crust. The bird quickly grabbed it and flew away. The saucy jay was immediately replaced by several squawking companions who were indignant that they had been discriminated against.

Todd leaned back against the trunk of a young fir, completely at ease. The tranquil surroundings erased all memories of the violent battle that had taken place just a few days before. It was only when he rolled on his side to throw some food of his own to the raucous group of birds that a piercing pain in his side reminded him. He carefully rolled on his back and cradled his head in his hands.

As he gazed at the azure sky, ringed with gently swaying tops of stately fir, he wondered what it was in the nature of man that made him constantly run from pillar to post, seeking greener pastures over the next hill, when if he just stopped long enough to look around he would realize he was where he wanted to be all along.

Darrel gently kicked the sole of his boot. "Suppose we should be saddling up if we're going to meet Tom tomorrow."

Reluctantly Todd got to his feet and moved to his horse. He wished this feeling of contentment could last forever, but he realized this was not life's way. Such moments quickly pass and have to be held and treasured for the brief time they exist.

CHAPTER

13

As the *Lucille* churned out of Portland's busy harbor, Captain Geyer hurried to the chart room and spread out his maps.

Lost in thought, he plotted their course: We probably won't hit trouble until we pass old Fort Vancouver, he surmised. The most likely place for the OSC to try and stop us would be near the Sandy River where they cut their firewood. Another might be beyond the Sandy, just below the Cascades. He marked each of these locations.

Staring ahead at the swollen river, Geyer mentally reviewed his options. First, instead of making one stop for fuel between old Fort Vancouver and the Sandy, he would make two, giving them enough wood to pass well beyond the OSC's fueling station. His two four-pounder cannons could keep a single ship at bay, but wouldn't be able to meet the challenge of two or more.

To get through a blockade, the captain had made other arrangements. The reason for his trip to Fort Astoria was to get not only the cannons but also materials he needed to build what he referred to as his "contraption." These were stored in the crates he had so carefully lashed to the main deck.

He had even considered the possibility of the OSC unleashing log rafts against them. In anticipation of this problem, the *Lucille's* hull was reinforced with two-inch thick iron plate. Henry Tines helped him work this out. They even added an extra serrated strip of heavy metal to the bow which was capable of withstanding a severe impact should Geyer be forced to ram another vessel.

Satisfied that all was in order, he made his rounds. They were nearing the Columbia River, and the cautious captain wanted to spend the night in the protected waters of the old Hudson's Bay fort.

After berthing, he paid a visit to the town of Vancouver. Shortly before midnight he returned, carrying the news of two locations on the Washington Territory side where they could find burnable pine.

By late morning the *Lucille* arrived at the first site. Scouts were placed a quarter mile downstream and a half mile upstream. They were to sound the alarm if they caught sight of any Oregon Steamship Company vessel not on its regular passenger run. Geyer assigned perimeter guards to protect the woodcutters from the possibility of an Indian attack, designating his stoutest men for the job of cutting and loading. While the others were going ashore, he asked four men to stay and open the containers he had been so secretive about.

When the contents were arranged neatly on deck, he supervised their assembly.

The ship's carpenter, who was involved in this process, took off his black knit watch cap, scratched the top of his scalp with blunt, cracked fingernails and asked, "What in tarnation is it, Cap'n? Looks like a derrick of some sort."

"It's kind of like a derrick," Geyer said. "It's a trebuchet. A medieval device that hurls missiles. Now let's see if it works. Roll one of those barrels over here and crack it open. We'll give it a try."

Open-mouthed, the crew watched in amazement as the sling hurled four-pound canonballs a hundred yards into the river. "Well I'll be keel-hauled. If that ain't the darndest thing I ever saw," said one crewman. The others were too

109

dumbfounded to even comment; their jaws had dropped and their mouths gaped open.

Well satisfied, Geyer had the propulsion covered with canvas and secured.

Estimating it would take another thirty to forty-five minutes to finish loading the wood piled on the bank, Geyer gave one pull on the whistle cord. This signaled the scouts and perimeter guards to drop back half their distance. As the last cord was being brought up, he gave two brief toots to signify they should return to the ship. When everyone was aboard, the *Lucille* slowly pulled into the rushing waters of the Columbia.

As dusk approached, the captain spotted an idle stretch of back water, sheltered by a spit of land that provided easy access to the mainstream.

"We'll anchor here for the night," he told his helmsman. "Cleary," he said, facing his mate who was standing nearby. "Double the guards. I want them checked every hour. If you find anyone asleep, throw him overboard and let him swim home."

If Cleary caught anyone dozing, he would do just that. The life of every man aboard depended on the alertness of the night watch. To be sure, he would make the rounds himself. And vary the routine so they wouldn't know when to expect him.

Next morning, mist surrounded the steamer, and delicate fingers of fog spread along the river bank that led to the inlet in which the *Lucille* rested.

The captain turned up the collar of his heavy seaman's coat and filled his chest with air, his breath fogging as he exhaled. This was his favorite time of day. Looking along the shoreline, his gaze stopped at a group of beavers busily gnawing the trunks of a stand of aspen. One tree fell with a small cracking sound, followed by a splash as it hit the water. Farther to the left a four-point buck, his horns still in velvet, cautiously approached the shore. Tiptoeing along he looked left, then right, occasionally twitching an ear or flicking his tail nervously. Assured there was no danger, he lowered his head and drank.

Suddenly his head came up sharply. He looked to his right, then bounded left into the dense woods. Captain Geyer could hear the delayed thump, thump, thump as he ran through the forest. Looking to the left of where the deer had been drinking, Geyer saw a flight of ducks coming in low for a landing; their brilliant green and blue plumage flashed in the morning rays of the sun, which was just now starting to burn away the ghost-like mist.

Not wanting to disturb the peaceful setting any more than necessary, he whispered huskily to the bosun standing nearby, "Never mind the whistle. Alert the crew by verbal command to move out." Holding the man's sleeve momentarily, he added, "As quietly as possible."

"Yes, sir," said the boatswain softly, hurrying off to spread the word. His hushed orders broke the silence, causing the energetic beavers to slap their tails in warning as they dived into the protection of the chilly water.

No matter how hard we try not to, the captain thought, one way or another the human race seems to foul up most everything it comes in contact with.

The *Lucille* eased into the flood-swollen Columbia and proceeded slowly upstream, its crew on the lookout for obstacles in the swiftly flowing current and for tell-tale signs of smoke that would signify the approach of an OSC steamer.

With the exception of two or three near misses by full-sized trees that had been uprooted and forced into the river by earth-tearing spring floods, the day went without mishap.

"Cyrus," Geyer addressed the messboy who had just brought him a mug of coffee, "ask Mr. Cleary to see me as soon as it is convenient for him to do so."

Within minutes Ryan Cleary came through the door of the wheel house. He touched the brim of his cap with two fingers. "Sir?"

"Cleary, in a few hours we'll be nearing the mouth of the Sandy. Before we get there we'll stock up on wood again.

And," he added, "take out a little insurance. Pick three of your best men. Include yourself. I want top hands, as we have a tough job to do that will keep us busy most of the night."

Pointing to the map before him, Geyer continued. "We'll pull ashore here. The OSC stops there, and this is the route the five of us will take." He cocked his head. "Bring Ben Long. He knows the area. Even though we'll have a full moon, it's easy country to get lost in."

Ryan Cleary nodded his understanding and turned to go, but was stopped by Geyer's voice. "We'll take that jenny palomino mule we have aboard, too. Have one of the cowhands rig up a pack that can hold two ninety-pound boxes. We'll also need three inch-and-a-half wood augers, a bucket of sealing tar and a gunny sack."

That afternoon the *Lucille* dropped anchor and the crew went about their task of replenishing the fuel supply.

As soon as it was dark Geyer, Ryan Cleary, Ben Long and two other seamen Cleary had picked — Percy Gelwick and Abe Tatum — met by the gangplank.

"Here's the plan," said Geyer, filling them in on the parts they each were to play. When Geyer finished, Ben Long whistled softly and the four exchanged glances of admiration.

"Remember," the captain cautioned, "success depends on our not being discovered. If you have any questions ask them now. I want no unnecessary talking or whispering from the time we leave until we get back."

He received acknowledgment from each man, indicating they understood.

"Ben, you lead off with the mule. Keep her at a slow pace. The drag rope will be attached to her packsaddle, and we can all hold on to that. If anyone has a problem on the way or if you hear anything, give two owl hoots and we'll stop."

As Captain Geyer had guessed, the full moon was of little advantage in the dark recesses of the broken ravines that cut through the foothills rising from the river. The damp undergrowth covered the sound of their footsteps and softened

112

the occasional stumble or fall made by one of the procession. Despite Geyer's admonition about talking, a soft grunt or occasional muffled curse could be heard as first one, then another of the group cracked a shinbone against an unseen sharp obstacle.

It was after midnight when they reached the Oregon Steamship Company's landing. Two stern-wheelers were berthed at the loading docks. There was no one about. Geyer had to know whether the steamers already had their load of wood aboard or were waiting to be loaded in the morning. He sent Percy Gelwick, the youngest of the four, to find out. Gelwick glided from cover to cover and agilely swung aboard the first vessel. A few minutes later Geyer saw his shadow as he crossed to the other ship.

Within twenty minutes Gelwick returned with his report. "They're about half loaded, Captain. No guards on either of the boats or on the wood pile."

"That means they'll finish loading shortly after dawn and will be on the Columbia right after that. We won't be able to slip by. Drill your holes at the top of the pile. They'll put that wood on first."

Each man had his assignment and went to work. In two hours they met again.

"Did you spread the shavings and smear mud on the tar spots?" Geyer whispered. Seeing affirmative nods, he motioned for his men to move out.

At dawn's first glow they were back aboard the *Lucille*, exhausted from their night's work. The rest of the crew wanted to know where they had gone, but Geyer ignored their questions and gave orders to get underway.

"This is the first round," he said to Cleary. "With luck we might make it. Take the long poles and push *Lucy* away from the bank."

Swinging into the choppy water, the *Lucille* shuddered as she hit the main current, pausing slightly while the paddles fought to gain a hold. As they reached the center of the Columbia, Captain Geyer noticed two columns of black

113

smoke rising above the trees around the bend ahead. "If we can see their smoke, they can see ours. Three-quarters speed," he shouted into the speaking tube. "Get those four-pounders loaded and ready for action!" he yelled to the men below. "And stand by the catapult!"

As the *Lucille* rounded the turn, he saw that the two steamships had positioned themselves so he could not get by. The OSC had picked their defensive position well.

"No other choice," he told Cleary. "If last night's efforts don't work, the only alternative we have is to try and bull our way through." Pulling the whistle lanyard, the captain gave a series of long blasts, a request to the other ships to part and let him by. Geyer signaled for full speed. Only two hundred yards separated the *Lucille* from the other boats when the boiler of the vessel on their port side blew up in a ball of orange flame. Without power it drifted aimlessly downstream. Carried by the current, it soon ran aground in the boulder-strewn rapids, steam hissing from its ruptured engines.

"One down," muttered Geyer. "Let's hope they didn't put all of the wood on that one ship. But if they did, at least the odds are even."

No sooner had these words left his mouth than an explosion rocked the second steamer. The blast dislocated its large stern wheel. Caught sideways in the river's turbulence, the steamboat rocked crazily and revolved 180 degrees, coming to rest backwards in the shallows.

"God Almighty, Captain," said Jerry Flowers, who was in charge of the cattle and was watching the action from the pilothouse, "What happened?"

"Seems like someone must have put dynamite in their firewood," said the captain, giving a series of jaunty toots on the *Lucille's* whistle as she passed the wreckage and churned upstream.

Geyer felt the odds were with him that news of his victory wouldn't reach the Cascades portage before he got

114

there, so the element of surprise would be on his side if he encountered any more OSC ships.

Because of their heavy load, they stopped again that afternoon to resupply the voracious appetite of the boilers. At this stop, he learned from a nearby settler that a rider had been dispatched from the Sandy to warn the OSC of his coming. Cursing under his breath, Geyer knew they were in for trouble. And he knew for certain where it would be: the location he had marked below Cascade Landing.

With his advantage of surprise now gone, the OSC had time to prepare. He was certain they would lie in wait for him just below the only stretch of navigable water where he had room to maneuver. If so they would have him boxed in, without a chance to defend himself to his best advantage.

For two hours he sat pondering the problem. Should he turn back? He had the lives of his men and the cowhands to think of. On the other hand, not getting the cattle through would be a crippling blow to the Columbia Cattle Company. Should he consult his crew and the cattlemen and take a vote? No, he decided, it's my choice, and I'll rise or fall on the consequences. Was it foolish to forge on, knowing full well the risk he was taking? It certainly would be no disgrace to return to Portland. No man alive could accuse him of cowardice, knowing the odds he faced. The turmoil in his mind was making his head ache.

"Dammit!" he shouted aloud, slapping the table with the flat of his hand, "I promised Todd and Tom the herd would meet them, and by God it will. Or we'll all go to hell in the trying."

His mind made up, Captain Geyer was himself once more: Confident, decisive and ready for action. Win, lose or draw, he would give it his best shot.

"Cleary!" he bellowed. "Full ahead. We're going on to the Cascades."

A bustle of activity followed his command, and again they swung into the raging mainstream of the Columbia River, the water curling from the bow in angry waves. The *Lucille*

115

responded as if she fully agreed with the decision to proceed.

If all went well, Geyer calculated they would reach the first stretch of rapids early the next day. That afternoon, now having been awake for thirty-six hours, he turned the ship over to Ryan Cleary and retired to his cabin. Tomorrow would be a big day, and he needed a good night's sleep.

Captain Geyer rose before dawn, completely refreshed. No doubt or indecision nagged him. His mind was totally absorbed with the task ahead. Resuming command from his first mate, Geyer told him to catch a few winks of sleep and report back at two bells. By dawn's light the *Lucille* was cautiously easing its way upstream.

There was little wind, and the *Lucille* strained eagerly against the mud-darkened river. Geyer watched an eagle soaring high in the sky. It dipped gracefully as if offering a salute. Patting the rail, he lovingly spoke to his ship. "Old girl, if we make it through this I'm going to rename you the *Heroic Lucille.*"

Promptly at 9:00 Ryan Cleary appeared on deck, freshly dressed and clean shaven. Glancing sideways at him, Geyer was secretly pleased by the care that Cleary had taken with his appearance, knowing a full-scale battle was ahead. Addressing his mate he said, "We should be there in the next few minutes. I doubt if the catapult will be of much use to us now. Keep it lashed down. Order the gunners to their posts, and break out the rifles. Our only chance is to. . ." He stopped in mid-sentence, stunned by the sight before him. For seconds he was immobilized with the impact of what his eyes saw but his brain told him couldn't be true. He rubbed his eyes in disbelief.

"By the gods, I don't believe it," he shouted, and uncharacteristic of his usual reserve, hugged Cleary. "The messenger must not have gotten through. We've caught them flat-footed!"

What he saw were four OSC steamers, three sternwheelers and a side-wheeler, all unprepared for the appearance of the *Lucille.* One was midstream and had just pulled away from the bank. Two were still loading wood, and a fourth was at anchor.

"Revise those orders, mate," he told Cleary, eyes flashing. "Unlash our contraption. Looks like we'll have room to use it after all."

As he gave these instructions, Geyer saw a flurry of activity taking place on board the four vessels. The side-wheeler was the one at anchor, and her boiler had not as yet been stoked. Now there was frantic activity to do so. The two boats that had been taking aboard fuel had cast off their docking lines. One was swinging into the main stream, and the other was struggling to hold its position against the rushing current.

Quickly sizing up the situation, Geyer realized the steamboat that had finished refueling was turning to face them too soon. Its boilers had not yet reached full capacity, and the paddle wheels were rotating at half-speed. He growled at his wheelman, "Hold your course, and when I give the word, turn us starboard as fast as you can."

The wheelman spread his legs for maximum balance and gripped the spoke handles. Sweat appeared on his forehead and stained his shirt as he saw the OSC ship, only forty yards away, coming toward the *Lucille* on the full force of the current.

"Now!" shouted Geyer, as the rival steamboat filled their cockpit window. A grinding crash followed as the reinforced prow of the *Lucille* neatly sliced into and through the paddle wheel of the other ship. Had the moment of impact been a few seconds earlier, both ships would have split apart and sunk; a second or two later and they would have missed each other completely, allowing the OSC vessel to regain control and attack from the rear.

"Check for damage!" Geyer shouted as he ran out of the wheelhouse to see the consequences of the collision. Looking beyond his stern, he saw his opponent floating helplessly downstream, its paddle wheel following in its wake.

Cleary reported back, out of breath and with a smile that spread from ear to ear. "No damage, sir."

The power of the impact had slowed them down, and it took the *Lucille* a few minutes to regain speed. During that time, the second of the two remaining stern-wheelers joined the one maneuvering to block their passage upstream.

Seeing this, Captain Geyer pounded his fist on an open palm. "Perfect," he said. "Perfect. Just what I hoped they'd do.

"Hold steady a hundred yards below them, Cleary, and we'll see if our rig does as well in combat as she did in practice. That's the *Andrew C* on the left and the *Morning Star* on her port side. Work on the *Andrew C* first. If we can knock her out, she should founder on the rocks."

The huge sling was readied and loaded, and the arm was released. The object it hurled sent up a visible splash twenty yards to the right of the *Andrew C.*

Meanwhile the crews aboard the opposing vessels had positioned themselves, and pinponts of fire could be seen from their small deck cannon.

The second missile was launched from the *Lucille.* It fell directly in front of their target, but several yards short.

"Get the range, men," Geyer shouted, "get the range."

The third ball landed directly amidship, and the fourth ball, launched only moments later, hit the smoke stack of the *Andrew C.* Air surged into the depths of the boilers, causing a massive draft that sent a mountain of flame and a shower of sparks into the sky.

"One more for good measure, then turn on the *Star.*" The fifth ball hit a paddle and, as Geyer predicted, the *Andrew C* drifted into the rock-strewn rapids.

"She's closing in, Captain," said Ryan Cleary as the *Star* moved downstream. "She's bigger than we are. If they grapple us, they can fire down on us."

Screwing up his eyes, the captain answered grimly, "You're right. We have to stop her before she does. Get those smaller balls out. The ones wrapped in rags. Soak them good in coal oil, and get the pitch torches going. Put four on the seat of the catapult at a time and set it for short range. When they get within distance, light them up and fire. Then load and fire as fast as you can." Holding Cleary's glance with his own, he added grimly, "Don't let the crew get careless. A fire aboard could end us here and now."

As Cleary left, a four-pound ball crashed through the wheel house, shattering glass and leaving a gaping hole in the wall where it exited. Almost simultaneously another landed near the catapult.

"Move! Dammit men, move!" Geyer yelled. "If they get the contraption we're done." His last words were lost in a double boom of the *Star's* cannon as it raked the deck with shot.

"Smart," said Geyer to the helmsman. "They're alternating shot with balls. One barrage of shot to slow the crew's return fire and the second to sink us." The following rounds verified his thinking as heavy balls tore into the *Lucille* once more. "Turn to face them. We've got to protect the paddles."

Once more, shot riddled the deck and pilothouse. One small ball passed through the captain's coat below the right armpit and another shattered the wheelman's shoulder. Leaping to his aid Geyer said, "Go below and get patched up," pausing only long enough to add, "And send someone up in case they get me next."

Noting his companion's hesitation to leave his post, he implored softly, "Hurry, man. I can manage."

Standing in shards of broken glass and peering through the jagged panes that once were windows, he saw the huge bulk of the *Morning Star* bearing down on them. The *Lucille's* engines were straining at full speed. Geyer spun the wheel to the left and braced himself.

To Captain Geyer's complete surprise the *Star* gently scraped by. There was no violent impact, no shower of shot and shell, no cursing, yelling boarders.

Ryan Cleary burst through the door followed by a replacement for the helmsman who took over the wheel. "Come look, Captain," Cleary gasped, and left. Not knowing what to expect, the captain followed.

His first glance was to the *Star*. She was swinging to face the current, her paddle wheels slowly losing ground to the relentless river. Fires blazed from stem to stern, and it was easy to see she was finished. Captain Geyer next looked for the side-wheeler, expecting attack from the OSC's fourth ship. It had not moved and was still at dockside, a white sheet waving from her flagpole. Geyer then walked the circumference of the pilothouse deck, silently assessing the damage.

"Any casualties?"

"Two dead and four wounded, Captain. We were lucky."

"Yes, we were lucky," commented Captain Geyer, "but the two dead men and the wounded weren't." Arms extended, he leaned against the rail and wearily closed his eyes. After a few moments he opened them. "Are we in condition to continue, first mate?"

"Yes, sir. No structural damage. The engine is purring along, the paddle wheel is in good condition and the hull is sound. We'll have the *Lucille* shipshape in no time."

"Then let's move on upriver. We won't have any more trouble from here on in."

In the fading light of dusk, they berthed at Fort Cascades. By morning the cattle would be unloaded and on their way.

That night as he lay on his bunk, Captain Geyer knew he had a major decision to make: join the drive up the Deschutes to meet Todd and Tom, or return to Portland. He tossed and turned. There should be no more trouble from the OSC. The stretch of the Columbia from the Cascades to The Dalles was served by a number of independent vessels, and the high-handed tactics of the combine were looked upon with disfavor by most of the merchants at The Dalles as well as the farmers in the area. It was only the lower river — from Portland to the Cascades — and the upper river — from Celilo Falls to the Snake River — that the Oregon Steamship

Company arrogantly exercised its control.

Geyer had made arrangements for the herd to be transported to The Dalles on the *Western Alliance*, whose captain, John Tucker, he knew and respected. Captain Tucker was fair and dependable — a man who dealt as impartially with the OSC as he did with his customers. That's why Geyer had chosen Tucker. The OSC would leave him alone.

The exhausted captain stared at the ceiling. The trip up the Deschutes was a tempting challenge. However, it meant that he would have to leave *Lucy,* and that would be a difficult thing for him to do. Being a steamship captain was in his blood. His mind wandered to the history of steamboating on the Columbia.

River boats had pioneered the development of traffic from The Dalles to Portland, and later from The Dalles to the Snake River and beyond to the Lewiston and Montana gold fields. He had made the trip to Lewiston only once, but like most river navigators could recall each important strip of water as if it were yesterday: Bradford's Island, a landmark named after the man who built a trading post to offer supplies and lodging to the earliest settlers; Memaloose Island, where the Indians buried their dead on raised wooden platforms; and the middle river, where towering spires of basalt rock rose straight into the air, high enough to cast permanent shadows over the dark current. All of these memories flooded back.

Geyer's pulse quickened as he recalled the excitement of his first trip to The Dalles, which was then called Dalles City. On that journey a trapper had told him the city got its name from the French word "dalle," which meant flagstone, and referred to those stretches of water above and below the growing settlement where rapids flowed violently over flat surfaces of hard, stratified rock.

The Dalles was now second only to Portland in size and importance. At one time it was the only town in Wasco, the vast county east of the Cascade Range that covered two-thirds of the state, bounded by California to the south and the Washington and Idaho Territories to the north and east.

Until 1859, the year Oregon gained statehood, the entire area was shown on maps as unexplored. Up to that time it had been pierced only by mountain men, an occasional military patrol, a handful of foolhardy miners seeking gold or lost wagon trains that had strayed off the Oregon Trail.

Geyer recalled the recent stories he heard before leaving Portland: Settlers by the hundreds crowding the streets, all fighting to arrange passage for the continuing journey west. Many being forced to sell their stock because the Oregon Steamship Company was charging as much for cattle and freight as they were for human cargo. There's an opportunity in itself, Geyer realized. He could pick up more cattle at distressed prices to add to those he had brought up the Columbia.

Rolling on his side, Captain Geyer put all conscious attempts to make a decision out of his mind. He knew that when he woke in the morning he would have the answer.

Early the following day, Geyer leaned against the railing of the pilothouse and watched the scene of milling cattle and shouting riders below. Squaring his cap on his head, he straightened and went to seek out Jerry Flowers, the head drover.

Geyer greeted Flowers, then came straight to the point. "I've made my decision not to go with you. Tell Todd and Tom that my saddle is on the water and not on a four-legged beast. I think there's money to be made running supplies up and down the Willamette. That's where I'll be until it's time to bring up another load of cattle. Also tell them that whatever I set up will be a part of the Columbia Cattle Company."

Geyer then told Flowers his thought about picking up more cattle at The Dalles. "I'll write a draft that you can use to buy them. I'll also take a load of passengers back to Portland. That will more than make up the cost of the cattle, and pay for our expenses as well."

Ending the conversation, he made one request. "Jerry, do me a favor. Leave a clean ship. We'll be hauling people this time, women and children among them. Swamp out well and spread as much clean straw around as you can find. It'll also help cover the smell somewhat." With a tight grin he added, "Maybe I can find a group that isn't partial to baths. Then they won't be able to tell the difference."

By late morning both jobs had been accomplished. Geyer had his passengers, and Flowers was ready to move up the portage road to meet the *Western Alliance*. Geyer and Flowers met again, this time to say farewell.

"Good luck to you, Jerry. Give Tom and Todd my best. Tell them I'll name our next two steamships after them."

"Goodbye, and good luck to you too, Captain," Jerry Flowers responded. "I can't say it was a boring trip. Cattle droving is going to seem a mite tame after these last few days."

Thinking of the rough journey that faced the cowman, Geyer gripped his hand firmly and answered seriously, "I hope so, Jerry. I truly hope so."

CHAPTER

14

Three days after they left Portland, Todd, Darrel Vaughn, Shorty Hansen and Reub Hassler passed through Lebanon and joined Tom Pickett. As Todd dismounted stiffly, Tom hurried to greet him, a concerned look on his face.

"Understand you were hit hard on your way to Portland. A Lieutenant Springer passed through here last week, and noticing our brand sought me out to tell me what happened. Said you'd been shot. He also told me you more than evened the score." Casting a quizzical eye over Todd, Tom added, "You don't look too much the worse for wear."

"In good shape," grunted Todd, still feeling the effects of his wound and out of sorts because of the long ride.

Noting Todd's frame of mind, Tom said, "Come on over to the chuckwagon. A little hot coffee along with some beef and beans should hit the spot about now.

"Captain Geyer get off all right?" Tom continued as they kneeled before the fire.

"Sure did," said Todd, filling his partner in on the OSC's second attempt on the *Lucille*.

"Do you feel up to leaving in the morning, or would you like to rest up for a day or two?" Tom asked, noting that Todd was a little testy.

"I can rest on the way," Todd replied curtly.

"Morning it is then. About a quarter mile away we'll pick up the Santiam River. We're on the right side, so won't have to cross until we get on up aways. From there the going will get rough. By the look of the water I'd say the snow is melting fast. If we don't have another cold spell we should be able to push right on through. There'll be mud and probably some rain, but that won't stop us."

Reub, who had been listening to this conversation, asked, "Seen any more sign of Frank Allen's bunch?"

"There's been a two-legged coyote skulking around," Tom answered. "Thinks we don't know he's there. Far as we can tell there's only the one. That doesn't mean there might not be more of them back in the woods or on ahead of us somewhere." Pausing to scratch a week's growth of whiskers, he added, "We best stay alert."

"You think they'll try again?" asked Todd.

"Wouldn't be surprised. They're an ornery bunch of polecats. They could hit us anywhere along the trail. Before the pass, or after we've crossed. I've told the boys not to spread out too thin and to keep in sight of one another. Two shots signal trouble. Don't need to worry about a stampede as the cattle won't have anyplace to go. The trail's not wide enough for them to wander, and they can only move in two directions — forward or backward. Besides, as rough as the country is, they'll be too tuckered out to do too much running."

"And too fat to run, too, from the looks of them," Todd observed.

"They've been eating well, no doubt about it," Tom replied. "If we don't push them they'll be in good shape when we arrive. Should be plenty of grass all the way. Now let's turn in. Tomorrow's going to be a long one."

Next morning Todd awoke to the rattle of the cook's pans. He lay there enjoying the smoky smell of the newly-aroused campfire and the low bawling of the contented herd. Comforting sounds and smells that combined with the trilled notes of the meadowlark, who punctuated the stillness of the

125

morning air with his melodic tune.

A light rain had fallen during the night, putting its damp coat on the ground and the oil cloth slickers of the sleeping cowhands. Shaking his hat and setting it comfortably on his head, Todd threw aside his bedroll, surprised then pleased that the pain in his side had not given him any major resistance. Another day or so and I'll be back to normal, he reassured himself.

Knowing that Todd was more exhausted than he had let on, Tom deliberately delayed the morning's start to give him an extra hour's sleep. Seeing Todd's refreshed condition, he knew the delay had been worthwhile.

"What's your druthers this morning, Todd — herd or drag?"

"You're the boss."

"How about drag, then. The critters should be easy to handle. Give you a chance to better see the country. This is a beautiful part of the valley."

An hour out of camp, Todd saw what his companion meant. Gentle hills rose to become imposing, majestic mountains, then tapered again to form complex ridges that met the rushing Santiam.

The river was dotted with bears who were hard at work harvesting salmon swimming upstream to spawn. In shallow areas the coarse-haired mammals would grab the red-bellied fish with their massive snouts. Then, their victims hanging from both sides of their mouths, jerking convulsively, they would lumber back to shore to sit on their haunches and devour their feast. Or drop the fish among their cubs, who were anxiously awaiting breakfast.

In faster water others worked in teams. One would stand straddle legged, facing downstream, then in a blur of motion scoop out a salmon and throw it ashore, where it would be snatched up greedily by its mate.

Reining alongside Todd's horse, Art Seaforth, a cheery, ruddy-faced 3C drover remarked, "Brown and black bear. They won't bother us or the cattle as long as we leave their

126

cubs alone. It's the grizzlies we have to look out for. You'll be able to tell the difference. They're bigger and meaner. Particularly this time of year 'cause they've been hibernatin'. I've seen them charge a man for no good reason at all. Even a young'un can knock a horse over, so don't let 'em get too close. If one gets among the herd he can create havoc. They kill just for the pure pleasure of it.

"Where one of those critters," he said pointing to a bear in the stream, "only kill what they eat. They normally won't attack another animal unless they're starved or rabid. They prefer fish, berries and roots. Love huckleberries. But a grizzly ain't like that. He's a born killer. Sometimes you can smell 'em. Most likely your horse will pick up his scent first. If he starts acting nervous and gets fiddle-footed, get out your rifle. Be sure to keep it loaded. I've seen them come at a man so fast that he barely had time to cock the hammer." Nodding his head at Todd's holster, he said, "Pistol won't do much good unless you get in a lucky shot. Takes a heavier charge."

"Thanks for the advice, Art. Much chance of wolves attacking the herd?"

"Not likely. They'd be most apt to pick off a stray calf or lost cow. Sometimes if they get real hungry they'll pack together, bold as sin, and make a try. There's lots of small animals for them to eat now, as well as deer. The snow's all but gone and their pickin's should be good, so I doubt they'll give us any trouble.

"The only other animal that might be a bother," Seaforth went on, "is the cougar. If he takes it in his head to go after one of these cows, he'll do just that. They like to work at night, so we'll keep two fires going. If he's around he'll make himself known. They have a scream that sounds like a woman being skinned alive. It's enough to make the hair on the back of your neck stand straight up. Won't have to worry about rattlesnakes until it warms up." With that parting comment he raised his hand slightly in farewell and rode off to chase some strays.

A mile farther upstream, beyond where the bears were

feeding, a natural dam had formed which impeded the progress of the salmon. The silver-hued fish were franticaly throwing themselves at this obstacle in an effort to reach the water above. The ones who succeeded continued on. Those who failed kept trying until they died from exhaustion. Such was the nature of their instincts. Todd could see those too spent to continue weakly rolling on their sides, gasping for air. Eventually these would roll feebly on their backs and float downstream, another casualty of nature.

Too bad Mr. Bear couldn't think this one out, Todd thought. He could save himself a lot of trouble. But then maybe he likes his meal alive and kicking.

They left the river and pushed through an area covered with blackberry bushes. The vines grew in patches as long as forty to fifty feet, and so high Todd couldn't see over them. The berries had not yet ripened and showed as hard, green kernels. Bees covered the blossoms of those yet to form. Wrens, sparrows and chickadees were active among the brambles, as were brown rabbits who scurried for cover under the thorny briars, then sat upright to get a better look at what had frightened them.

Stopping his horse, Todd stood in the stirrups to stretch out the cramps in his legs. Tom, who had been riding fifty yards ahead, turned and rode back to him. Pulling alongside he whistled to Art Seaforth and waved him over. "Take our place for awhile, Art. I want to show Todd something." With that he spurred off. Todd followed.

They rode a good fifteen minutes in silence, then Tom dismounted at a small spring. Lying flat on his stomach, he drank from a pool whose sides and bottom had a coating of what looked like rusty iron. The spring bubbled out of the ground, filled the pool, then disappeared again into the earth through a small fissure.

"Try some of that," Tom said, wiping his mouth on the sleeve of his shirt.

"If you drank it I guess it's safe," said Todd, kneeling and wrinkling his nose. "It smells downright bad."

Looking at Tom dubiously, Todd cupped his hand, filled it with the liquid, and took a tentative sip.

After another drink he considered for a moment. "It's different. Can't say as I like it, but then can't say as I dislike it, either." Taking a final mouthful he added, "A little goes a long way."

"The settlers call this Soda Springs. I've heard they come as far away as a hundred miles to fill up their barrels and jugs. Some swear it will cure anything, but most use it as a spring tonic in place of sulphur and molasses. It's the minerals in the water that discolor the rock and cause the funny smell and taste. In any case, I've never known it to hurt anyone, and who knows — maybe it's good for you."

That night they camped in the pocket of a sway-backed ridge. It rained again. A harder rain. And colder. Returning to the fire after his late shift, Todd spread his hands to gain as much warmth as he could for his numbed fingers. He was chilled to the bone.

"It's goin' to get colder than this before we get to where we're goin', hoss," a voice came out of the darkness. It was Jeff Donnel.

Donnel, a heavy-boned man with craggy features and bushy eyebrows that covered alert, wide-set eyes, had been riding with Tom Pickett since the Columbia Cattle Company first started. A silent man by nature, he usually kept his thoughts to himself. This was one of the few occasions he had had any converstion with Todd; not because he didn't like Todd, as Todd knew, but because this was his way.

Donnel moved closer to the fire. "The higher it gets, the wuss it gets. I don't think these old mountains realize that spring has arrived."

Holding an enamel cup of hot coffee in both hands to warm them, Todd, shaking with cold, replied, "They say what gets worse eventually has to get better."

Nodding at this sage advice, Donnel grunted and spat a huge stream of tobacco juice into the flames, completely smothering one burning ember. "Couldn't sleep fer the cold.

129

Guess it must be my age creepin' up on me. Might as well roll my gear. It'll be gettin' light soon anyway."

Todd finished his coffee, wondering why it was that when it was near freezing, a metal cup would be too hot to put to your lips but the liquid itself would already be cold. Contemplating this strange law of physics, he went to rouse the cook.

Encouraged by one of the hands, the lead steer stepped out and the day's drive began.

Todd could see why the river they had followed was so high. Swollen tributaries and feeder creeks tumbled down steep mountain sides and cascaded around massive rocks to join its progress west. The roaring waters made conversation impossible. Wet foliage soaked their legs, and giant fern fronds slapped moisture onto the rest of their clothing. Dampness permeated the air like a clinging fog. Even when they were beyond the deafening noise of falling water, its trickle could be heard everywhere.

Todd noticed, too, that the sun seemed to spend less time in the sky. The canyon walls rose higher and the days grew shorter as they moved into the depths of the mountain range.

Art Seaforth returned with the news that they would have to ford the river soon if they were to keep on course.

Tom and Todd went on ahead to search for a crossing that would give both cattle and horses decent footing.

"Looks like as good a place as any," said Tom, choosing a spot below two huge rocks that appeared to be a shallower section of water. Playing out his lariat, Tom tied one end to his waist and handed the coil to Todd. "Wrap it around the cantle of your saddle, will you? Just in case I hit a hole. I can't swim." With these words he carefully walked his horse into the stream bed. Todd moved closer to the bank, feeding out rope as Tom needed it.

Without warning, Tom's horse stumbled into deep water, throwing its rider into the ice-cold stream. The horse pawed frantically to gain higher ground, lost its footing and swam wide-eyed to the opposite side where it clambered out. Reacting to Tom's plight, Todd quickly hauled in the rope. Tom was half dragged and half crawled out of the water. Trembling uncontrollably, Tom was already turning blue from the effects of his dunking. "G-g-g-get a f-f-f-fire st-st-st-started, f-f-for I f-f-f-freeze t-t-t-to d-d-d-death."

Todd quickly unlaced his bedroll. Putting it around Tom's shoulders, he took off Tom's wet hat and replaced it with his own dry one. Then he built a fire.

"D-d-d-damn," stuttered Tom as he hunched over the flames, trying to soak up their meager warmth, "I l-l-like m-my b-b-baths a l-little w-w-warmer th-th-than th-that."

Whistling over Tom's horse, who had walked downstream and cautiously but safely crossed back, Todd pulled off Tom's bedroll and got out a dry shirt wrapped in an oil slicker.

Shocked at first by what could have been a serious accident, Todd bit his tongue to keep from laughing as he helped Tom change clothes.

Darrel Vaughn, riding point, arrived just yards ahead of the herd that followed. Taking in the whole situation at one glance, he asked with a twinkle in his eye, "Find a good place to cross, Tom, or are we all going to have to take a dunking?"

"Why don't you just go ahead and find out. But don't go any farther upstream than where Todd's horse is standing," Tom replied through still chattering teeth.

Knowing Tom's penchant for practical jokes, Vaughn looked at Todd, who gave a barely noticeable nod of agreement. Assured by this gesture, Vaughn turned and entered the stream, followed by the lead steer.

That night, as his boots dried by the fire on two sticks stuck in the ground, Tom moved his feet toward the coals and said, "Next time it's somebody else's turn to check for deep water."

CHAPTER

15

It was a dull, lifeless day. The leaden sky was broken only by a single shaft of light on the distant horizon. To Todd it seemed as if the heavens had been painted in one sweep of a giant paintbrush that left a sameness of color on the hills and valleys through which they rode. The wind blew from the southwest, bringing with it varying changes in temperature and weather. Sleet-like rain fell, followed by swirls of icy snow. As Todd pulled his hat lower to shield his face, the chilled moisture turned to hard balls of hail that soon covered the ground with a blanket of white.

Todd was raising the collar of his sheepskin coat to protect his neck from the icy pellets when he spotted Shorty Hansen working his way toward him. Shorty had been scouting the track and his report was brief and to the point. "Rough country ahead. Steep and narrow."

Tom had ridden up to join them and caught Shorty's remarks. "When we get there we'll keep one man out front to pick his way," he offered. "If there's not enough room to ride flank, the lead man can take the steers through single file and the rest of us will follow."

By mid-morning they were riding into some of the roughest country Todd had ever seen. Walls of solid granite alternated with steep slopes of shale. Loose, exposed boulders clung precariously to the surface of these inclines, seemingly defying gravity.

"Slide country," Tom commented dryly. "Keep your fingers crossed. We'll string the cattle out. Darrel can take the lead. His horse is sure-footed as a mule, and Darrel's not the type to take any unnecessary chances."

Working along this way, they came to a point where the trail became so narrow that Darrel had to dismount and lead his roan. Noting the careful approach Vaughn was taking, Tom commented, "This is one time I wish the cows weren't so fat. Their sides stick out so much that if they rub against the hill they might start the earth to moving."

Thinking he was joking, Todd started to reply with a humorous remark, but the look in Tom's eyes stopped him. Tom was dead serious.

A good hundred yards beyond the narrow path, the terrain opened to form a fan-shaped meadow. Pointing toward this, Tom said, "We'll gather and regroup there once we all get across."

As the last cow started over the trail to join the main body of the herd that was now contentedly grazing on the other side, a sharp crack split the air. Its report rebounded off the high walls of the canyon.

Todd, who had been watching Darrel and waiting for his signal to cross, saw him drop from his saddle. Two explosions in the shale banks above and in front of them followed. Glancing up, Todd saw what appeared to be a fat stick, about a foot long, sail end-over-end in the sky. It landed, bounced once, then exploded in a bright flash with a blast that made his ears ring. He could barely hear Tom's warning shouts. "It's dynamite! Head for cover!"

Beyond the avalanche that followed, Todd saw a group of riders appear, surround the herd, and move them out of the valley.

"Sweet mother," Tom said, flinging his hat to the ground after they had regrouped, "they dynamited the mountain, took our herd, and here we sit! I'll hand it to the buzzards. They may have the cattle now, but when we catch up to them they'll sing a different tune."

Looking around he asked, "Did anyone see what happened to Darrel?"

"I did," said Todd. "He was shot off his horse."

Kicking his hat viciously, Tom, who rarely swore, said, "dirty, God-damned sons-a-bitches."

Walking to the slide, they each could guess what the other was thinking. "Well, there's no way through that," said Tom finally, biting off each word, his eyes burning with an inner fire. "We'll just have to backtrack and detour up that box canyon we passed. I figure we've lost a good two days." Bitterly he added, "If Darrel isn't dead now, by the time we get to him he may well be."

There was little talk as they retraced their previous route. Each rider was preoccupied with his own thoughts: Tom, silently cursing himself for allowing this to happen; Todd, hoping Darrel had only been slightly wounded and would survive; and the rest of the crew discouraged by what had taken place.

Each step they took backward was like a bitter drop of gall on the tongue of Tom Pickett. His mind centered on what he would do to the people who had stolen their beef once they caught up with them.

Three days later they found Darrel Vaughn. He was dead.

It was apparent that he had died slowly and painfully. The bullet had hit him in the back, going out through his rib cage. Vaughn had crawled a few yards from where he had fallen and tried to pull a shelter of leaves over himself to ward off the night chill. It was obvious from the type of wound he had suffered that he did not live to see morning.

Looking down at Vaughn, Tom said through lips tightened with anger, "He was a good man. They don't come any better. The back-shooting cowards who did this to him are going to pay."

They buried Darrel deep in the ground and covered his grave with large rocks in the hope of keeping wild animals from it. No services were held. They all stood in silence, heads bared and bowed, until Tom spoke. "Let's find them." Grimly they mounted and followed the still-visible tracks of the herd.

"Eight riders, I'd guess," said Tom, analyzing the sign. "And you can bet your bottom dollar they're wearing the FA brand."

For two days they traveled, stopping only when it became necessary to rest their mounts.

"Tom, I know you want to catch up with those coyotes we're following. We all do, but we're going to have to start getting smart." This advice came from Reub Hassler. "I reckon they're not so dumb as to think we won't come after them. They probably left some men behind. In this country it would be easy to pick us off. Like shooting fish in a barrel."

"I know, Reub. I've been thinking the same thing. Here's what we're going to do. We'll wrap our horses' legs and hooves to protect them from the rocks and travel at night."

"Tom, that's impossible," said one of the cowhands.

Eyeing him coldly, Tom replied. "Maybe. Maybe not. They won't be expecting us to ride in the dark, and that's our best chance of catching them without getting dry-gulched like Darrel. Have you got a better idea?" In the way Tom asked this, the rider who had made the objection knew better than to reply.

"Tom, we won't make any time that way," protested another. "It'll slow us down."

"It might. But as Reub said, they're sure to post guards. If we can sneak by them at night, we can make up the time we lost by riding all day."

Noting that the crew were exchanging worried looks, Tom hitched his pants and said, "Any man wants out can turn back right now and there'll be no hard feelings."

"Guess that ain't in our nature, Tom," Jeff Donnel replied, echoing the sentiments of the group. "We ride for the Triple C and we'll do what has to be done."

135

Eyeing his men appreciatively, Tom said, "When they expect us to bed down, we'll build a bigger fire than usual, leave enough wood on it to burn most of the night, and sneak off."

The next morning, Tom was hunched over the ground, studying a set of prints. "Looks like we've gained on 'em. They're less than a half-day ahead." Looking around and noticing the shape his crew was in after a rough night of alternately walking and riding, he said, "Let's hole up in that grove of willows and sleep for a couple of hours."

Todd, grateful for the opportunity to rest, dropped off immediately. A light sleeper, he woke twice. Both times he saw Tom pacing up and down, waiting impatiently for the two hours to end so they could get started again.

In the outlaws' camp the strain was beginning to show. The first to complain was Ance McDowell, a surly, barrel-chested FA rider known for his quick temper and belligerent manner. Standing before Jose Rivera, the man Luis Baca had put in charge of the group, McDowell let his feelings boil to the surface. "We just ain't making good enough time. These cattle are too tired and too fat to push."

Rivera, looking down from his horse, resented this challenge to his authority. In a cold, flat voice he asked, "What do you suggest we do, McDowell?"

"I got no answer. I'm just stating fact."

The rest of the group, now gathered for their morning meal, had agreed with McDowell that Rivera should be approached. Progress with the stock had been slow, and it was only a matter of time until their pursuers caught up with them. That they would be followed, they had no doubt.

"We could leave the herd," said one.

Rivera, seeking out the speaker with his cold, coal-black eyes, leaned forward, his forearm on his saddle horn. "Oren," he said in a voice full of menace, "you want me to tell Luis Baca that we left this herd, or do you want to tell him yourself?"

136

"Not me," said the speaker.

"Then I guess we're just going to stick it out. McQueen and Flaherty are watching our back trail. If the Columbia riders get anywhere near, they'll stop them. Or give us enough warning to do the job if they can't."

"Maybe so, maybe not," McDowell muttered. "I'm keeping one hand on my .44 just in case. I think this is going to end up in a fight."

"If so I'd rather fight them than Baca," said John Oren, the rider who had suggested leaving the herd. The mumbled comments indicated the other riders agreed.

"Look, Tom," Todd said to his partner while cinching up his saddle. "You're letting this thing eat at you too much. You need some rest. When we meet up with Allen's bunch you're going to have to be thinking straight."

Giving an extra hard pull on his own cinch strap, Tom's red-rimmed eyes flared with the heat of anger as they looked into Todd's. "I'll rest when we settle with Darrel's killers, and not before." Swinging into his saddle, he challenged. "Anyone have a change of heart after last night?" Without waiting for an answer, he said, "Then let's be off."

Two hours later Tom dropped back to join Todd. "They're pushing those cattle too hard. If I know that old brindle steer, pretty soon he'll just sit and they won't go nowhere. I've been watching his tracks, and he's already stopped the herd several times. Looks like this is our chance. I'll range on ahead and scout out their position. If I draw any fire, don't come a'running. Work your way in carefully." Eyeing Todd meaningfully, he added, "There's no sense in both of us getting killed."

By early afternoon Tom had returned. "Just as I figured. The cows have slowed down on 'em. They need to rest and they need to graze. There's six men with the herd, so two are missing. Probably in the hills behind us." Pausing to take a long drink of water from the canteen Todd handed him, he continued. "If we can take them without any gun-

137

fire, then we can just sit tight and wait for our two ambushers to show up."

Seeming to be his old rational self again now that action was at hand, he handed the canteen back to Todd. "Thanks. My throat was dry as a thistle. I've been thinking on a plan and I'd like your opinion."

After hearing Tom's proposal, Todd said, "Let me play the part of sacrificial lamb. I think it should be you or me, and they know you. They don't know me, so I might be able to fool them."

Tom pondered this suggestion for a minute. He knew Todd was right, but he also knew the chance Todd would be taking. Reluctantly he looked up. "Agreed. But be careful!"

The outlaws were sitting around their supper fire. Suddenly Jose Rivera jumped to his feet, spilling his plateful of beans. Drawing and cocking his six-gun all in one motion, he pointed it toward the outer perimeter of darkness and shouted, "Who's there?"

At first sign of alarm the rustlers scattered, dropping their plates as they stumbled over one another to get out of the ring of light.

"It's me. Todd Howard," was the reply. "I'm alone and unarmed."

"Come in so we can see you. Slow-like. And don't try anything fancy," Rivera growled. At the same time he spoke to Ance McDowell and John Oren. "You two circle the camp and see if anyone else is out there."

Todd appeared out of the shadows leading a limping horse, his holster and rifle scabbard empty.

"Start talking!" Rivera exclaimed.

In a hoarse, exhausted voice, Todd replied, "All the rest are dead — under the slide. I didn't know my way back so I just kept coming." Looking at the pot of beans, he added, "Can I have something to eat? I haven't touched a bite for days."

"Search him first," Jose Rivera told the FA rider nearest Todd. "We'll find out if he's lying when Ance and John get back."

After he had been carefully checked for hidden weapons, Todd went to the fire, scooped a full helping of beans onto an extra plate and ate ravenously. Between mouthfuls, he spoke to Rivera. "I'm not lying. I'm the only one left. If I weren't alone, do you think I'd ride into your camp?" Pausing just long enough to let this thought sink in, he went on. "I lost my rifle and handgun when my horse fell. I was hoping to follow you through these mountains without showing myself, but I figured I'd starve to death first. If you kill me, at least I'll die on a full stomach."

After three helpings of beans and repeated refills of coffee, Todd leaned back, rubbed his stomach and said, "Whoo-ee. My stomach was beginning to think my throat had been cut."

Out of the corner of his eye, he saw Jose Rivera talking to his men. Todd knew they were discussing his story.

McDowell and Oren returned and reported to Rivera. "We circled the camp three times. Went out a mile-and-a-half. Other than his tracks, we didn't spot a thing. He's alone all right."

"That being the case, what do we do with him?" the rider who had searched Todd asked.

"Let's sleep on it. We'll decide in the morning," Rivera replied. "Oren, you stand first watch. Tie him to that tree over there — good and tight."

Rising to his feet, Todd said, "That's agreeable to me. I'm dead tired." When he spoke he stumbled through the fire as if too exhausted to control his saddle-cramped legs. In doing so, he sent a shower of sparks into the air.

Lying on the rim of a hill more than two miles away, Tom spotted the signal he had been waiting for. Todd had said to watch the fire for anything unusual.

Slipping quietly down the slope, he joined his companions who were waiting in a draw another quarter of a mile back.

"Looks like it's time to saddle up. I don't want any shooting unless it's absolutely necessary. I'll take whoever is watching Todd. Shorty, you and Art take the night watch. The rest of you men pick your candidates. If we move out now, we can be there in two hours. They should be settled down by then. When you hear two trills of a nightbird, move in."

Carefully they worked their way toward the rustlers' campfire. Giving his men time to get into position, Tom waited until those still moments of the night that precede the break of day. Then he whistled his sharp call.

Todd's guard had dropped off to sleep, relaxed in the knowledge the man he was guarding was securely trussed. In three quick steps, Tom was in front of the dozing man. He crashed the barrel of his revolver hard across the outlaw's temple, then turned swiftly to see if his help was needed elsewhere.

The camp had been caught completely by surprise. Shorty and Art had disposed of the second sentry, who was now sprawled flat on his face. The rest of the FA riders were also out cold, struck down by the Columbia crew, who gave them no chance to cry out in alarm.

"Tie 'em up tight and dump 'em by the fire. Be sure to get all their guns and knives. And take their boots off. A man doesn't feel as cocky in his bare feet. Besides, it's a good place to hide a knife."

"They sure don't have any sense," exclaimed one Columbia rider. "No one's even watching the herd."

"I guess they figured the cows were too tired to go any-where," Tom said. "And they probably are. But just in case, two of you see that they stay put. If those missing riders come by and you have a chance, take 'em. Otherwise ride off and let 'em come on into camp. We'll get a little surprise party set up in case they return.

"Sorry, partner, first things first," said Tom, stooping to cut Todd's bindings and release the bandana that had been tied around his mouth.

"Am I happy to see you! I figured my goose would be cooked about breakfast time."

Tom answered, "I think I was more worried than you were. I figured they'd shoot you on sight."

"My biggest problem," said Todd, "was getting down those three helpings of beans and all that coffee. I wasn't half as hungry as I tried to make out. And getting the horse to limp was a problem, too, until I thought of lodging a rock in his shoe."

"Well, you did a good job," Tom replied. "Now let's get some answers to a few questions."

To those who had recovered consciousness, Tom asked, "Who's the boss here?"

"I am," Jose Rivera answered sourly.

"Get him up and drag him to that tree over there." Tom indicated a distant pine to two of his men. "I've got a few questions I want to ask him. Private like."

"Now," said Tom, when they were out of earshot of Rivera's men, "supposing you just tell me who put you up to this."

Returning Tom's stare, Rivera sneered, "You'll find out soon enough anyway, so I don't mind. It was Luis Baca, Frank Allen's foreman. Our orders were to steal your herd, kill you, or both."

"Well, that was your mistake," said Tom Pickett. "You should have done both."

"What are you going to do with us?" Rivera asked insolently.

"What they do to any murdering cattle thief. Hang you."

"It'll take a better man than you," Rivera retorted. "Frank Allen casts a big shadow. Before this is all over, we'll see whose neck stretches at the end of a rope."

As dusk dissolved the shadows of men and horses, Tom had the Three C crew build up the camp fire and arrange

141

their captives.

"Tie them in a sitting position, gag their mouths, and put them close enough to the blaze so they'll be seen, but far enough away so you can't see they're bound up. Then we'll wait and hope those other two back-shooting skunks show up. Pick a hiding place and keep out of sight."

Three hours later, the camp was hailed. "Come on in," mumbled Tom.

As he rode into the light, the first horseman saw the trussed figures of his cohorts and reached for his gun. Turning his horse he bumped into the second rider, who was following closely behind.

"Hold up," advised Tom, stepping into view. "You're covered. Drop those irons or we'll drop you." The rest of the Columbia riders showed themselves. Seeing they were out-gunned, the two riders dropped their weapons and raised their arms.

"Now get down," Tom ordered. "If either of you so much as wiggles an ear, you'll both be dead before you touch ground." With this threat facing them they slowly dismounted. "Now tie them up, gag them and put them with the rest of their kind. I don't want to hear one word from any of them," Tom said. "Let them make peace with their maker tonight. Tomorrow morning we'll do what has to be done."

As the two remaining FA hands were bound, Jose Rivera threw them a hateful glance. He had counted on them as his ace in the hole.

After breakfast next morning, Tom pulled Todd aside. "I know you're new to this country, and this seems hard, but we must hang these men. No one will think the worse of you if you want to ride on ahead."

"Tom," said Todd, "I'm not looking forward to the sight, but what has to be done has to be done. Don't forget, Darrel saved my life. He was my friend, too."

As they rode off, they left behind eight bodies, their necks stretched by their own weight, hanging from the stout limbs of two sturdy pine trees.

CHAPTER

16

Luis Baca was pleased. The meeting with Grey Wolf had gone well. For ten repeating rifles, two hundred rounds of ammunition and a share of the beef Baca planned to rustle, the Indian had promised to work under his direction.

Baca laughed silently at the thought of what he had pulled off. He was the only contact between the Oregon Steamship Company and Grey Wolf. And Grey Wolf would be taking orders from Luis Baca, not Frank Allen. As soon as Jose Rivera took care of Pickett and Howard, and joined him with the Columbia Cattle Company herd, he would make his move against Allen.

As he rode, Baca reviewed the plan that had been agreed upon with the Indian leader. Grey Wolf and his band of eighteen renegades were to harass all settlers within a fifty-mile terminus of the Santiam Pass. They were to kill any homesteaders and take their stock. Baca knew that such actions, once passed along by word of mouth, would paralyze movement of cattle and immigrants through the pass. Once the Santiam was shut down he would turn his efforts south — to the passes from Eugene City — thus closing off all major routes from the Willamette Valley to Central Oregon. He did not worry about drives from The Dalles. The OSC and Jack Bartels would do what was necessary to maintain control over Columbia River traffic.

Grey Wolf had voiced concern about General Crook and the Indian peace treaty, but Baca had assured him that Crook's victory over the Umatillas and Shoshones had been far to the east and south, and that the influence and power of the Oregon Steamship Company would keep Crook out of the Deschutes area. At this news the Indian had grunted his pleasure, for not only was he looking forward to killing and looting, but he also had a personal score to settle with the Warm Springs tribe who had aided the Army in their battles against his tribe, the Paiutes.

Luis Baca's lips tightened cynically as he recalled Grey Wolf's reaction to his statement that General Crook would not bother him. Baca knew differently. But his devious mind had concluded that by the time Crook got word of what the Indian band was doing, and reacted, the Indians would have served their purpose. In fact, if Crook did not act soon enough, Baca was prepared to eliminate the hostiles himself once they had done his dirty work. By that time Baca would be in full control and his influence would be enormous. Straightening in the saddle at the thought of the power lying within his grasp, he threw his head back, bared his teeth and yelled for the pure joy of the moment.

Luis Baca had met privately with Grey Wolf, as was their agreement. To be on the safe side he stationed his men less than two hundred yards away, giving them instructions to rush to his aid if he needed help.

At his cry the waiting FA riders appeared at a full gallop, their weapons out. Seeing Baca riding alone and unharmed, they surrounded him in a cloud of dust.

"What's up?" one grimy-faced rider asked. "We thought for sure that was the yell of an Indian as he lifted your scalp."

"No problem, compadres," Baca replied. "Grey Wolf is going to cooperate, and will start tomorrow by burning out the homesteader who is living on the old military camp by Black Butte."

Gesturing toward Raoul Gomez, the only man in his outfit who looked more like a working vaquero than the hardened killer he was, Baca said, "Gomez, when Rivera gets here, head back through the pass. Don't say a word to anyone you meet. Let them continue on so we can take their stock. Once you get to Lebanon spread the word that the Indians are on the warpath again and it's not safe to cross. If you see any military patrols tell them nothing and get back here to warn us. Got that?"

"Sure, boss. I'll leave when you give the word."

"Good," said Baca, pleased with himself. "Now all we have to do is wait for the Indians to do their job and Rivera to meet us with Pickett's herd."

Nine days after the hanging, the Triple C riders reached the summit of the Santiam Pass. Tom Pickett and Todd Howard were riding together. It was chilly and the lake they were passing reflected the dirty grey color of low, moisture-laden clouds. A few white caps, stirred by the wind, dotted its surface. The coldness of the water reflected from spots of newly-formed ice along the shoreline.

Minutes earlier they had been riding in the warmth of the sun. Now they felt the wind's bite as it cut through their outer clothing. The sky filled with dark, churning clouds, but spring was working its magic and minutes later the clouds dispersed and the sun appeared once more. A small group of ducks swam nervously toward the center of the lake: four females in neutral brown plummage, led by a drake with a cobalt blue head whose shoulder and coverts of deeper hued greens and blue-greens flashed gaily in the sunlight. His concerned quacking followed in the V-wake of the trail they made through the water.

Tom Pickett was the first to speak. "From what I've been told, it should be fairly easy going 'til we reach the Deschutes River. The country we're heading through now opens up soon. The timber disappears once we pass Mount Jefferson," he said, indicating the towering snowcapped peak

145

to their left. "About halfway between here and the Deschutes is old Camp Polk. It was used by the Army during the earlier Indian raids, but was abandoned a while back."

They were crossing a small stream that had cut its way through a pine-bordered meadow when Tom pulled his horse up. "Thought I heard something, Todd. Let's check it out." Spurring their horses, they raced to a knoll on which stood a marginal stand of jack pine. Reining up, Tom cocked his head. "Gunfire. And right over the next ridge. Head back and get some help. I'll check out what's going on."

Todd kneed his gelding and left.

After cautiously working his way up a shallow gulley, Tom tied his cow pony to a bush and wriggled his way to where he had full view of the scene below.

In the center of an open field stood a lone cabin. About thirty yards behind the cabin was a dilapidated barn and lean-to shed. Whoever had built the rough, one-room dwelling knew what he was doing. It was more like a stockade than a house. Rifle holes replaced windows, and the walls were two-logs thick. A sod roof was supported by heavy beams. From his vantage point Tom could only see one well-fortified door, but he guessed there would be a second one on the other side. Most settlers, afraid of fire or being trapped, usually had an alternate escape route.

A band of hard-riding Indians, their war paint visible even at this distance, was circling the house. Three were kneeling before the door, attempting to ignite some scrub-wood with a burning pitch brand. When the brush caught fire, one of the savages threw the torch on the roof of the cabin. The Indians raced back to the shelter of the stout log barn. As they dove for cover, a rifle was thrust out of one the small openings. Tom saw a puff of smoke and heard the loud boom of a Henry. A second shot came from the other side of the cabin.

Right after the Henry had fired and disappeared inside, the three Indians ran from the barn, their arms loaded with dry straw. The Henry appeared and boomed again,

146

sending one of the Indians sprawling.

Tom swore under his breath in frustration. In a few minutes it would be too late. Already he could see flames eating at the door. If it wasn't for the sod roof the whole structure would be ablaze by now.

Hearing a rush of horses, he turned. Todd and most of the crew were racing up the slope. Tom hurried to his horse. They arrived just as he seated himself in the saddle. Quickly explaining the situation and the terrain, Tom said, "There are at least fifteen of them."

"And twenty-two of us," Todd interjected.

"So we'll hit them from two sides." Dividing the group with a vertical sweep of his arm, Tom said, "Those to my left go with Todd. The rest come with me. Circle outside and close in. Hold your fire until you're on them. The closer we get, the better our chances are."

The group split and charged over the rise. Grey Wolf was the first to see them. He raced to warn his warriors, a series of shrill shrieks coming from his throat. He arrived at the same moment the Columbia riders opened fire.

Their first volley dropped three Indians. Todd's group had ridden through the hostiles' circle and turned to charge again. Tom and three other men rode down the two unmounted Indians who had helped set the fire.

As they swept over the demoralized renegades, Tom fired point-blank into one who was trying to reach his horse. Whirling in his saddle, he fired at another whose mount had stumbled and fallen. He cursed aloud; he had missed. The brave who had gone down was trying to remount. As the warrior vaulted astride his paint, a shot caught him in the back. The momentum of his leap and the impact of the bullet sent the Indian tumbling over its neck. Looking to his right, Tom saw Reub Hassler grinning in satisfaction as he lowered his smoking rifle.

Todd rode up, braking hard as he jerked to a stop. "Looks like we've routed them, Tom."

147

Giving a satisfied nod of his head, Tom quickly checked the Columbia crew as they formed a circle around him and Todd. "What's the score?" he asked.

"Ed Freeman got his horse shot out from under him and did a cartwheel, but he says nothin's broken," one rider reported.

"Lloyd got hit in the leg but the bullet went clean through. The way he's cussing, I guess he'll be all right in a day or two," Shorty Hansen offered.

"Any others get hurt?" asked Todd.

"Think I might have a cracked rib or two," said Fred Hudspeth, his voice rasping. "One of those heathens hit me with a war club so hard I couldn't move a muscle. Good thing he was in a hurry to leave or he might have finished the job."

"What damage did we do to them?" asked Tom.

"Eight dead and at least three wounded," Todd replied. "Elmer is checking it out now."

A triumphant whoop interrupted their conversation. The two occupants of the cabin were hurrying toward them. Todd was shocked to see that one of them was a woman. In her early fifties he guessed. She was holding onto her skirts with both hands to avoid the soft mud flying up from her boots. An old Patterson Colt was strapped around her waist, sweat stains streaked her calico dress, and her bonnet had slipped off her head and hung at an unnatural angle. Her hair, which had been tied in a bun, was in wild strands and her face was streaked black with burnt gunpowder.

Striding ahead of her was a large, raw-boned man of about the same age, whose lips portruded out of his bushy whiskers like two ripe cherries; lips that matched the color of his round, red cheeks. He was dressed like most of the crew: a pullover wool shirt and heavy pants tucked into high boots. A felt hat covered his head, under which a heavy growth of white-streaked brown hair stuck out. He too was sweat-drenched. His face and clothes showed the marks of black powder and ashes from the fire he had stopped to put out.

148

"Hot damn, are we glad to see you!" the man bellowed. "My name's Archie Ridley. This is my wife Emily. Em was fixin' dinner when they hit us. I was in the shed unsaddling our mare. Just barely made it. Wouldn't have," he said, affectionately putting his arm around his wife, "if Em here hadn't spotted them when she came out to tell me it was time to eat. Went right back into the cabin, got her Colt and came out blastin' away. Kept them off my back long enough for me to skeedaddle for cover."

While Archie Ridley was telling his story, Todd noticed that Mrs. Ridley's face had flushed a fever pink. He thought it was because of the excitement and her husband's compliments, until she said, "Land sakes, I must look a mess." She brushed at her skirt with her hands, then started to tidy her hair. "Come inside the house. I'll fix some coffee."

Just like a woman, Tom thought. Almost killed and the first thing she thinks of is her appearance, then making coffee — as if we had just stopped by for a social visit.

Todd, being more observant, had noticed the slight edge of hysteria in her voice. Taking off his hat he said quietly, "Ma'am, you look just fine. And a hot cup of coffee surely would hit the spot."

After they had shared a giant pot of chickory coffee, Tom sent four punchers back to bring up the cattle. Mrs. Ridley, meanwhile, had gone to work cleaning and binding Lloyd Simi's bullet wound. After this, she tore a clean flour sack into strips and bandaged Fred Hudspeth's ribs. As she was tending to the wounded, Todd and Tom discussed the battle with Archie Ridley.

"It don't make sense," Ridley commented. "Since General Crook's big victory there's been no trouble. None at all. Besides, we're only a few miles from the Warm Springs reservation. They're friendly and normally would let us know when hostiles are around." Pausing to take another drink of coffee and to give his mind a chance to sort out these facts, he went on. "They had new rifles too, which is mighty peculiar. Maybe they were after our stock. If so it's a good thing they're gone."

By way of explanation Archie Ridley added, "Our stock — not the Indians. Our two boys moved them out early yesterday morning. We came across the pass with two other families. Liked this place so well we decided to stay. In the pass we met a fellow by the name of Barnes who had settled in The Ochocos. Raved so much about that part of the country the others decided to go there. They sent word that they were gatherin' some cattle to drive up to the gold camps at Canyon City and did we want to send some of our beef with theirs. That's where the boys went."

"We're heading that way ourselves," Todd said. "Why don't you come along with us?"

Visible relief showed on Archie Ridley's face. "Sure appreciate the offer, son. I guess it would be smart to move to where our friends are."

"Can you leave first thing tomorrow?" Todd asked.

"You bet," Ridley enthusiastically replied.

They left the next morning at dawn. An hour out, Todd dropped back to pay his respects to the Ridleys and found Archie in a talkative mood. "Been trying to recall where I've seen your brand before, and it came to me sudden-like at breakfast. We were about four days out of Sheridan when a rider came by to look us over. He was with a herd headed for Portland and said they were being followed. Sounded like he was expecting trouble. Nice fellow. Had your mark on the left stifle of his horse. Later we crossed trails with an army lieutenant who was huntin' some renegades and told him about your situation. Said he would take a look."

"Been thinking about your name too," Ridley continued before Todd could comment. "It's the same as one of the fellows who came from Sheridan with us. Clay Howard."

"Arch," said Todd, "I've never met this Clay Howard before, but if you're the ones who sent Lieutenant Springer to help us out, I guess as far as you owing us for yesterday, the slate is clean." Todd related what had happened on the drive to Portland, including the Oregon Steamship Company's unsuccessful efforts to stop them from moving cattle up the Columbia River and the ambush in the pass where Darrel Vaughn was killed.

"If our cattle that went up the Columbia reached The Dalles, we should be meeting up with them this side of the Deschutes. If they're not there, we'll wait two or three weeks, then move on. Probably east or southeast. In any case, I doubt if we have seen the last of the OSC."

"Sure sorry to hear about your trail boss," Ridley said. "He seemed like a right nice fella. The Lord works in funny ways. Seems He takes the good ones from us more often than He takes the bad. Sometimes it's mighty hard to understand."

While Todd and Archie Ridley were holding their conversation, twenty miles directly south Luis Baca had just gotten word from one of his scouts that the Columbia drive had made it safely through the pass and had foiled Grey Wolf's assault on the Ridley homestead. The scout also reported he could find no sign of Jose Rivera or his men.

Baca was in a rage when he called for Raoul Gomez. "Forget our previous plans. I don't know what happened to Rivera but we can't wait for him. We have to stop the Columbia drive now. Knowing Grey Wolf, he'll be as mean as a hurt rattler and striking at anyone getting in his way. Pick up his trail. Tell him to attack tomorrow and that we'll help. Promise him another rifle for each scalp they take. I want everyone on that trail drive dead by sunset tomorrow."

CHAPTER

17

Dawn exploded over the desolate countryside. Desert animals stirred to life as the first rays of light sought out and erased the shadows left by the darkness of night. The herd, encouraged by the yips of the drovers, started slowly then picked up momentum as they moved east through a vast expanse of dusty, blue-green sage. The route they followed was broken by lava-encrusted dips and hollows that sloped gently downward to meet a broad monochromatic plain.

Unknown to the cowmen, this barren land had once been a shallow sea floor composed of semitropical swamps where mammoth crocodiles lazed, rhinoceros fed and sheep-like miniature ponies came to drink.

It was during this age, the Age of Mammals, that giant volcanoes violently thrust through the earth's crust to form the spectacular Cascade Mountain Range, whose tops burst to spread hot, molten lava eastward, smothering entire rivers and valleys. Following these fiery explosions, the exposed craters spewed forth tons of pumice dust that blotted out the sun, choking and burying all forms of plant and animal life until all that remained was a vast, lunar-like landscape.

Several thousand years later during the Ice Age, the face of the land was reformed as giant glaciers slowly crept southward, cutting and notching imposing mountain peaks and forming deep, tortured valleys. After another million years the air cleared and the atmosphere again warmed, leaving massive fields of trapped ice that would eventually thaw and become great landlocked lakes.

Such was the geological nature of the country through which Todd and Tom pushed the Triple C cattle. Formed by violent and tempering influences, it was a land that attracted men with temperaments to match.

Despite the fact that everything seemed tranquil and in order, Todd was uneasy. He couldn't put his finger on the reason why, but some inner voice seemed to be sending out warning signals.

Alert, but relaxed by the warmth of the mid-morning sun, Todd filled his lungs. The fragrant, spicy odor of the sage, mingled with pungent alkali dust, was pleasant to his senses. The change in climate, once they had crossed the timberline, was dramatic. The spongy, damp earth had turned dry and dusty. The lush green vegetation of the Willamette Valley and Santiam Pass was replaced by trees and plant life, stunted by lack of adequate water, in shades of grey, grey-green or greyish blue. In the pass their clothes had been spattered with mud. Now they were caked with a powder of white dust. The sun, which they had seen for only a few hours each day, now beat down on them unmercifully from early morning until late afternoon.

Jeff Donnel had ridden ahead to scout their route. He returned and pulled in beside Todd, his dust trail following him and enveloping them both. Donnel reported they would soon be entering a stand of fescue, "Higher than the bellies of our horses," he stated as he untied his neckerchief and mopped the sweat from his face and neck.

Squinting against the unclouded brightness of the glaring sun, Todd removed his hat to shade his eyes and looked up. He had noticed two buzzards an hour ago. Now eight or nine were making lazy circles in the sky.

"I noticed them too," said a voice breaking into his train of thought. It was Shorty Hansen. "Probably dead game, but just to satisfy my curiosity I think I'll ride over and take a look."

"Was thinking of doing the same thing myself," Todd responded. "I'll join you."

Ten minutes later they were threading their way through a narrow, rock-strewn ravine. As they entered a clearing, two vultures were silently observing a bloody object on the ground. At their arrival, the unattractive birds flapped clumsily into the air. As Shorty Hansen dismounted, Todd started to comment that it looked like an animal all right. Then a drawn-out moan sent a cold chill up his spine. Despite the heat of the day, goose bumps crawled over the surface of his skin. He shuddered involuntarily.

"Great Jumpin' Jehosaphat!" Shorty cried out. "It's human."

Kneeling beside the gruesome object before them, Todd swallowed hard as an acrid taste rose in his throat. It was a man. Or what was left of a man. The contents of a pack, which had been strewn about, indicated he was a miner — one who had been savagely mutilated. The hamstrings of his legs had been cut through and his wrists had been slit to expose the muscles, which were tied with rawhide thongs to nearby juniper bushes. His stomach had been slashed open and filled with sharp-edged pumice rocks.

"He's trying to say something," Shorty said. Together they leaned forward, both unaware they had stopped breathing in order to better hear.

"Indians," the man gasped in a bubbled whisper, "and a white man...jumped me after breakfast...said...heard white man say they were after a herd...noon." With what must have been a superhuman effort, he reached out to them. "No family. Pain awful...kill me. Please."

Todd looked up and saw Shorty drawing his pistol. Just then the miner gave a convulsive sigh, shuddered and died. "Thank God," said Shorty, as he replaced the handgun, his face bathed with sweat.

Todd made a difficult decision. "Shorty, I hate to do this but we're going to have to leave him here. Unburied. If what he says is true, the herd's in danger and we can't waste a minute."

"No other choice, boss," said Shorty, eyeing the buzzards. "I guess he wouldn't have minded, knowing the stakes."

It was almost noon. The Triple C riders, alerted to trouble, were riding through the meadow Jeff Donnel had sighted earlier. Todd felt it was a bad spot to be in but agreed with Tom that they had no choice. "Keep moving and look for a place to make a stand," had been Tom's advice. "I'll ride point, you take drag. Shorty and Reub can watch our flanks."

When the sun was at its zenith, Grey Wolf attacked. The Indians had been lying in wait in the tall grass. Rising to their feet, those with rifles opened fire. The others used their bows or tried to pull the drovers out of their saddles and finish them off with tomahawks and knives. As the battle raged on all sides, Todd rode from man to man shouting instructions over the melee. "Keep together. Move the herd forward! Don't circle! We can fight our way out! Without horses they can't catch up!"

Suddenly, as if to belie his last statement, a painted figure on a spotted appaloosa charged through the field.

Todd whirled to face him. The warrior was dressed in a loincloth. His jet-black hair was tied ponytail fashion. Two eagle feathers stuck in a thong headband hung downward over the left side of his face. A beaded knife belt encircled his waist,and he brandished a rifle whose newness reflected in the sun.

With a piercing scream the savage charged. Todd spurred his own horse into action. Seeing this, the Indian pulled his mount to a stop, raised his carbine and fired. The shot, intended for Todd's chest, hit Todd's horse in the head. The animal stumbled and fell, throwing Todd to the ground.

Sensing an easy kill, the renegade kneed his pony and

struck Todd as he was struggling to his feet. Todd reached for his six-gun and clawed at an empty holster. As he frantically looked for his pistol, he heard another shriek.

Before Todd could collect his wits, his adversary was on him. Instinctively he rose and leaped back. As the Indian swept by, Todd grabbed his wrist and set his heels. Off balance, the Paiute tumbled from his horse. In the blink of an eye he was on his feet, arms spread, knife in hand.

Suddenly, like a great tawny cat the savage hurled himself at Todd, who barely managed to step aside. As he did he threw a wild punch that hit the Indian on the temple. Stunned by the blow, the red man hesitated then lunged again.

This time Todd was ready. He blocked a knife thrust with his left forearm and hit the warrior full in the windpipe, dropping him to his knees choking and gasping. Todd stepped forward and angrily kicked him in the head. "That's for the miner." The Indian rolled on his back, unconscious.

Going to his horse, Todd removed the riata and bound his attacker. Then he took his rifle from its scabbard and tried to coax the Indian's pony closer.

After several unsuccessful attempts, he finally managed to catch the reins. The horse shied nervously and pulled away. It had been years since Todd had ridden bareback, and the rifle was an encumbrance to mounting, as were his boots and chaps, which were made for stirrup and saddle. He grabbed the mane in his left hand and awkwardly leaped onto the back of the skittish animal. After a moment of nervous bucking, the spirited appaloosa settled down, responding dutifully to pressure from Todd's knees and heels.

Riding to higher ground, Todd surveyed the scene below.

The Indians were setting fire to the dry grass, and a perimeter of flame was licking its way toward a Columbia crew in full retreat. Heavy grey smoke rose into the sky, obscuring the sun and covering the battlefield in a dusky amber mantle. Somehow the crew had managed to keep the the herd from scattering. The drovers had broken out of the grass and were heading for the safety of a low-banked river. A burst of gunfire greeted them. At first Todd thought some of his own cowhands had managed to reach the shelter and were providing support for their fleeing comrades. Then he realized the firing was directed at the Columbia riders by a group of white men.

It took only a moment for the truth to hit him.

Frank Allen's riders were at the water's edge, and they were working with the Indians! That's why the hostiles were on foot. They were pushing the Triple C into a trap!

From his vantage point Todd saw a possible out. It was a slim one, but it might work. However, if he didn't move quickly, it would be too late. Already the herd was starting to mill and his men were dismounting in confusion. He dug in his spurs. The pony, unaccustomed to being rowelled, took two short, jerky leaps ahead then bounded off at a dead run.

When Todd reached the crouched line of warriors who were slowly following the fire, one, hearing his approach, turned and lifted his rifle. Todd fired first. The shot caught the half-naked brave in the chest, throwing him to the ground like a discarded rag doll. Todd's sudden appearance caught the rest completely by surprise, and he was through their lines before they could stop him.

As his mount sprinted forward, Todd saw that his men were shooting the cattle to form a breastwork. He waved frantically. Fred Hudspeth, thinking it was an attacking renegade, raised his rifle.

"Don't shoot!" shouted Art Seaforth, who was standing by him. "It's an Indian bronc but the rider don't look like a redskin." Then as Todd drew closer Seaforth pounded Hudspeth on the arm. "Damn my eyes, it's Todd." Turning first right then left, he yelled, "Hold your fire! It's Todd Howard coming in. Let him through!"

A cheer erupted from the throats of the besieged crew as Todd joined them. Before anyone could speak he called out, "Where's Tom?"

"Don't know," a voice answered. "We haven't seen him

since the Injuns fired the grass. Maybe he's on the other side of the herd."

Taking no time to brief the men as to their situation, his instructions were curt and to the point. "Mount up. We're going to charge those bushwhackers at the water. Get the cattle running and keep pushing them until they're across the river. Gun down anyone who gets in the way. I'll pass the word along to the others."

Not waiting for a reply, he whirled and disappeared in the smoke. He reached another group of his men behind some carcasses, returning the fire coming from the river.

"Seen Tom?" yelled Todd over the explosions of the weapons.

"Nope," said a bloodied rider. "But the homesteader and his wife are with us." As if to punctuate this statement, Todd heard the loud report of Archie Ridley's Henry.

"Pass the word. We're going to run the herd through that bunch and cross the river."

"We may not make it," a voice shouted back.

"That's a chance we'll have to take. If we stay here, we're through anyway. And so are the cattle. Get moving!"

The men mounted and worked the panicked beef. Spooked by the noise and confusion, and no longer blocked from an escape route, they surged forward. This tactic caught the rustlers completely by surprise. Most of them, unable to escape, were trampled or drowned as the frenzied cows swept over their position.

Those who got away headed toward a band of riders about a quarter-mile downstream. Shorty and Reub joined Todd. Stirrup to stirrup, they watched.

"Looks like when them fellas hitch up and the Injuns get here, that'll be all she wrote," said Shorty.

"Afraid you're right," Todd replied.

"Game's not over yet," Reub responded in a cool voice. "Looks like we're being dealt a new hand."

Looking at him quizzically, Todd followed Hassler's nod.

"That new bunch are goin' after the rustlers."

Wiping away the sweat that was blinding his vision, Todd looked again. Reub was right. Their ambushers had swung to the west bank and were exchanging shots with the group crossing the river.

A handful of the new arrivals went after Allen's men, but the bulk raced on to engage the Indians. When the last shot echoed away in the distance, a rider trotted their way.

"Well I'll be hog-tied," said Shorty, first to recognize the horseman. "It's Jerry Flowers."

Halting his dun and leaning over the saddle horn, a grinning Flowers greeted them. "I told you we'd be waiting for you, but didn't expect you'd be bringing company. You must live right. This is the best spot to cross within fifteen miles. We arrived four days ago. Our cows are about three miles northeast of here."

Seeing the serious expressions on the faces of the three, he turned somber, awaiting a response.

Todd spoke first. "Jerry, we don't want to seem ungrateful, we've just had the wind taken out of our sails. Thanks for your help."

"We'll get the rest of the cows across," Flowers said. "Where's Tom?"

"We don't know, Jerry," Reub Hassler said softly. "No one's seen him since the Indians hit us."

"He'll turn up," Jerry Flowers answered positively, but with a hint of worry in his voice. "He always does." Kicking his horse, he rode off.

"Reub, Shorty," said Todd, "we've got work to do. Shorty, round up a few hands. Check on our men and cattle. If Mrs. Ridley is all right, ask if she would mind seeing to our wounded. Also send a couple of men to give the miner, or what's left of him, a decent burial. That's the least we can do after what he did for us." Almost as an afterthought he added, "Take a count of the Indians and rustlers. Those that are dead, bury. Any survivors put under guard." Looking to

Reub Todd said, "Pick two of our sharpest-eyed riders. We'll look for Tom."

By early dusk the herd had settled down. Shorty gave his report to Todd. "We lost two men: George Gentry and Lee Pickleseimer. Four wounded. Lloyd Simi was hit again — got lung shot and is in bad shape. The rest are patched up and will be back in the saddle after a night's rest. Mrs. Ridley is tending to them.

"We're short eighteen cows. Had to shoot six to put them out of their misery. As for the Indians, eight are dead." Pausing significantly, Shorty added, "Other than the one you had hog-tied, we didn't find any alive. Found the body of a white amongst them. Looked like an FA coyote. Five of Allen's gang were killed. Art Seaforth and a couple of the boys are watching the three who didn't get away." He looked questioningly at Todd. "Any word on Tom?"

Todd threw a pebble he had been toying with hard at the ground. "Not a sign. First thing tomorrow, we'll take every man we can spare and scour the countryside. We won't leave here until we find him."

CHAPTER

18

His senses were trying to tell him something, but his sleep-drugged mind refused to respond. It was several seconds before he realized someone was shaking his shoulder.

"Todd. Todd, wake up."

Todd saw Reub Hassler's outline above him in the dim light of early morning. Other sleeping riders were being aroused, and an air of quiet urgency moved through the camp.

"Something's up," Reub whispered as Todd pulled on his boots. "Shorty and Fred spotted two Indians skulking around the herd. Looks like we're in for another round of trouble."

Wide awake now, Todd buckled on his gun belt. "Look to Mrs. Ridley and Lloyd, will you, Reub. Leave a man with them."

"Mrs. Ridley can take care of herself," a voice behind him spoke out. "She can shoot better than most men, and a few more Injuns won't rattle her."

Todd saw Archie Ridley had joined them. "Was I you, I'd be careful about shootin' at Indians 'til I knew if they were friendly or not. Might be some Warm Springs bucks checkin' out what the big do was all about yesterday."

"Good idea, Arch," Todd replied. "Let's go take a look."

From the crest of a partially-hidden coulee, Archie and Todd scanned the terrain that ran from the river beyond the grazing cattle. Ridley spoke first, so quietly that Todd had to strain to hear.

"There's two of 'em workin' down the draw left of that lightnin-struck juniper. One more on the ridge beyond that odd-shaped pile of rock. They're lookin' us over all right."

Peering at the blackened juniper bush, Todd saw two shadowy forms; then something by the rocks Archie had mentioned caught his attention. It could have been the wind stirring some leaves, the jerk of a chipmunk's tail, or the scratching movement of a small bird as he foraged for insects. But Todd's eye was quick to catch the difference. He had located the third Indian's hiding place. Had he missed this small disturbance he could have looked in vain. Impressed with Ridley's ability to spot the Indians so quickly, he made a slight turn to compliment him.

Speaking even more softly than before Ridley cautioned, "Don't move. There's someone behind us and unless I miss my guess, we're lined up in his sights." Turning casually and spitting a stream of tobacco juice in the dust, he slowly rolled back onto his stomach. "Yep," he said. "No more than fifty yards to our rear, and he has us cold. Do exactly as I do."

Pushing his Henry beyond reach, Ridley waited for Todd to do the same. Sensing Todd's resistance, he spoke urgently. "This is no time to argue. Just trust me." Todd slid his rifle forward. Although the morning had as yet not lost its chill, sweat was running down Todd's neck and beading his face.

"Now, keep your hands above your shoulders, fingers spread, and get up slowly. Don't make any sudden moves, and above all, don't go for your hand gun." Ridley rose to his knees, his fingers splayed and his arms raised. Todd involuntarily jerked as Ridley shouted a series of gutteral words he did not understand.

The Indian behind them replied in three grunted syllables. Archie Ridley got slowly to his feet. Still confused, Todd did the same. Archie's face split in a grin that went from ear to ear, his clear blue eyes danced with a mixture of joy

162

and relief. Todd turned to see the brave who had been covering their backs casually trotting toward them, a rifle at his side.

Ridley uttered a series of monosyllabic words, at which the red man grunted another reply.

"I know a little Warm Springs talk," Archie said. "They're friendly and intend us no harm. I told him we'd been attacked by some renegades and a band of rustlers yesterday. He said they came with many riders to see what caused the smoke."

Walking ahead of them, the Indian gave a signal and the two Indians in the draw and the one behind the rocks rose from their concealment, like ghosts materializing. One quickly sprinted away. The other two stood fast. Minutes later a giant cloud of dust rose from behind a hump-backed ridge and a column of riders appeared. The group was almost completely obscured by the cloud of alkali dust they were creating.

"Indians don't ride like that," Ridley exclaimed. "Them's cavalry troops, or I'll be go to hell."

The column turned toward the herd and the Columbia drovers. Two riders detached themselves and galloped toward Todd and Archie.

The first horseman was an officer, the second a civilian riding an Army mount. As they drew closer Todd recognized them both. The military man was Lieutenant Dennis Springer. Only he was wearing the bars of a captain. The second rider was Tom Pickett.

Reining in, Springer saluted smartly and said, "Good to see you again, Todd." Turning his gaze to Archie he added, "And you too, Mr. Ridley." After these greetings he spoke to the Indian in the combined dialects of the Des Chutes and Wasco tribes, obviously praising the brave, who accepted the compliments stoically, then turned and jogged off toward his companions.

Meanwhile Tom had leaped off his horse and ran to greet Todd.

163

Todd said, "I thought you might be dead," at the same time Tom said, "I thought you had been killed." At this coincidence they both broke into laughter, alternately hitting each other to show their affection. Theirs was a relationship that went beyond the bounds of a mere partnership; it had developed into something more rare and precious — a true friendship.

The sacredness of the moment suddenly broke, and Tom shook hands with Archie Ridley as Todd approached Springer. "I see something new has been added to your uniform, Captain," said Todd. "Guess you must have caught those Indians you were after."

"Those and more besides. I was detached to General Crook after the last Bannock uprising. That's where I got to know the Warm Springs tribe. They were assigned to us as scouts. I got along with them so well that General Crook assigned me to this area. A promotion went along with it. Incidentally," Springer asked, "how's the hole in your side?"

"Healed shut," replied Todd. "I've never felt better in my life." And indeed, at this moment he never had felt better.

"Now," said Tom, "tell me what I've missed, and I'll fill you in on where I've been."

They walked back to the herd, arriving as Todd finished his account of what had taken place the preceding afternoon.

After a warm and exuberant greeting from the crew, Tom told his story.

"When the Indians hit us, I was cornered downstream by three of them. The only out was across the river. They entered the water after I did, so I got across first. They turned back, not wanting to be caught by my fire in midstream, I guess. I circled north to recross the river and join the herd. That's when I saw Frank Allen's crowd moving in."

Stopping to carefully choose his words, he went on. "I was torn between the desire to fight my way through to you or to go get help, but common sense told me I wouldn't make it if I tried to join you. I remembered Archie saying

164

his two boys had left just before we arrived, so I went looking for them. Never saw the Ridley boys but I did run into Captain Springer here," he said, jerking his thumb in the captain's direction. "Would have been back sooner but my horse stepped in a chuck hole and broke his leg. That's why I rode in on an Army mount."

At this point Captain Springer interrupted. "When we found Tom he must have walked five miles. Our scouts were out investigating the smoke and there he was. Good thing they crossed his trail," he added wryly. "He had another forty miles to go to reach the settlement in The Ochoco."

Stooping to refill his cup from a battered coffeepot that was resting on the coals of a late breakfast campfire, he focused his attention on Todd. "My scouts spotted that Indian pony in your corral and went to look at your captive. I don't know if you're aware of it or not, but you caught yourself a real prize. His name is Grey Eagle, and he's a subchief of the Paiutes. We've been trying for months to catch up with him. We'll be more than happy to take him off your hands. The rustlers too."

"Guess we'd appreciate your doing that," said Todd, looking at Tom who waved his agreement. "You could do us another favor too. We have a badly shot-up rider that needs attention. Sure would appreciate it if you could have Doc Bynum take a look at him. He did a good job on me; maybe he could patch up Lloyd."

"Todd," said the regimental doctor, who had just joined their party and heard Todd's remark, "I already checked to see what I could do. He died this morning before we got here. I'm truly sorry."

Todd took the news hard but Tom's reaction stunned them all. Raw anger flashed from his eyes, and his face became distorted with rage. He spoke to no one in particular but in a cold, toneless voice that all could hear, said, "Allen, you'll answer to me personally for the deaths you've caused. I swear to it. One day we'll meet and when we do, you're a dead man."

165

CHAPTER

19

For the first time in weeks the Columbia crew had a good night's sleep, thanks to Captain Springer who assigned his scouts to guard the herd and camp. His offer to do so had been warmly received by the exhausted drovers.

The next morning Todd, Tom, Reub Hassler and Archie Ridley joined the young captain for a leisurely breakfast of Army rations. Their conversation centered on two subjects: the Indian situation and the nature of the country in Central and Eastern Oregon. Captain Springer was doing most of the talking. A rough, hand-drawn map was spread in front of him.

"You shouldn't have any more trouble with the Indians. There are still a few wild bucks on the loose, but their chiefs are getting them under control. That's no iron-clad guarantee though. It's strange what can set them off: a medicine man, a strong leader, or a killing of one of their own by a nervous settler or a hot-tempered miner. The Shoshones in Idaho are still hostile, as are the Sioux around the Bozemen Trail in Montana. Every time the Indians in these parts hear about a victory there, they get restless. But right now this whole country," he indicated the area he was discussing by sweeping his hand over the map, "from The Dalles south to the California border, and east to Idaho, is quiet. And we intend to keep it that way."

Pointing to a dot on the map called Warm Springs Station, he said, "This is where I'm headquartered." Moving his finger down, "This is where we are now, at Indian Ford, and here's where you cut through the Cascades. If you swing south there's a good place to cross the Deschutes. It's not more than three or four hours away. Once you get across, there are a number of options open. Straight east to The Ochoco, or the John Day area beyond that; south 'til you hit the Klamath Reservation; or southeast to Goose Valley."

Tapping his finger on the line indicating the Goose Valley route, he continued. "If you go this way keep north of the Walker Mountain Range. By staying near Crooked River, which joins the Deschutes here and runs from here," he traced the river's course, "you'll have good water all the way to Camp Harney."

Jabbing his finger at a point on the map that was marked by what appeared to be a musical note but actually was a small box, atop which was a rough caricature of a pennant, he commented, "Camp Harney was established after the Bannock treaty. Below it is Harney Lake. It's fine cattle country. Plenty of water but a mite swampy in spots. An ideal location if you want access to California, but it's a ways from the Idaho-Montana gold fields."

He touched the map again. "This area south of Crooked River looks good now, but will be bone dry in summer and most of fall. About the only thing that thrives are jack rabbits and rattlesnakes. I'd avoid that section."

Pausing to fill and light his worn briar pipe, Captain Springer looked questioningly at the group who were either seated, kneeling or sprawled on the ground. His alert hazel eyes watched closely for any reaction.

Todd asked the first question. "Where are the Canyon City gold fields?"

"Here," Springer pointed with his pipe. "East of Camp Watson on The Dalles Military Road, just below the John Day River."

167

Archie Ridley was next. "Heard talk they're going to build a bridge over Crooked River."

"That's right," Springer replied. "Near where Ochoco Creek joins it. Just west of Barney Prine's store. It's supposed to be completed sometime next year."

"Captain," Tom interrupted, "if you had a bunch of cattle and were looking for a place to settle in and grow, where would it be?"

Without a moment's hesitation Captain Springer said, "Here," tapping his pipe stem emphatically at a point on the map, "in Ochoco Valley. Either at Mill Creek or on Ochoco Creek. Good grass and lots of timber. The water's plentiful year 'round, and the rimrock and mountains provide shelter from bad weather. The snow's not too heavy in winter and the valley is protected from freezing winds. Besides," he added, "Ochoco Valley is growing. The town there will be a full-fledged city some day. Was founded two years ago and already they're talking about a school. The way it's positioned, most people figure it will become the hub city for Central and Eastern Oregon. Probably will, too. It's located within twenty miles of the geographical center of the state."

So close had Todd and Tom become these past months, and so alike in nature, that their thoughts ran along the same vein. It was almost as if their actions came from a single mind. There was never any argument when one made a decision without consulting the other, because that would have been the decision each would have made. This, and their friendship, was the true strength of their partnership. There were no petty jealousies, no egos to be pampered, and no unexpressed bitterness tucked away to fester internally before poisoning the mind with imagined and groundless doubts and fears. This relationship manifested itself once more as they read each other's eyes.

"The Ochoco it is then," said Tom.

The rest of the day they spent burying the dead and as Archie Ridley put it, "licking our wounds." Over a noon meal Jerry Flowers related the story of his trip to the Cascades with Captain Geyer; first going through the dynamite in the firewood incident, then the fireball catapult. He ended with Geyer's promise to name his next two vessels the *Tom Pickett* and the *Todd Howard.*

"Damndest thing I ever saw," Flowers said, recounting the battle below The Dalles. "Water roaring and boiling as if it were coming straight from purgatory. A big steamboat bearing down on us, smoke belching out of her stacks, guns roaring and tearing big chunks out of the *Lucille,* and all the while the captain standing there cool as a cucumber, giving orders. I thought for sure we had bought the farm. Then all of a sudden it was over. The steamer that was going to ram and board us hit with barely a glance and drifted on downstream — all afire and explodin' like some fireworks I saw once at a Fourth of July picnic in New Albany." Scraping the uneaten remains of his plate into the small fire, he shook his head and looked up. "I've never seen anything like it."

"Just be glad he's on our side," Todd remarked. His statement was received with a chorus of "Amens."

"Say, Todd," Tom said, his eyes dancing with amusement, "I'll bet we're the first cattlemen to have steamboats named after them."

That afternoon as they were checking out the herd with the Army captain, Tom rose in his saddle and pointed at the activity of some of Springer's Indian scouts. They were spreading their blankets and fur coverings over a field of anthill mounds. "What in tarnation are they doing that for?"

"A spring ritual," Springer replied. "They call those their ant blankets. The mounds are full of red ants. They'll eat the lice and vermin that have infested the Indians' furs and bedding all winter."

"And we call them dumb savages," said Tom.

"The only people who call them dumb savages are those who haven't had to fight them. The West Pointers who have education coming out of their ears change their tune in a hurry after they've been licked a few times. At least the smart ones do. Just tell Colonel Steptoe, General Wright or

169

General Crook that they're dumb, and you'll get a look that will freeze you right in your tracks.

"As a matter of fact, the Indians use the same tactics against us that we used against the English in the Revolutionary War. And we won that war." Looking toward the small band of braves, Springer continued. "If all of their tribes banded together like the original thirteen colonies did, they could win too. They've never had a shortage of smart leaders. Paulina was one. So were Red Cloud and Cochise. Those to keep your eye on now are Chief Joseph of the Nez Perce; Quanah Parker, a Comanche who is trying to unite the Kiowas and Cheyennes; a young buck called Geronimo in Arizona; and Sitting Bull, a Sioux in The Dakotas.

"I've enjoyed our visit but now I have to be off. If you do settle in the Ochoco country, our paths will cross again." Saluting smartly, the captain turned his mount and cantered away.

"A good man," said Todd.

"Agreed," replied Tom. "I guess we both owe him."

Two days later, after crossing the Deschutes, Todd, Tom and the Ridleys stood at the edge of rimrock that towered over the pleasant valley in which the small settlement of Prine was nestled.

The bright morning sun had burned away the blue haze surrounding the distant mountains. Glistening silver fingers, which were spring-swollen creeks, rushed to feed a larger river whose convoluted banks wound snakelike in a northerly direction. Directly in front of them was a cluster of unpretentious buildings. Beyond that, plateaus of rimrock parted to show a mountain range still partially covered in snow.

"Quite a sight, ain't it?" said Archie. "That's Crooked River below us. It's easy enough to see why they call it that." He followed its course with the stub of what had once been his index finger. "It winds north, then west until it meets the Deschutes. Over yonder," he pointed, indicating a group of mountains on their right, "is the Maury Mountains. Named

170

after Colonel Reuben Maury by one of his men who was through here on an explorin' trip. Some of the bunch from Stephen Meeks' lost wagon train of '45 camped just north of those mountains." Pausing reflectively Archie continued, "A tragedy, that train was. Lots of people died because of Meeks' mistake. They found a baby's grave at the foot of them mountains just a few years back. It had been marked by a note in an empty whiskey bottle."

Excited at the prospect of visiting the small settlement and seeing her sons again, Emily Ridley interrupted. A light breeze stirred the wide cap of her shade bonnet as she pointed out a wisp of smoke. "That's Barney Prine's blacksmith shop and store. He started the town. But Elisha Barnes, Wayne Claypool, Ewen Johnson and William Smith were here first. They settled a few miles farther east. On Mill and Ochoco Creeks."

"A wise move on Barney's part if you ask me," said Archie. "His location for a store was better. See that mountain northwest of us?"

Todd and Tom turned to look, nodding simultaneously.

"That's Grizzly. There's a road runs this side of it all the way to The Dalles. Follows the same trail as used by the Indians for hundreds of years. Then later by the Army. A stage service makes the run now. Yep," said Archie, pausing to scratch his whiskers, "that Prine is a smart 'un all right. His store sets smack dab on the trails that cross for Eugene City and Lebanon to the west, Canyon City and the John Day Country east, Linkville to the south and The Dalles up north."

"Is Canyon City near John Day?" asked Todd.

"Shore is."

"Where's Linkville?"

"Below Klamath Lake. Sets on the east side. They call it Linkville 'cause it links up Oregon and California."

"Why do they call this The Ochoco?"

"Ochoco is a Paiute word meaning willows. The river banks are covered with 'em."

171

Sitting up straight in his saddle to ease his back muscles, Ridley grinned wickedly. "What Em didn't tell you was that Barney Prine not only has a blacksmith shop and a store, he also sells whiskey. It ain't what you're used to in 'Frisco and Portland, but it's the best you'll find around here."

"You men and your priorities," said Mrs. Ridley. "What I want first is a hot bath, a change of clothes and a chance to catch up on the latest gossip. It's been too long since I've heard any woman-talk."

From the rimrock's edge Todd watched the cattle being worked down the lava rock slopes. He breathed deeply; the tangy, sage-spiced air was like a pleasant narcotic that helped wash away his cares. He had never known air so pure or sweet. Each breath seemed to fill every recess of his lungs, energizing his entire body.

A sharp call shook him out of his reverie. It was Tom. "Hey, partner, do your lollygagging later. The cattle are nearing the river, and we're going to need all the help we can muster to get them across."

Todd mounted slowly, reluctant to break his mood and feeling of well-being.

From a distance Crooked River had appeared tranquil and lazy. Up close it was anything but. Brown, roily water rushed by, carrying with it uprooted shrubs and small trees that would make the crossing not only challenging but also dangerous. On the other side a crowd of people had ridden or walked from town to greet them. They were waving and shouting instructions that couldn't be heard over the roar of the water.

Jerry Flowers was the first to realize the significance of the gestures. "I think they're trying to tell us to put the herd upriver and work them diagonally across." At that moment, one wagon on the opposite bank headed upstream and one down. At some distance apart both stopped. The drivers stood up and pointed at each other.

"That's just what they're trying to say, Jerry," Tom replied. "They want us to push off upstream and land on the bank where the river swings east again."

The animals were driven bawling and crying into the turbulent stream. Art Seaforth, who had taken the lead, was bent over, holding onto the neck of his sorrel with both arms. His cowpony had entered deep water and was swimming to the other side. Finally it found its footing and scrambled out. As it did a faint cheer was heard from the onlookers who rushed to meet the soaked rider. The steers followed and as the last one staggered onto solid ground Tom yelled out, "Looks like our turn is next, Todd. Want to go first?"

"After you, Tom. You're good at finding the holes. I figure if there's one out there, you'll hit it."

With a loud "Yippee," Tom hit the river at full gallop. Partway across, his horse must have realized what it was getting into and stopped, sitting on its haunches in the gravelly bottom. Tom fell backwards into the main current. His mount then rose and made the crossing riderless.

Todd guided his horse in more gently and came alongside of Tom as he rose up, hatless and sputtering. "Grab onto my horse's tail and we'll take you across." Tom did as Todd suggested, falling to his knees after they clambered out on the opposite bank. The crowd was in stitches after this exhibition, and even Tom was laughing.

As they struggled out of the mire caused by the cattle and headed for dry ground, an imposing, thin, wiry-looking man with broad shoulders stepped forward and held out his hand. He was wearing a heavy black wool suit with matching vest, a white shirt and string tie. His dark hair was parted in the center and hung over his ears on both sides. A neatly trimmed mustache that merged with a Van Dyke beard covered the lower half of his otherwise clean-shaven face. His dark, piercing eyes glinted with pleasure.

"Welcome to Ochoco country, friends. My name is Barney Prine. As soon as you've dried out, come on up to my store. It would be my privilege to buy you all a drink."

"Much obliged," Tom replied. "I'm Tom Pickett, and this is my partner Todd Howard. We came over the Santiam

Pass from Lebanon and hope to settle here. I'll sure take you up on your offer. That water is colder than it looks. I could use something to warm my innards."

After the townspeople left, Tom sat down to drain his boots. As he was squeezing the water from his socks, Archie Ridley walked up with his sons and two older men.

"Todd, Tom," said Archie. "I want you to meet my boys and the fellas I came from Sheridan with. This here's Horace Singleton, and this is Clay Howard. I was just goin' over what happened to your herd on the way to Portland, and the trouble we had at our place and Indian Ford."

Clay Howard, who had stooped to shake Tom's hand, turned toward Todd. As he did his genial expression died and was replaced by a look of sheer disbelief. The blood drained from his face and his knees buckled. He grabbed at Archie for support.

"Are you all right, Mr. Howard?" Todd asked anxiously.

Clay's voice almost failed him. He managed to stammer, "Yes. Quite all right, thank you." Then in a stronger voice, "Archie tells me your name is Howard. Todd Howard."

Archie Ridley and Horace Singleton looked at each other curiously. They had never seen Clay Howard ill a day in his life, and his ashen appearance concerned them. "Are you feeling under the weather, Clay?" Horace asked.

"No, just a momentary thing. I'm feeling better now," Clay replied in a voice that was closer to normal. "Guess I'd better find Ellie. She was afoot in town and probably is wondering about all the commotion." Without another word he turned and left.

"Strange," said Archie. "I've never seen him act like that."

"Maybe too much alkali water," Horace replied. "Takes awhile to get used to."

That night as they were lying in bed, Clay reached out and took his wife's hand. He held it tightly. "Ellie, the likeness was unbelievable. My imagination I suppose, but he looked so much like Mary I found it hard to even breathe."

CHAPTER

20

Todd and Tom were sitting in Barney Prine's combination store and saloon. The dunking Tom had taken two days before was still the main topic of conversation in town, and they were joking about it now.

They had made their decision where to settle: on Ochoco Creek, about twenty miles due east. Tom and Todd had scouted the area the day after they arrived. It was a perfect spot. The valley they selected was surrounded by gentle slopes whose sides were timbered with stately pine. Thick, lush grass grew waist-high in the meadows that lay adjacent to the creek, which they were told ran the year 'round.

Both partners filed claims for 160 acres. Jerry Flowers signed for another 160 which was to be held for Captain Geyer. These claims were registered under the partners' own brands, but all of the land would belong to the Columbia Cattle Company. By filing individually the Triple C owned a total of 480 acres. However, as their land was in public domain, they had access to thousands of acres on which to graze and build their herd.

Todd eagerly looked forward to the challenge ahead. He knew that this was a country that would either make or break them. As he started to propose a toast to the continuing success of their enterprise, Shorty Hansen burst through the front door. His face was flushed with excitement and he was panting heavily. "Better come quick!" he shouted. "Ty and Earl are getting stomped down at the bar in Monroe Hodges' hotel."

Ty Blackwell and Earl Bond were two of the Columbia's best riders. They were both easygoing and quiet by nature, so if they were in a fight Todd and Tom knew it was probably not of their own making.

"There's only the two of them against five others," Shorty gasped, out of breath from his run. "One of the locals went to find some of our crew and caught up with me in Heisler's store. Said I'd better get some help over there pronto, as they were takin' a real beating."

Tom, who had been seated on a tilted barrel with his back braced against the log wall, rocked to his feet and raced for the door. Todd followed.

As they neared the hotel Tom spoke to Shorty. "Watch the rear door. Give us some backup if we need it. Todd and I will go in from the street side." He was relieved to see Art Seaforth and Hugh James headed in their direction. The one thing he didn't want was to start off on the wrong foot with the locals. No matter who caused the fracas, he intended to settle it amicably. It was in this frame of mind that he stepped quickly but easily through the canvas-draped doorway, Todd at his side.

What he saw made him change his mind. His hand dropped for his pistol and stopped. Ty Blackwell was standing protectively over the prone body of Earl Bond. Blackwell was holding a broken whiskey bottle by the neck in one hand; his other arm bloody and useless at his side. Facing him was a greasy-looking rider whose Bowie knife glistened dully in the dim light. The knife was covered with blood, and an evil smile was frozen on the face of the man who held it. His stance indicated he was about to use it again.

Todd heard an indrawn hiss of breath and felt Tom's hand on his gun arm. "Easy, Todd. It's a setup."

A laugh filled the room. "Welcome, compadres. As soon as Gonzales finishes the job he started, you can be next."

176

Todd turned slowly, his hand still poised over his holster.

On the right side of the speaker, in the shadows of the room, were three dirty, unshaven outlaws, their revolvers drawn and cocked. "I am Luis Baca. We met before. At the Deschutes River. You held the high cards there, but we are holding them now."

The name Baca exploded in Todd's head. He stood frozen, unable to move. Nothing else that Baca said registered. Just his name. Todd's mind churned. There must be thousands of Bacas in the world, yet could it be possible that . . .

He didn't have time to finish his thought. Tom pushed him aside, drew and fired.

Pandemonium broke loose. The sharp reports of hand-guns were punctuated by a louder blast from the direction of the bar. The single window exploded in a shower of glass, and additional light sent its dust-laden rays through the billowing smoke of spent powder.

"To your left, Todd," Tom shouted. Rolling on his back, Todd sent a bullet at an indistinct shadow rushing toward him. He could tell by the sound of lead hitting flesh that his shot had found its mark. The shapeless form stumbled and fell.

Tom was behind an upended barrel. Without looking at Todd he said, "Art and Hugh just came in, so there are four of us now. Plus Shorty. Someone's using a shotgun but he's on our side. I think it's the bartender." As Tom finished speaking, the rear door flew open. There was a flurry of shots, then silence.

Peering cautiously over the barrel, Tom called out the names of his companions, receiving an answer from all but Ty Blackwell and Earl Bond. Slowly they rose to their feet. Bodies were sprawled in every position. From the corner he heard Art cry out. "Ty and Earl are still alive."

Cautiously working their way along the narrow corridor wall, Todd and Tom reached the back door. They found Shorty outside. He hadn't been shot, but he had been viciously

177

pistol whipped. There was a red bruise on his forehead and his upper cheek was cut and bleeding.

"One of them got away, and unless I miss my guess, it's Baca," said Tom.

Coming up behind them Hugh James said, "You're right on the money. There are four bodies inside that don't belong to us, and the bartender says Baca ain't one of 'em."

Walking back to the bar, Tom stopped before the bartender, who was busily cleaning the barrels of his Greener with an oily rag. "Thanks. Your support is appreciated."

"My pleasure. This is a clean town and Mr. Hodges runs a respectable place. Be glad to have you and your boys in for a drink anytime."

At the front door Tom stopped Todd. "It's likely Baca will either head for the stable or the river." Pulling out a double eagle from his pocket, he said, "if it's heads I take the stable. Tails you get the river."

The coin flipped in the air and landed at their feet. "Tails it is," said Tom. "Better take Art with you."

At the water's edge Todd had to shout to be heard. "Art, you go upstream. I'll work down."

Within a few minutes Todd found Baca's bootprints in the mud.

Drawing his pistol he slowly continued on, instinctively crouching to make himself a smaller target. The tracks continued until they reached a stand of willows. Here they ended. Dropping behind a water-soaked log, Todd watched for any sign of movement, occasionally glancing over his shoulder to be sure Baca had not circled to catch him from behind.

Something in the sagebrush across the water caught his eye. It was a coyote sneaking downhill. His movements made Todd suspicious. Normally a coyote trotted toward his destination with a purpose. This one was being more cautious, frequently stopping to look furtively to its rear. Following the animal's backward glance Todd saw a dark shadow pause, then pass into a large crevice some two hundred yards away. Only one animal made an outline like that — man. Baca must have crossed here and was now below the rimrocks that towered above the valley.

Removing his boots with one hand and holding his gun in the other, Todd eased into the river. In midstream he was caught in a back eddy and to his surprise was deposited gently on the opposite bank — only thirty yards below where he had started.

He drained his boots and put them on again. Then he checked his Colt and examined the loads. Satisfied that everything was in working order and that the barrel had not filled with mud as he crawled ashore, he took his bearings and worked toward the spot where he had seen the shadow. When he reached the bottom of a rock-strewn slope, he paused to catch his breath. The way up would be a tortuous one and he would be exposed, but there was no other choice.

He was halfway up the rise when he saw a puff of smoke and heard the whine of a bullet. Ducking behind an outcropping of rock, he fired once in return and sprinted to the next available cover — an old, gnarled juniper tree. Save your ammunition, he told himself as he replaced the expended round. The distance is too far to be effective with a side arm. With this last thought in mind, Todd sprinted up the hill and threw himself at the base of the rimrock cliff. Forcing air into his tortured lungs, he listened and waited.

Todd was slightly above the point where he had seen Baca disappear. There was no way for either of them to scale the face of the vertical stratified rock, so the gunman had to be either in front of, or slightly below him. The dipping afternoon sun cast elongated shadows over the terrain, providing darkened places of concealment where his foe could lie in wait. Todd knew this, but he also knew he did not have time to go back for help. It would be dark soon and Baca could make good his escape. This vast expanse of desert land, broken by ancient river beds and rocky outcroppings, provided a thousand places to hide.

With his back to the wall of fractured stone, Todd edged slowly along its narrow base of loose rock, planting his weight carefully first on one foot then the other. To keep his balance, he had stretched both arms out and was leaning against the barrier behind him.

He was in this position when Baca rose in a fissure thirty feet directly below. Baca had a triumphant smile on his face as he raised his gun to fire. The still air carried his piercing cry, "Rot in hell, amigo."

CHAPTER

21

Back in town, when a building-by-building search failed to locate any trace of Baca, a posse formed to find him. Four riders had already left to check upstream. Eight others were waiting for Tom Pickett to finish saddling his horse.

Clay Howard, who had just ridden into town, cantered over to this group. "What's all the commotion about?" he asked.

"There's been a shootin' at Hodges' bar," Jay Pettit, a bewhiskered old-timer answered. "A bunch of no-goods was layin' for the Columbia crew. Durn near killed two of 'em, and reworked the face of another. The Columbia boys turned the tables and got all but one. Todd Howard and one of his hands left about an hour ago to look for him. We're fixin' to head downstream. Want to join us, Clay?"

"May as well tag along to help." Getting off his horse, he walked over to where Tom was tightening the cinch on his saddle.

"You and Todd known each other long?"

"Several months."

"Where's he from?"

"Frisco," answered Tom.

"Know anything about his background?"

"Nope. Only that he comes from a wealthy family. His folks are named Fields. He claims that's his middle name, but

181

I expect he added the name Howard to prove to them he could make it on his own."

Stopping to squint suspiciously at Clay, he asked, "Why all the questions?"

"No particular reason. He just looks like someone I knew a long time ago. Someone very close to me."

"Well, Todd's become close to me too. He's the best partner a man could have. And I don't want to see him planted six feet under by that no-good skunk he's chasing."

"Just who are we looking for, anyway?" Clay Howard asked.

"Frank Allen's foreman, Luis Baca," said Tom, rising to his saddle and spurring his horse toward the river. In doing so he missed the stricken look that came over Clay's face.

The rest of the posse had already mounted and were waiting for the conversation between Tom and Clay to end. When Tom galloped off, they turned and followed him.

Clay Howard stood rooted to the spot at the mention of the name Baca. "It couldn't be. It just couldn't be," he muttered as he headed toward Prine's small store. Clay was not a drinking man, but at this moment he badly needed a drink and time to collect himself.

Wall-eyed Jay Pettit was an old Army scout. Some people swore he could follow a horse thief for a hundred miles through a raging blizzard. In any case, he had no trouble reading the sign along the river.

"Here's where your friend and his sidekick parted," he told Tom. "Todd Howard's tracks turn right." Silently Pettit rode ahead, his body bent forward to peer over the horse's neck. What he saw in the disturbed soil told him everything that had taken place.

Pointing out two sets of footprints, Pettit shouted above the noise of the water. "They both crossed here. A couple of you better work down on this side, just in case. The rest of us will go on over."

The horses entered the flow one at a time. When they had all gathered on the opposite bank, Pettit picked up the trail again. Partway up the slope he stopped and got down.

"Some activity here," he said to Tom, who had joined him. "Somethin' made him jump for that nearby shelter of rock. No blood, and he didn't fidget around much." Getting to his feet he walked to an ancient, misshapen juniper, where he stooped and picked up an object from the ground.

"Cartridge case. He fired one shot." Looking up at the rest of the riders, who now surrounded him, he nodded to the escarpment above. "That's no place for a horse. We'll leave someone here with our mounts. If we need 'em we can always come back."

As they were drawing bunch grass straws to see who would stay, one shot echoed from the rocks above. They stood stock-still, waiting for more to follow. When there were none, Pettit said aloud the old adage they were all thinking. "One shot, one kill. Two shots, probable kill. Three shots, no kill."

When Baca raised his gun, Todd cried out. "Wait! Before you shoot, there is something I have to know."

"And what is that, dead man?"

Todd's words tumbled over one another. "If you were...if you ever...if you knew a woman named Mary Baca?" Seeing no visible reaction, he blurted out, "She was my mother."

Baca's eyes became slits. He hadn't thought of his wife in twenty years. And now he was being confronted by someone who claimed to be his son. A son who bore no resemblance to him in any way, and one he didn't need or want. Unemotionally, he stared at Todd. "Then your name is Baca. Like mine?"

"No. It's Howard. Todd Howard. I'm named after my grandparents."

"And where is your mother now?"

"She died when I was born."

"Tell me, Todd Howard, do you believe that when you go to heaven you will see this mother of yours, Mary Baca?"

"Yes, I do."

183

The tone of Baca's voice was ice-cold as he pulled the trigger. "Then tell her that Luis Baca sends his regards."

Todd braced himself to take the bullet. There was no time to draw his own weapon. Even if he tried, the movement of doing so would cause him to lose his balance and fall on the razor-sharp rocks below.

A split second before Baca fired, Todd saw a blur of movement. By some miracle, the lead struck just inches from his head. Its impact sprayed him with rock splinters. Transfixed, Todd watched the scene beneath him.

A terrified Luis Baca was struggling away from a large diamondback rattlesnake that had struck him full in the face, evidently disturbed when Baca rose from his hidden position to fire. Holding one hand over his punctured cheek, Baca stumbled backward. His only thought was to get away from the hideous creature whose vacant and expressionless stare seemed to be trying to impose its will on his own. The reptile's forked tongue flicked in and out as it coiled, then struck again. With a whimper Baca threw himself sideways and crashed through a thin crust of lava into a pit that had been formed in another age by an air pocket caught in a flow of molten rock.

His disappearance was followed by a shriek of sheer terror. Todd's heart beat wildly as he climbed down the jagged lava cliff. He avoided the snake, who slid silently into an opening at the base of the pit where Baca had been standing. Creeping warily to the edge of the cavity he looked down, not knowing what to expect.

An indescribably nauseating and vile smell hit him full in the face. But it wasn't the smell that struck Todd dumb; it was what he saw. Luis Baca had fallen into a rattlesnake pit. Hundreds of venomous rattlers, who had wound themselves together into a huge ball as earthworms do, were viciously striking at the uninvited intruder.

Baca was sinking in a sea of rattling tentacles. His face and neck were already swollen from dozens of venom-filled bites. Raising one hand he pleaded, "Help me." Instinctively

Todd reached out his hand, which Baca grasped, then pulled. "Now we will die together," he hissed.

Todd momentarily lost his balance. Lances of pain shot through his body as he was hit. First by the fangs of one snake, then by another.

Jerking his arm free, Todd looked on numbly as Baca sank below the surface of squirming reptiles. Then he stared at his bitten arm in a state of disbelief. Taking out his pocket knife, he cut at his shirt-sleeve and tore it away.

One set of punctures was on his upper wrist. Clumsily he slashed shallow cross cuts over the two, tiny red spots that stared back at him. As blood and clear venom oozed out, he put his lips to the wound, sucked rapidly, and spat the blood and poison out of his mouth. He repeated this procedure several times, then searched frantically for the second bite. His heart sank as he realized it was on the back side of his upper arm, where he couldn't reach it. Knowing any further effort was hopeless, Todd focused his attention on two brown, diamond-marked shapes gliding toward him. A third had already coiled. Its rattles whirred angrily.

Todd reached slowly for the gun in his holster, hoping that his arm would remain free from paralysis long enough to take care of this immediate threat. He knew any sudden movement would cause the snake to strike.

"Holy Mother of God! Don't move, son. Not an inch." These words were followed by three quick shots. A split second later Jay Pettit was beside him, kicking three wriggling snakes toward the open pit. The bodies were bloated and puffed where the lead had entered, and the snake that had been coiled was viciously striking at itself where Pettit's bullet pierced its body.

Tom and two others Todd didn't recognize jumped into the small clearing. Stopping only long enough to take in the whole scene and utter an oath, Tom fell to his knees at Todd's side. Picking up the knife Todd had dropped, he found the area Todd couldn't reach and made a series of small cuts around the edges of the swelling. Putting his own lips to Todd's arm, he drew out as much poison as he could. Then he asked urgently, "Were you bitten anywhere else?"

"Just the wrist, I think, but everything happened so fast I can't be sure," Todd croaked weakly.

A quick examination showed there were only the two bites. Squatting to check the wounds, Pettit made a comment. "Looks like the one he couldn't reach has gotten into his system. Reckon we'd better get him out of here.

"Hank, have Elroy bring the horses up as close as he can. Then head for the river and find something we can get this fella across on." Turning to Tom he said, "Looks like we'll have to carry him. He ain't in any condition to walk."

"Hoist him on my shoulders, then, and let's go." Tom answered.

By the time they reached the river, Hank Petersen, the man Pettit had sent on ahead, had lashed together some birch logs. They placed Todd on these and tied him down.

"Tom, give me the end of your lariat. Then you and Buster Geohegan get across and haul him over. Hank and me will follow. He's goin' to get a dunkin', but it can't be helped."

Tom did as he was told, uncoiling a long length which Pettit tied to the makeshift raft. Once across, Tom and Geohegan wrapped the other end around a stout poplar trunk, gripping tightly as the float drifted into the current. The force of the turbulent water was too much for them, and they desperately braced their heels as they began sliding toward the tree which was their anchor.

"Hang on, dammit," yelled Pettit as his horse clambered up the bank. Leaping from the saddle, he grabbed onto the rope and helped them pull. Their combined efforts succeeded, and Todd swung to shore.

While Tom and Buster Geohegan draped Todd face down over Tom's horse to drain the water out of him, Pettit went to work cutting a travois from the willows along the bank. By now it was dark, but there was a full moon, so they were able to see their way as they trudged wearily back to town.

186

Clay Howard was still sitting in Barney Prine's store. He had taken his first drink quickly, but the second one sat untouched in front of him.

The four riders who had gone upriver came in. Art Seaforth was with them. The subdued crowd spoke in hushed tones. Several of the group tried unsuccessfully to draw Clay into their conversation. Finally, respecting his privacy, they left him alone.

Archie Ridley, who had been silently nursing a drink at the bar, walked over to Clay's table, pulled up an empty chair and sat down.

"Clay, you've been actin' mighty strange lately. Are you sure you're feelin' up to snuff?"

Reaching for his drink, Clay answered, "I'm fine, Archie. It's just something that happened a long time ago. It involved a man named Baca." He reached his arm across the table and firmly grasped Ridley's forearm in a strong grip. "Thanks for your concern. It's a thing I have to work out in my own way."

An excited shout came from the open door. "They're back!"

In an instant the saloon emptied. Clay Howard, who was the last to leave, rose slowly to his feet. Staring vacantly at his unfinished drink he sighed, "Mary, oh Mary, if I only knew where you were and if you're still alive." Feeling the full weight of his age for the first time in his life, he left to join the others.

As he stepped out onto the weather-hardened street, Ridley met him.

"Clay, Baca's dead. Killed by rattlesnakes. They brought Todd Howard in. He's been snake-bit too, and is in bad shape."

Pushing his way through the group, Clay Howard looked down at the pain-racked man on the pole sled. Wild, unruly chestnut-colored hair fell over a fair-complexioned face whose features were perfectly chiseled. Full eyebrows set off

187

a pair of serious brown eyes. As Todd grimaced, two dimples appeared at the corners of his mouth.

Suddenly Clay knew. The resemblance was too close to be a coincidence. The man on the makeshift stretcher had to be Mary's son. His grandson.

CHAPTER

22

The noisy crowd that surrounded Tom and Todd shoved and pushed at one another as they jockeyed to get a better look at the figure on the litter. When Tom bent over to check Todd's condition he was jostled to the ground. Angrily he fought to his feet. His patience snapped as he shouted over the din of voices. "Give him room. Somebody get a doctor."

One of the onlookers replied, "We don't have one. Had to send for the Army doc over at Warm Springs Station to take care of the men of yours that was cut up in the bar fight. They're at the hotel. Want to put Todd in with them 'till the sawbones gets here?"

"No," interjected Clay Howard in a booming voice, himself once more. "He can stay with us. Ellie has worked on snake bites before and can do as much as any doctor can. Bring him to our place." Turning, he walked briskly toward Deer Street and the home he had built on the outskirts of town.

Clay pushed open the door of their rustic three-room log cabin and stepped inside. Ellie was stooped before the fireplace, stirring the contents of a large iron kettle that hung over the open fire. She started to speak but stopped when she saw Clay's expression and the half-dozen men who followed him. Two were carrying Todd.

"Ellie, get the spare bed ready. We've got a guest who's

tangled with some rattlesnakes."

Rushing to an adjoining room she unrolled a feather mattress, then hurriedly got out some clean sheets and a fresh quilt. "Bring him in here," she called, at the same time giving instructions to Clay to light the candle on the stand by the bed.

"He's a mess, Ma'am," Tom Pickett said. "I'm afraid he's going to dirty up your clean bedding."

"Never mind that," Ellie snapped back. "It can be washed. Take his boots off. Clothes, too. Then put him under the covers." Raising her voice she addressed Archie Ridley. "Pull that stew off the fire, Archie, and put on a big pan. We're going to need hot water.

"These the only places he was bitten?" she asked as she examined the four tiny holes Tom had pointed out. When he answered that they were, she spoke to her husband. "Clay, I'll need to fix a hot poultice. Fetch those herb leaves in the cupboard, and when the water gets to boiling drop in the two empty liniment bottles we've been saving."

Turning, she took her apron by both hands and flapped it at the group crowding into the bedroom as if shooing chickens. "The rest of you git. We've work to do and can't get it done with everyone standing around gawking."

Silently they left. All except Tom and Archie, who was busy tending to the hot water. "That means you too," she said to Tom. "There's nothing you can do and you'll just be in the way." Before Tom could reply, she knelt by the bedside. As far as she was concerned he was already gone. Realizing this, Tom quietly took a seat in the corner.

When she had finished washing Todd's wounds, Ellie asked for one of the liniment bottles. Clay brought it to her, wrapped in a clean towel. She took this in her left hand and put the mouth over the worse of the two punctures. A few minutes later Clay brought the second bottle. This one she took with her right hand and, handing the first bottle back to her husband with her left, immediately applied it to the same area. Clay dumped the first bottle back in the boiling water and the same procedure was repeated with the bites

190

on the wrist. Ellie stopped only after she was satisfied that the suction of the steaming hot bottles had removed all of the surface poison. Next she mixed a poultice that smelled strongly of kerosene and mustard, and smeared it on the infected areas. This done, she tore a clean flour sack into strips and bound the arm from shoulder to wrist.

Getting up, she filled a wooden bucket with cold water from the water barrel and dropped in two clean cloths. Wringing one out, she folded it neatly and placed it on Todd's forehead. Finally she spoke. "If you're going to stay, make yourself useful. Keep a cool rag on his forehead." Tom suddenly realized she was speaking to him. "Yes, Ma'am," he said meekly, leaping up to do as he was told.

Ellie Howard gave a long sigh as she replaced a wisp of hair that had strayed and fallen over her face. "We've done all we can. If the fever isn't any better tomorrow and the swelling doesn't go down, that arm will have to come off."

Swallowing hard, Tom bit his lip and nodded. A one-armed man in this country would be better off dead.

Ellie went to the basin on the stand by the back door and poured some hot water into the cold she had dipped from the water bucket. After washing her hands, she took the basin of water outside and dumped it on the matrimony vine that was growing by the kitchen window. Then she dried her hands on her apron. "I suppose the stew has gotten cold. I'll heat it up and fix some cornmeal bread."

"Thanks, but I'd better head for home," said Archie. "Em will be expectin' me." Tom, whose stomach started growling at the mention of food, gladly accepted Ellie Howard's invitation to stay for supper.

Simple as the fare was, Tom ate until he thought he would burst. Inconspicuously he loosened his belt a notch, then undid the top button of his pants.

During the meal Ellie and Clay had been exchanging meaningful glances. Tom thought it was because of his table manners and flushed with embarrassment. Being a bachelor, he did not realize that married people have a way of communicating that does not require words. After years of living together they learn to read each other's expressions, gestures and even body movements. The closer the relationship and the longer the marriage, the more impossible it is for one person to hide his or her feelings, or even thoughts, from the other.

Silently as if by mutual agreement they both rose and went into their bedroom. Behind the deerskin hide that provided some privacy Tom heard a whispered conversation. He did not want to leave without thanking Mrs. Howard for the dinner, yet at the same time he felt like an intruder. As he drank his coffee, wondering what to do next, they re-entered the living area. Ellie went to sit on the stool by Todd's bed and changed the cloth on his forehead. She gently bathed his face with the other. Tom could see tears coursing a path down her pale cheeks.

Clay Howard cleared his throat. Tom refocused his attention on the burly, gentle man. Tight-lipped, Clay began. "Tom, you may think us a couple of silly old fools, and Lord knows you may be right, but ever since I first saw Todd I've had this funny feeling I couldn't shake. It kept gnawing and working at me." Searching for the proper words, he stumbled on. "That's why I was asking you so many questions about Todd and where he came from. Ellie and I just talked it over and she has had the same feeling ever since we brought him to the house." Here Clay paused and took a deep breath. "We think Todd's our grandson."

Tom was stunned. He looked at Clay to see if he might be joking. Then he glanced at Ellie Howard, half expecting her to object to her husband's foolish notion. She was sitting holding Todd's hand in both of her own, her attention riveted on his face.

Carefully thinking out his answer, Tom turned to Clay, a note of sympathy in his voice. "Both of Todd's parents are alive and living in San Francisco. I know he has gotten letters from them, and he talks about them. Mr. Howard, this is not what you want to hear, but he couldn't be your grandson."

"Tom, don't ask me why, I just know he is. For one thing, he's the image of our daughter. She left because we didn't approve of the man she married. And my middle name happens to be Todd." Going to the fireplace, he bent to pick up a blackened pot of coffee and returned to the table. After pouring Tom another cup he put the pot down, slumped into his own chair and continued.

"The name of the man our daughter married was Baca. Luis Baca." Looking down at his cup of coffee, he said stubbornly, "It's as if the man who took our daughter away brought us back a grandson."

"Mr. Howard," said Tom, his voice hoarse from the deep emotion he felt. "I still think you're mistaken but I'd like to help. What can I do?"

"Bless you," replied Clay. "I guess the first step would be for us to contact the Fields in California. If you know their address, Ellie and I will get a letter written tonight. It can go out on the stage tomorrow."

"Todd carries a bundle of mail in his saddlebag. I suppose he wouldn't mind if I gave it to you." Tom rose to his feet, shifting awkwardly from one foot to the other. He looked hard at the hand-hewn plank floor before he spoke his mind.

"Mr. Howard, you and Mrs. Howard are nice people. I guess you know what you're doing, but you're going to be mighty hurt if you find out Todd is not your grandson."

"I know, Tom, but if we're ever going to have a moment's peace in our lives we have to know for sure."

Tom nodded in agreement and walked to the door. Stopping he looked back. "That was a great supper, Ma'am. Thanks for having me. I'll be back with the letters shortly." Without waiting for a reply he went out into the night.

The Howards' message to the Fields was simple, sincere and to the point. They explained who they were, the circumstances that led to their daughter leaving, who she married and what she looked like. They also stated straightforwardly that they believed Todd might be their grandson, despite the

193

fact they had been told the Fields were his parents. They told the Fields that Todd had been bitten by rattlesnakes and was staying with them until he was better. They made no mention of Luis Baca's death or their fear that Todd might lose an arm.

All through the night Ellie and Clay took turns sitting up with Todd. By morning he seemed better, but he was still running a high temperature.

Shortly after dawn, Clay took the letter into town and left it at Barney Prine's store to be picked up by the stage. Then he returned to stand vigil with his wife. Tom dropped by at midmorning and, seeing that he could do nothing, left after staying only a few minutes.

That evening Todd's fever broke. With a sigh of relief Clay patted Ellie's hand. "Looks like he'll be able to keep that arm, El. Thanks to your nursing."

Too tired and wrought-up to speak, Ellie Howard looked at her husband and nodded, her eyes brimming with tears.

When Tom Pickett had stopped by earlier, the Howards suggested that Todd not be told about their feelings until they heard from the Fields. Tom breathed an inward sigh of relief. He was in full agreement. It would have been awkward for Todd to recover in the home of two people he barely knew who claimed to be his maternal grandparents.

By the third day Todd was sitting up in bed. Ellie never left the cabin, and catered to his every need.

"You remind me of a mother hen clucking over her brood," Clay told her jokingly one evening as she was serving Todd some hot broth and fresh biscuits. "Worse yet, you're going to have him as fat as a wart hog."

Todd, unaware of the reason for so much attention, replied from the bed. "He's right, Mrs. Howard. I must have gained five pounds yesterday alone. It's about time I got up and started working some of it off."

"You'll do no such thing," Ellie Howard scolded. "The military doctor said you should stay in bed for at least a week

194

or you might have a relapse. Putting a little meat on your bones won't hurt you any. You're as thin as a rail."

Todd relaxed and sank back against the big feather pillows that supported him. He felt comfortable with the Howards. As comfortable as he felt with his foster parents in San Francisco.

He wondered what the Fields were doing at this particular moment. Probably gathered around the supper table reviewing the days events. Jamie Fields would be dressed in a formal business suit with matching waistcoat and an immaculate white shirt. His hair would be well-pomaded and neatly combed. Tess would be attired in a dress of the latest style from one of the fashionable shops on Montgomery Street, every strand of hair neatly in place. She would be listening attentively to her husband, asking casual questions before telling everyone what had transpired with her that day. Once their subjects had been exhausted, it would be Katy and Ann's turn to talk.

At the thought of Ann, Todd's pulse quickened. She had been on his mind constantly these past few days, and in private moments he would open the locket and gaze longingly at her picture.

When he was able to use his arm he would write to his family, and Ann, and tell them where he was. Also, he needed to contact Mrs. Blevins in Portland and ask her to forward his mail. He was sure there would be several letters from the Fields, and hopefully some from Ann as well.

Todd vividly recalled Ann's parting words before he left. "How can you leave me? You know I love you." At the time he had cavalierly dismissed them. Now he ached to tell her how much those words meant to him. Would he ever see her again? Did she still feel the same, or had she even forgotten that she said them? No, Todd recalled, in her last letter she had written, "My feelings for you have not changed. It is important to me that you know this. I miss you more than you can imagine." Still, in his absence she might have become infatuated with someone in San Francisco. Visions of Ann being in love with a handsome, wealthy young man raced through his head, consuming him with a feeling of jealousy. He was so engrossed in this daydream that he hadn't noticed Tom's entry. It was only when Tom repeated his name that he snapped back to reality.

"What?" asked Todd, his eyes refocusing on the face in front of him, which was now split by a wide grin.

"Mrs. Howard said I could have your piece of fresh apple pie if you don't want it. But now that you're among the living again, I guess you will."

"Yep, I guess so."

"You're looking better."

"I'm feeling better. Only don't tell Mrs. Howard or she'll throw me out. The cooking here is so good I'm trying to convince her I need to stay in bed another week or two."

"Don't you believe him, Tom," Mrs. Howard said from across the room. "We've practically had to hogtie him to keep him down as it is."

Lying back, Todd winked at Tom. "The real reason I wanted to get up was to go to the outhouse. It's kind of embarrassing using the thundermug with a lady in the house."

At this statement Tom roared with delight. Ellie Howard quickly turned so they couldn't see the blush and smile that spread across her face. "I've seen better bottoms on heifer calves," she replied.

This statement brought gales of laughter from the two men. Wiping his eyes with his thumb and middle finger, Tom couldn't resist adding, "I've seen better bottoms myself, but not on heifers."

"Here, Mr. Bottom Authority, see if you like this," said Ellie in mock severity as she put a piece of hot apple pie before him. Taking another plate to Todd, she spoke to Tom. "If you promise to see that he doesn't get out of bed, I'll get you both a slice of fresh cheese."

Making a crossing motion over his chest, Tom said, "I promise. Cross my heart."

Satisfied, Ellie left for the cold pantry over the spring,

196

which was located about fifty yards from the cabin.

"What do you think of the Howards?" Tom inquired casually.

"Tom, it's strange you should ask that. They treat me as if I was part of their family. And strangely enough, I feel as if I am. I don't know how I'll ever repay the Howards for what they've done.

A thoughtful look passed over Tom's face as he replied, "I don't think they expect to be repaid. They're doing it because they want to."

"That's the way it comes across to me, too."

Seeing Ellie Howard coming down the path, Tom changed the subject. When she entered, they were discussing the Upper Ochoco and the cabin Tom was having the men build for their winter shelter.

Todd had been with the Howards for almost two weeks. Despite the Howards' objections that he shouldn't be working, he insisted on helping Clay replace the rye grass and willow roof with heavy shakes that Clay had sawed to length and split by hand.

Ellie made frequent trips outside to be sure Todd was not overexerting himself. Each time she left with the admonition to her husband not to work Todd too hard, "as he just got out of bed." At dinner she made sure Todd didn't work that afternoon by telling Clay he should visit Horace Singleton to see how their cattle were doing on summer graze. Clay Howard took the hint good-naturedly and left while Ellie was washing the dishes.

"Mrs. Howard," said Todd, "I'm going to walk up to Prine's store. I'll write another letter to my folks there and leave it for the next stage."

"Fine, Todd. Would you mind checking to see if my curtain material has arrived yet? And ask Barney if he needs any eggs. We've got more than we can use."

As Todd left the log cabin, Ellie went to the door. There was a catch in her throat as she watched his movements.

197

With each step he bounced jauntily up and down. His toes pointed to the outside so that his tracks made a narrow V-shape. It was as if she were watching Mary go off to school. Was this her imagination, she wondered, or was her mind playing tricks on her? These last few days had been among the happiest of her life.

Suddenly, she dreaded the arrival of the letter that might tell them Todd was not their grandson.

Todd entered Barney Prine's small ten-by-fourteen-foot willow log building, and made his way to the counter around an obstacle course of unopened crates and barrels. He spent the next half hour chatting with the energetic proprietor about horse racing, then bought some paper and asked to borrow the store's quill pen and some ink. Taking these to a corner table, he sat down to write.

In his letter to the Fields, Todd explained how much the Howards had done for him, and that under their care he had completely recovered and would be joining Tom at their ranch before the week was out. He described the incident at the hotel with Luis Baca, and his shock at hearing the name.

He also recounted his face-to-face encounter with the outlaw: "When I mentioned I was Mary Baca's son, there was absolutely no recognition of her name. He displayed no emotion whatsoever. In fact, his only interest was to know if my name was Baca. When I told him I was named after my grandparents, he asked if my mother was still alive. That's when a rattlesnake struck him. I was bitten trying to help.

"I doubt if I will ever know whether Luis Baca was my father or not. But I do know this: he didn't look at all like me, or act as if he knew my mother. The important thing is, if he was my father I am not like him in any way that I could see. Luis Baca was an evil man, and deserved to die the way he did."

What he wrote to Ann was much more personal. He told her of his worries: that they had almost lost the herd twice, and that such a loss would have been financially devastating; that the hardships were worse than he had ever

198

anticipated, and that there had been times when he considered giving up and returning to San Francisco. But his feelings of self-doubt changed to optimism as he described the beauty of the land, the opportunities the future presented, and how comfortable he felt "with honest people, hard as nails, who are not afraid to take a chance to change their own destiny."

He struggled, but it was difficult for him to put into words how much he cared for her. He did say that he thought of her every day, and closed by adding, "I have so many things to share with you. I miss you more than ever. I hope your feelings about me have not changed. Love, Todd"

Two days later Todd was preparing to leave. He couldn't explain his feelings, but he was reluctant to go. Ellie Howard hugged him hard, released him, held him tightly again, then drew back shyly. Clay Howard, wanting to show more affection but unable to do so, settled for a lingering handshake. Tom had brought Todd's bay and was unobtrusively watching this scene.

Ellie suddenly put a hand to her face. "Land sakes, I almost forgot." Holding her skirts up with both hands she hurried back into the house, returning with a large baking soda tin. Opening the lid, Todd saw that it was full of fresh pan cookies.

"Don't eat any now or it will spoil your supper," Ellie admonished.

This was too much for Tom, who laughed and remarked, "If you knew what he was going to have tonight, you'd say don't eat your supper, it will spoil the cookies. I'm afraid after the way he's been treated here, his meals are going to come as a real shock."

When they reached the Howards' gate, Todd paused to look back and wave. Clay Howard had one arm wrapped tightly around his wife, who was crying into the corner of her apron.

CHAPTER

23

In Portland, the directors of the Oregon Steamship Company were holding an emergency meeting. They had gathered in Homer Siebold's private office, whose large, cut-glass windows overlooked the Willamette River. The stately grandfather clock that had belonged to Siebold's father, and had accompanied him around the Horn from New Bedford, chimed the hour of 5:00 p.m. Its sonorous tones seemed to emphasize the solemn mood of the group. Although it was only two weeks until the first day of summer, a chilly rain was falling outside.

Siebold rose from his straight-backed chair and spoke to the men who were seated around his conference table. "There's no need to tell you why we're here. Certain," he said, stopping to clear his throat, "incidents have disrupted our earlier plans. Captain Geyer's success at getting his cargo to The Dalles, despite our efforts, has made us the laughing stock of our competitors as well as the settlers along the Columbia. This, plus the fact we have been unable to stop the Columbia Cattle Company from reaching Wasco County, has seriously jeopardized our efforts to control the rangeland east of the Cascade mountains."

Standing erect to his full height of a gaunt six feet, he stared at each of them through shrewd, calculating grey eyes, his wizened face and full mutton-chop whiskers a caricature of his Boston ancestry.

"Gentlemen, as president of the OSC I find the situation as it now stands intolerable. It is my personal opinion that if we are going to maintain our authority we must act. And act quickly." Before seating himself he paused, then said, "The matter is open for discussion."

Robert O'Conner rose to speak. His position as shipping and receiving agent in The Dalles had been greatly enhanced by the increased migration of families to the Willamette Valley. He now owned the largest mercantile store in The Dalles, and most of the choice land that spread south and east from Front Street along the military road to the Army post. Like the others around the table, he had worked hard for his position of power and was in no frame of mind to lose it.

O'Conner was brusque and to the point. "It seems to me, Homer, that we are overreacting to Geyer's success in getting one load of cattle up the Columbia. Let me remind you, he made that trip and quit. Since then no one has made any further attempts to challenge our authority." As he sat down he glanced at the faces around the table, relishing the nods of approval he saw.

Jim Nikol was the next one to his feet. "I agree with Bob. Whoever controls the Columbia — and we do — also controls the fishing industry. I haven't been hurt by Geyer's try. The boats I don't own know they have to do business with me if they want to sell their salmon. Our real problem has been stopping the valley ranchers from getting their cattle across the Cascades. Either we'd better give up the idea of expanding into Eastern Oregon, or find someone who can get the job done properly."

Frank Allen angrily jumped to his feet to defend himself, but before he could speak was interrupted by Henry Tabor.

"Jim's right," said the stocky lumberman. "If we didn't call the shots on the Columbia, my business would be in big trouble. What with the demand for lumber in 'Frisco and the

201

boom in Portland, profits have never been better."

Focusing his attention on Frank Allen, another member of the board spoke out. It was Cecil Hershey, who had become the largest feed and seed grower in the Willamette Valley. "Frank, what Henry says makes sense. The river trouble seems to be over, but we have lost control in Eastern Oregon. Nobody's blaming you, exactly, but I guess we'd all like to know if anything is being done to solve the problem."

Allen, a shorter and less imposing figure than his associates, usually made up for the inferiority he felt because of his size by sheer bluster. And today was no exception. He knew that his future status as a director of the Oregon Steamship Company, and the prestige and power that went with this position, depended on what he was about to say.

Putting on his most sincere expression, he blatantly lied, yet mixed enough fact with fiction in the hope of making his story believable. He tucked his thumbs behind his wide leather belt and spread his feet. "I don't disagree with anything that's been said so far. If there has been a delay," — and he emphasized the word 'if' — "in our plans, it has to do with Pickett and Howard getting their cattle across the pass into Central Oregon."

Changing positions, Allen leaned intently over the table, his eyes flashing and his fists clenched so that the knuckles of both hands rested on the highly polished surface of the black oak table. He emphasized every word he spoke, pausing slightly between each one to make his delivery more effective.

"The man I sent didn't follow my instructions. He double-crossed us." Seeing he had everyone's full attention, he straightened and resumed his conversational tone. "I told you the man I was going to put in charge was Luis Baca. I also told you he was competent and trustworthy. He was neither. But I hedged my bets. I had a man with him who was reporting to me. He told me Baca intended to let the Columbia stock through and take them for himself. Baca deliberately let men loyal to us be ambushed and hung, after

202

they told him they would not go along with his plans. To cover his tracks he joined up with an Indian named Grey Wolf. He planned to send word back that Grey Wolf had taken the herd. The man I sent to watch Baca didn't get back with the news in time for me to stop Pickett and Howard, but once I found out what had happened, I sent a hand-picked crew to track Baca down. When they find him, they'll kill him."

O'Conner interrupted. "Seems to me that's like closing the barn door after the horse is stolen."

The silence that followed was broken only by the loud ticking of Siebold's clock. They all looked at Allen, waiting for his reply. While he had been talking, Allen was desperately trying to think of an answer that would both satisfy his associates and provide a solution to the problem. Now he had it!

Turning to hide the look of relief that crossed his face, he folded his arms and lowered his head as if reflecting on an answer. He wanted to shout, "You fools, do you think you can better Frank Allen? The best of you all?"

Instead he slowly faced them, straining not to let the signs of triumph show, his voice held dramatically low. "My instructions were that once they killed Baca, they were to kill Pickett and Howard and any other ranchers in the area. Then take their herds."

Audible gasps followed his statement.

"May I remind you, gentlemen, the last time we met to discuss this matter you asked me what needed to be done. At that time I said we had four choices: control the water, stir up the Indians, rustle the cattle or kill their owners. My recommendation then — and no one disagreed — was that if killing was the best solution, that is what we should do."

The babble of conversation that followed made it necessary for Homer Siebold to rise and call for order several times. Once he had everyone's attention he said, "It gives me some concern that this action may be precipitous and might cause us some embarrassment. Dennis, as the governor's secretary how do you think the governor and legislators will react?"

Mitchell rose to his feet, his slender white hands grasped the silk lapels of his frock coat. He reflected on the question before answering. The others leaned forward to hear his reply.

"With so few people in Wasco County now, I really don't anticipate a problem. The fact that a handful of cowmen have lost their lives trying to settle in an untamed county shouldn't be too hard to gloss over. I say Frank is to be congratulated. He saw what had to be done and did it. In fact, I would like to move that we approve his actions."

"Second," shouted Henry Tabor.

"In that case, all those in favor raise their right hand," said Siebold.

The vote was unanimous.

When the meeting broke up the first to leave was Arnold Boden. As usual no one had asked for his opinion. In fact, most of the board had simply ignored his presence. He stepped unnoticed out of the room, bitter and resentful at the way he had been treated.

Allen headed for the nearest saloon. His mind raced as he walked. That had been a close call. Now he had to put into action those things he told the other directors he was already doing. He would leave first thing in the morning to gather his men. His next thought brought a sardonic grin to his face. He would delay the drink he had in mind and have it with Jack Bartels. Bartels hated Pickett and would welcome the opportunity to get revenge for the licking he had taken. If he played his cards right, Bartels might even be talked into joining him in Eastern Oregon.

Turning at the corner of Morrison, Allen walked south on First Street. He turned left again at Yamhill and proceeded to Front, where a line of sailing vessels were being unloaded. His destination was the Red Dog, located near the corner of Salmon.

As Frank Allen elbowed his way through the batwing doors of the popular saloon, the heat from a potbellied stove combined with the sour odor of the bar hit him full in the face. Squinting through the blue haze of the smoke-filled room, he looked for Bartels. Not seeing him, he walked to a vacant spot at the counter and signaled an aproned bartender, who acknowledged his presence with a nod. After filling and serving three previously ordered mugs of beer, the sallow, middle-aged barman came over. "What's your poison?" he asked as he wiped his hands on a stained bar rag.

"Some information," answered Allen.

Narrowing his eyes warily, the bartender appraised Allen for several seconds before he spoke. "What kind of information?"

"I'm looking for Jack Bartels. I understand he hangs out here."

The bartender folded his gartered arms, threw back his head and roared. "Not any more he don't. Ever since he got whupped he's been drinkin' at the Waterfront. I expect that's where you're apt to find him."

Nodding his thanks Allen turned, retraced his steps and went outside. Pulling the collar of his wool Mackinaw around his ears and settling his hat more securely on his head, he turned right and headed for Jefferson Street. The chill of the river joined with a cold breeze from the dark fir forests that surrounded the growing port community to create a numbing wind. Suddenly it started to pour. Allen tucked his chin into the warmth of his raised lapels and reached up with his right hand to hold his coat together. He had lost the top button months ago and had never bothered to have it replaced.

Allen knew of the Waterfront Saloon. It had a rough reputation. The locals avoided the place like the plague, considering it no better than the worst dives on San Francisco's Barbary Coast. The unwary who went there for a drink usually came to the next morning on a ship bound for the Sandwich Islands or with their pokes missing and a lump on their head. A few never woke at all. Their bodies were dumped in the Willamette River to be swept downstream.

As Frank Allen thought of this, he shifted the weight of his gun belt and pulled his handgun slightly out of its holster to be sure it wouldn't stick if he needed to use it in a hurry. How should he best approach Bartels? The fact that Bartels could no longer hold his head up in the Red Dog would certainly rankle him. Allen would play hard on this fact.

The laughter and signs of merriment that had emanated from the saloons he passed in the busy, well-inhabitated section of Front Street gave way to darkness, and a stillness which was broken only by the creaking of vessels at anchor and the lapping of water against the pier. This section of Portland had no gas lamps and the few people he saw were hurriedly moving to their destinations, casting furtive glances around as they went. Allen picked up his own pace, one hand on his gun butt, the open collar forgotten. This was no time to be careless. He kept as far away as possible from the shadow-darkened recesses of the alleys.

Stopping before the entrance of the saloon he was seeking, Allen glanced up and down the street. The windows on both sides of the door were tightly shuttered, allowing only faint rays of yellowish light to escape from the interior. The door itself was oversized, and on its front was nailed a steam-ship's navigational wheel, reputed to be from one of the steamers that had plied its trade from Astoria to Portland before it had been beached by rough weather on the rocks where the mouth of the Columbia River meets the Pacific. Two two spokes of the wheel were broken and three handle pegs were missing.

Pushing the door open, Allen stepped inside. All talk ceased as the occupants turned to inspect this newcomer. A single ship's lantern burned over the bar, which at one time had been part of the bridge of a sailing vessel. Sparring hung haphazardly from the ceiling, and a well-worn mainmast in the center of the room supported a sagging roof. A rusty, dented lantern sat on a beam over the door through which he had just entered. Its flickering light threw Allen's distorted shadow before him.

Walking slowly and carefully to the bar, Allen quietly addressed the bartender, a dirty, one-armed ex-seaman with a vivid red scar on the left side of his face that covered the spot where an eye should have been. "I have business with Jack Bartels."

"Newcomer to Portland, are ye?" the bartender asked, his voice raised loud enough for all to hear.

"No, I just do my drinking somewhere else. And the only conversation I want is with Bartels."

Squinting at Allen with his rheumy good eye, tobacco juice drooling out of both sides of his mouth onto a week's growth of whiskers, the bartender tilted his head toward the back of the saloon. "Ye'll find him playing cards in back."

"Tell him Frank Allen is at the bar and would like a word with him."

The bartender walked to the far end of the bar. Leaning on his one good arm he massaged his stump, spat over the counter onto the bare floor, and replied insolently. "If ye want to see Jack Bartels, I guess ye'll jest have to announce yourself."

Their conversation had been followed by the crowd, and this comment brought forth some raucous laughs and a few insulting side comments.

With deliberate, measured strides, Allen went to the door the barman had indicated. Stopping before it, he raised one foot and kicked hard. The door flew inward on its hinges.

Five men were in the room, seated around a table covered with cards and chips. Half-empty whiskey bottles, glasses, and tin cans that had been cut in half to serve as ashtrays littered the patched felt surface. The occupants leaped up at the crash, knocking over chairs and spilling their drinks. The smoke in the room was so thick that Allen could not distinguish Bartels among them until one of the obscure figures spoke.

"It's all right, I know him." Coming forward, Jack Bartels said deferentially, "Mr. Allen. What are you doing here?"

"I was hoping to have a word with you, Jack."

"Sure, Mr. Allen." Looking around the room Bartels

207

asked, "Boys, do you mind if we talk?" Knowing this was a private matter, the others pocketed their chips and silently filed out.

Allen took a seat and repeated the same basic story he had told the OSC directors, embellishing only those points he thought might incite Bartels' anger toward Todd Howard and Tom Pickett.

After Allen had finished, Bartels picked up a bottle of whiskey and held it out to Allen, who shook his head. Bartels put the bottle to his mouth and took a long pull.

Putting the whiskey down, Bartels licked his lips, wiped his mouth with the fingers of a grimy hand, and said, "You've got yourself a taker, Mr. Allen. I've got a debt to settle with those two and this looks like the chance to do it. You can count Sid Bacon in, too. He does what I tell him."

"Good. I'll have that drink now."

Reaching over to get a glass which had been used by one of the departing players, Bartels threw its contents on the floor and filled the tumbler, which he passed to the cattleman. Pouring a healthy measure for himself into another glass, he raised it in a salute.

"Here's to the end of the Columbia Cattle Company."

After finishing this toast, the slight OSC director bent forward. "How soon can you start?"

Leaning back in his chair, Bartels scratched his chest and rubbed his protruding stomach. "First thing tomorrow morning suit you?"

"It does," said Allen, rising to his feet. "I'll leave at first light to pick up my men. We'll meet you below Cow Canyon off the Grizzly Mountain stage road. From there we'll travel east and headquarter near the south fork of the John Day."

His business finished, Allen walked to the door, stopped, and looked back at Bartels, who had remained seated. "By the way, I forgot to ask. Can you handle a horse?"

"Yes, and I'd ride to hell and back for a chance to stick a knife in the bellies of Howard and Pickett."

CHAPTER

24

Todd Howard and Tom Pickett turned off the dusty main street of Prine and headed east. When the last building faded from view Todd pulled up, stood in his stirrups and inhaled deeply. It was good to be back in the saddle again. With each lungful of fresh air, his spirits rose.

An hour later they crossed Mill Creek. Tom pointed up the valley through which the stream ran. "That's where the first settlers staked their claims. To our right are the mountains Archie Ridley said were named for Colonel Reuben Maury. He commanded the First Oregon Volunteer Cavalry. They were organized to keep the Indians under control when the Union Army withdrew its troops to fight in the Civil War. The lost wagon train of '45 passed by those mountains, just east of here at a place called Camp Creek. Barney Prine told me some of the metal he uses in his blacksmith shop came from the wagons they had to abandon. Straight ahead of us is the Ochoco Mountain Range. That peak you see between the break in the hills is called Lookout Mountain."

"You've sure learned your history," Todd said, complimenting Tom.

"Yeah, I guess so. Folks around here are proud of The Ochoco, so you pick up a lot of information. The place kind of grows on you."

The broad, open valley through which they rode was protected by a mesa of fault-block mountains whose gentle slopes were dotted with isolated stands of scrub juniper. Ancient lava cones, mantled by three centuries of dust that nourished their sage-dotted surface, rose up like giant anthills.

Two miles past Mill Creek the valley narrowed. Rolling hills became tree-lined draws. The stunted, irregular-shaped juniper gave way to stands that grew tall and straight. Again their passage opened. Broad meadows spread before them, backed by the full beauty of the Ochoco Range.

An hour later the valley closed in once more, like the shape of a giant hourglass, narrowing then expanding. Ochoco Creek, whose banks were lined with willows, tamarack, birch and aspen, wound lazily through the bottom land, forcing them to recross its shallow bed. Lupine, haleboro, wild astor and desert hawk's-beard colored the fields. Mule deer and wild game were so plentiful that Tom broke his silence and remarked, "Looks like we can save our beef and butcher only when we get tired of venison and birds."

Overhead an osprey scanned the rippling stream for his midday meal. The delicately feathered tips of his wings were spread wide to better guide and sustain his vigilant search.

As Todd and Tom worked their way past a beaver pond, Todd spotted an orange-hued coyote casually trotting up a rise. A fat ground squirrel hung from its mouth. Stopping his horse to watch, Todd saw the doglike animal approach a crevice in a rocky outcropping. There it was greeted by three yipping balls of fur, each snapping voraciously at the meal their mother had brought to her den.

As their route turned northeast, the juniper gave way to stands of sugar pine and dense growths of shorter jack pine. Farther ahead the valley broke into ridges of stately Douglas fir and towering ponderosa. Noting this, Todd added his own comment. "Reckon we don't have to go far for building material, either."

"Yep," answered Tom. "Nature's a good provider when she wants to be. She takes care of her own. Like those beaver who have been working on the birch saplings yonder. They not only use the wood for building their dams, but also for food. And it's their dentist. Their teeth don't stop growing, so they gnaw on the wood even when they don't have any use for it. Otherwise their upper teeth would grow right through their bottom jaw." To qualify this last statement he added, "At least that's what Barney Prine told me."

Off in the distance a gathering of white cumulus clouds covered the top of the mountain toward which they rode. Tom pointed this out. "That's Lookout. The one we saw when we started out. Never stays the same. I could sit and watch it all day long."

As if cued by his remark, the cloud cap lifted, showing a majestic table-topped peak that was still carrying occasional spots of shadow-protected snow, the last remnants of violent winter storms. The sun's rays moved slowly across the face of the mountain, highlighting one ridge and darkening another, until the shadowed areas turned a purplish blue, then into strips of vivid green as the lighting rearranged its own patterns. They stopped briefly to stretch, then remounted and continued on. The creak of their saddle leather, the occasional blowing of their horses who expressed displeasure at not being able to graze the tender grass, and the calls and cries of the wild birds were the only sounds they heard. It was magnificent country, still unspoiled. The way God had created it.

"That's our stock up ahead," said Tom as they broke through a stand of willows. "They're spread out for another five or six miles."

When they neared a peak whose sides were covered with blackened and charred trees, the result of a decade-old lightning fire, Tom gestured up the draw to their right. "There's our luxurious ranch house," he laughed, pointing to a frame of logs that was the beginning of a crude shelter. "Come cold weather we'll have it finished. Right now the boys

211

are working on a corral for the horses. That comes first. Then a barn to store hay for winter."

They pulled up at a pine corral. The crew who weren't out riding herd paused in their work to wave, then wander over. Reub Hassler was the first to arrive.

Taking off his stained, weather-beaten hat, Reub scratched his thinning brown hair with black and broken nails. Then he wiped the sweat from his hatband with a red kerchief, replaced his hat and squinted up at Todd. "Glad to see you up and about. Looks like you haven't missed any meals at the trough," he observed, referring to the weight Todd had put on.

"It's mighty good to be on two legs," Todd replied. "After the meals I've had, I don't know whether I'm up to eating Cookie's grub or not."

By now the rest of the crew had gathered around, calling out friendly greetings. Sliding from the saddle Todd shook hands with each one. Shorty Hansen eyed him cagily. "Guess you'll be glad to hear we ain't seen any rattlers in this neck of the woods."

"Better news than you think," said Todd, suppressing a shudder. "The next one I see, I'm giving wide berth to. Say, it looks like you fellows have been doing all the work while I've been taking it easy."

"Yeah," said Shorty. "But there's still a lot more to do. We can use another pair of hands."

Todd pulled the saddle off his mount and said, "Where do I start?"

"Since you're the rested one, how about giving me a hand notching some corner posts for the barn," Tom replied.

Three weeks later the corral, barn and winter cabin were finished. However, until cold weather set in, the cattlemen preferred to sleep outside. Shorty Hansen summed up how they all felt when he made the statement, "Who wants to sleep indoors when the stars make a perfectly good roof." Todd agreed. Some nights as he was lying on his back gazing at the heavens, he felt as if he could reach up and touch them.

With the buildings done, the cowhands turned to branding cattle. The stench of singed hide and hair filled the air.

"What with the new calves, I figure we should have about 400 head apiece," Tom said, his face blackened by the smoke of the sage fire they used to heat the irons.

It was Art Seaforth, sitting astride his horse and holding a tight rope on a bawling heifer, who first saw the rider. He waited until the young cow had been marked, then shook his riata loose from its hind legs and called out, "Someone comin' in from the west, and he ain't lettin' any grass grow under his feet." Looking up, the dusty punchers saw a single horseman race down a swale about a quarter-mile away.

"Something's wrong," said Tom. "A man wouldn't push his horse like that in this heat unless there was trouble."

As the rider drew closer, they saw it was Jay Munro, one of Horace Singleton's hands. Munro rode up and in his haste to dismount he stumbled slightly as his feet touched the ground. Todd could see from the lather on his horse that he had been ridden long and hard. Without any preliminary greetings Munro asked, "You fellas had any trouble?"

"Nothing unusual, Jay. Why do you ask?"

"Someone hit us yesterday evening. Shot up the night watch and ran off with damn near half the herd. Same thing happened the night before at Hal Murphy's spread on McKay Creek. They got better than a hundred head off him. We followed their sign north toward Antelope but lost 'em in the rocky section this side of Trout Creek."

"Was it Indians?" asked Tom.

"Nope. Shod horses ran those cattle, and it weren't no two-bit outfit, either. Must have been at least thirty, maybe forty riders."

"Did anybody get a look at them?" Todd asked.

"Nary a glance. They hit our two hands at dusk, and it weren't 'til the late night watch went to relieve 'em that we found out what happened. One dead, the other had his skull creased. He was still out cold when I left. We couldn't do much 'til daylight, and by then they were long gone."

Tom pursed his lips and stared into space as his mind digested what he had heard. Then he spoke. "Looks like all the outfits around here had better get together."

"My boss has already talked to Clay Howard and Archie Ridley. They feel the same way. I was to tell you there's a meetin' tonight at Howard's place."

"Tell Horace we'll be there," said Todd.

"Best I get goin' then," said Jay Munro.

"You had a hard ride. How about some coffee and beans?" Todd offered.

"I'm obliged, but we're gatherin' in our cattle and I best not linger. Mr. Singleton will need every man."

"That mare of yours looks pretty tired," said Tom, casting an appraising eye over Jay Munro's horse. "Take one of ours. I'll ride yours back tonight and we can switch at the Howards'."

"Thanks, I'll do that. I didn't have my thinkin' cap on straight. She's plumb tuckered out, that's for sure. Good horses are hard to come by, and only a damn fool would ride one to death."

As he left, Todd, Tom, Shorty and Reub gathered in a huddle. "Looks like we'd best get our cattle branded fast," said Tom. "Then pull them in where we can keep an eye on 'em."

Directing his gaze at Reub he added, "Todd and I will ride into town after we get this batch of steers finished. Give Munro's paint some water and grain, then tie her up in the shade. Shorty, round up the strays. Bring them to the big meadow and hold them there until we find out what's going on. Double the guard and keep a sharp eye out for trouble. We should be back by midnight."

After grabbing an early supper, Todd and Tom started for town.

The light had just begun to fade when they rode up to Clay Howard's cabin. From the number of horses tied to

214

the hitching bar, it was obvious they were the last to arrive. They dismounted and led their cow ponies to the watering trough. While the horses were having a drink Todd took the opportunity to look around.

A number of changes had been made since he was here last. The kitchen was now in a separate room, which made the living room larger. New calico curtains hung from the windows, and there was a trellis for the growing matrimony vine. Marigolds in full bloom surrounded the house.

Todd and Tom stepped through the front door and were warmly greeted by Clay Howard. Ellie had been serving coffee and at their appearance hurried into the kitchen. They said their hellos to the men they knew, then turned to meet two men they didn't recognize. Clay introduced them.

"Todd, Tom, this is Hal Murphy and Elmer Johns. Hal has the place north of here on McKay Creek that was raided. Elmer's spread is on the Deschutes."

After the four had shaken hands, Clay asked, "You two hungry? Ellie can fix something."

"We've had supper, but thanks," Tom responded. "It looks like we're the last to arrive, so I suggest we get down to business."

Horace Singleton, who had sent Jay Munro to alert Todd and Tom, spoke first. "I'm afraid we don't know much more than we did when Hal and I sent riders out to get in touch with all of you. We lost one man, as you know. The other finally regained consciousness. He couldn't tell us much. They must have laid in wait for him and Ted Berry — our man who was killed — because neither had a chance to draw leather. We sent a rider to Warm Springs to alert the military, but we're out of their jurisdiction so I doubt there's much they can do to help us."

Looking around uncomfortably, Horace Singleton nervously shifted his weight from one foot to the other. A quiet, self-effacing man, he was not used to being the center of attention. Realizing he had nothing more to say, he abruptly sat down.

"Thank you, Horace," Clay said. Turning to Hal Murphy, whose herd had been rustled first, he asked, "Can you give us any more information, Hal?"

The tall, lean rancher whom Todd and Tom had just met stood up. Stuffing the fingers of both hands in his back pockets, he shifted a quid of chewing tobacco to his left cheek and spoke out angrily. "I can't add much to what Horace told you. They took us the same way." Removing his right hand from a back pocket, he pulled at the lobe of his right ear. "Only difference was we didn't have anyone on guard. Had our cows in a box canyon. The grass was good, so we figured they wouldn't wander.

"The rustlers struck late in the afternoon. Got fifty steer and twenty-five pair." He added bitterly, "None of them branded. We were going to do that the next day. We followed their trail but lost them in the rocks. That's when we bumped into Horace, who was looking for his own beef." Raising his voice an octave louder, his eyes radiating his feelings, he exclaimed, "I've got too much invested in them cows, and in getting them here, to take this lying down."

Clay Howard spoke softly. "We all understand your feelings, Hal. That's why we're here. We don't intend to just sit by and do nothing about it."

Archie Ridley jumped to his feet, his voice charged with emotion. "Well, we sure as hell ain't goin' to catch 'em sitting around this table jawin'. I say let's get our men together and go after 'em." Sitting down he folded his arms defiantly, looking around the table and nodding his head at each man, confident that they would agree with what he had just said.

It was Todd who answered. "Archie, until we know who and what we're chasing, it won't do any good to ride off in all directions. If we did, our herds would be left unguarded."

Archie Ridley's crestfallen expression indicated that Todd's point was well taken.

Singleton agreed. "Todd's right. There's nobody readier than I am to get my cows back, but we have to know what

216

we're up against before we make our move."

At this point the meeting disintegrated into a series of loud, individual arguments. Leaning across the table and taking Clay Howard's arm, Todd raised his voice over the din. "If you can quiet them down, I have a thought or two."

Reaching around, Clay took a cowbell off the wall, one Ellie used to call him when he was out in the field. Clanging this loudly he finally got everyone's attention. "All of this is getting us nowhere. Todd here says he's got an idea. I dare say that if he has we should listen to it. Go ahead, Todd."

"There's not much doubt in my mind that Frank Allen and the OSC are behind all this. But we don't know for sure, and until we do we're just guessing. I'd like to suggest we hire some Indian scouts from the Warm Springs reservation to move around in the hills, see what they can find, and report back to us. From what Captain Springer says, they don't miss much. In the next day or two Horace's rider will be back from talking to the Army, and we'll find out what they know. Meanwhile we can best put our time to use getting our cattle out of the hills and branded."

Seeing these comments were well received, and not wanting the meeting to deteriorate again, Clay quickly moved to accept Todd's ideas.

Archie Ridley, somewhat chastened by the dampening of his earlier outburst, seconded the motion and suggested the Indians might be willing to trade their services for beef. The motion and Archie's idea were unanimously approved by the cattlemen, who were relieved to have arrived at a course of action.

After the meeting Clay approached Todd and asked if he could stay for a while after the others left.

"Sure thing, Clay. I was planning on saying hello to Ellie anyway."

While Clay was shaking hands with the last of his guests Tom left with Horace Singleton to exchange horses. Todd strolled into the kitchen. He started to say how much he missed Ellie's home cooking when he noticed a stricken

217

look on her face. Without a word she turned and nervously began fussing with some dirty dishes in the sink.

When Clay entered, Ellie gave an audible sigh of relief and hurried to her husband's side.

In an attempt to put Todd at ease Clay said softly, "I guess if Ellie had known earlier that you were coming, she would have done some baking. But she didn't hear about the meeting until late this afternoon."

Todd, realizing that something was bothering the Howards, said he would settle for another cup of coffee. Then he sat at their bare pine table and looked down at his hands, which were clasped in front of him. His voice broke the awkward silence. "I must have done something to hurt you folks. I don't know what it was, but I guess the reason you asked me to stay is because you wanted to talk about it."

Taking the seat across the table, Clay looked at Ellie then back at Todd. "It's nothing you've done, it's something we've done. We should have told you before, but didn't want to say anything until we found out for sure."

During this conversation Ellie had walked across the room and was standing behind her husband. Her two hands were biting into his shoulders.

Reaching into his shirt pocket, Clay pulled out three folded letters. One had been opened and contained an object of some sort. The other two were sealed. Sliding the open letter to Todd, Clay said, "This letter, which contains a locket, is to us. The others are to you. I know this all sounds strange, but after you read them you'll better understand.

"Ellie and I would like to ask you one favor. That you wait until you get back to your place before you look at them."

Sensing that Todd might be thinking some tragedy had befallen the Fields, Clay hastily added, "I can assure you nothing has happened to your family. They are all well."

"If that's what you wish, then of course I will do as you ask," Tom replied solemnly. "I know that whatever you did, it was with the best of intentions."

218

Todd felt uneasy as he left the house to join Tom, who was waiting outside. He knew a major change had just taken place in his relationship with the Howards, and he hoped the letters would explain why.

When he got to the ranch Todd hurried to the vacant bunkhouse. He lit the lantern that hung over the rough plank table, raised the wick for more light, and sat down. He placed the three letters in front of him. Then he reached for the one that had been opened and set aside the locket it contained. It bore the distinct handwriting of his foster mother and was addressed to the Howards.

The first two paragraphs dealt with her deep concern about Todd and their desire to be kept informed of his condition.

Todd paused, glad that he had written to let them know he recovered with no ill effects. Then he continued reading.

I am sitting down this evening to write, as Mr. Fields and I know you are anxious to receive a reply as soon as possible.

Although Todd is as dear to us as if he were our own son, he is our foster son.

His mother Mary was my best friend. She died in labor, giving birth to Todd. I knew very little about her husband, other than his name was Luis Baca and that he had abandoned her shortly after they arrived in San Francisco. She spoke often of her parents, who were living in the Willamette Valley in Oregon, with great love and affection. (Todd was named after her father, whose middle name was Todd. If she had a girl, she wanted her to be named Eleanor after her mother.) I truly believe that she wanted to write to them when her husband left but was too ashamed to do so. If you are her parents, you would know how proud and independent she was.

Mary was forced to work as a laundress to earn a livelihood. This is where we met. She could have made more money at any of the establishments along the Barbary Coast, but her moral standards were too high to do so.

Everyone who knew Mary loved her dearly. Shortly after her death a rider was dispatched with a letter addressed to her family in Sheridan, Oregon.

This letter carried the news of Todd's birth. It was sent by Mrs. Heinreich Schwartz, who was also with her when she died.

When her parents never answered, I took Todd as my own child. Shortly thereafter I met and married Mr. Fields, who also accepted Todd as his son. We love Todd as much as if we were his real parents.

With the exception of the enclosed locket, which contains daguerreotypes of her mother and father, Mary left no personal effects. From your description of her and the man she married, it sounds as if Mary could have been your daughter. The pictures should verify this one way or the other.

I have never shown them to Todd. Probably for selfish reasons, but also because we did not know if his grandparents had rejected him. If they had, we wanted to spare him this pain.

I am sending a separate note to Todd. You might also want to let him read this letter.

We are thrilled that he may have found his maternal grandparents. If the locket proves this to be so, would you please be kind enough to inform us at your earliest convenience.

With the greatest respect,
Mrs. Jamie Fields

Todd picked up the locket and opened it. There was no doubt whatsoever. The frozen images that stared back at him were those of a younger Clay and Ellie Howard.

CHAPTER

25

Todd picked up the second letter, which was also in Tess's handwriting, and tore open the flap.

Dearest Todd:

First let me say how much we miss you. All of us have been praying for your full recovery, and we are anxiously awaiting word from either you or the Howards that will put our minds at ease. As I am writing this letter to you, Ann is writing one of her own.

I am assuming that you have read my letter to the Howards, so I won't repeat myself. We never kept the fact that you were not our true son a secret from you, and for this I am thankful. Should the Howards be your grandparents, our hearts would be filled with joy.

Your mother was a warm and sensitive person. I see many of her traits in you. My one regret is that she never lived to see the fine son she brought into this world. Life works in mysterious ways. After her tragic death, your birth gave my life new meaning and direction. Had it not been for your love, I would have given up all hope for a better life. My prayers are with you. Your happiness is very precious to me and to your father.

I know that it is difficult for you to write more often, but we do worry when we don't hear from you.

Love,

Mother

Todd rose, walked to the open bunkhouse door and gazed at the shimmering sky. After collecting his thoughts, he returned to the table. His heart beat faster as he studied the delicate handwriting on the last envelope. Hurriedly he unsealed it.

Todd dearest,

Father read the Howard's letter to all of us at the supper table tonight. What wonderful news that you might have found your grandparents after so many years!

I am so happy for you. Call me silly, but I know somehow that the Howards are your own mother's parents. It is apparent from their letter that they are forthright and honest people. I am going to tell you a secret, but don't tell mother or father that I told you. Father said if the Howards are your grandparents, he feels you should be referred to by the family name of Howard. I know that this decision is a hard one for him to make, but he is doing it out of love for you. When he said this, he wistfully added that he hoped you would still keep the name Fields in your full name.

Now you have no legitimate excuse for not proposing to me! Although I have not mentioned it to them directly, I am sure that Mother and Father are aware of my feelings for you, and I know they approve. It is improper for a lady to propose, so you must do so. But don't worry, I know you are too busy to come to San Francisco. So I have found a way to solve this problem. Father is considering a lumber investment and mentioned that he has been thinking about traveling to Portland on business later this year. When he heard about your accident, he definitely decided to make the trip so that he could see you. I shall talk him into letting me accompany him. Perhaps you could meet me there. If not I will hire a mule and go to Eastern Oregon!

As you can see, I won't take no for an answer. In fact, I shall go see Mr. Woo in Chinatown tomorrow. He is known to cast spells on people, and I will give him a small retainer to be sure you think of no one but me.

If our first child is a girl, we shall name her Mary after your mother. The first boy we shall christen Jamie, after my father. The other six you can name!

I think of you constantly and have never taken off the necklace you sent me from Portland.

I love you,
Ann

At the bottom of the letter she had randomly written Mrs. Todd Howard several times, followed by a P.S.:

See, I'm already practicing how to write my new name.

Todd pulled the locket that Ann had given him out of his pocket. He undid the catch and gazed at her portrait. She did indeed have the capacity to cast a spell over him. The half-smile turned into a mischievous grin, and her blue eyes glistened with laughter as the sun glinted off her honey-hued tresses, the way it had that day after his nineteenth birthday on San Francisco's Nob Hill.

He knew one thing for certain: he wanted her to be his wife and would meet her in Portland to tell her how he felt.

Todd folded the letters and placed them in his bunk chest along with the locket containing his grandparents' pictures. Tomorrow he would write to the Fields and to Ann. He now understood why the Howards had acted so strange. It might take a little time for the three of them to get over any initial shyness, but Todd knew in his heart that this would happen and that a comfortable relationship would follow.

In the distance a coyote began its mournful howl to signal the beginning of a new day. Todd stretched lazily, turned down the lantern and left the cabin. The white faces of the nearby herd lifted from their grazing to gaze at him curiously as he walked to the creek to wash his face.

Tom knew Todd had not been to bed, and studied him closely when they met for breakfast. He also realized Todd and the Howards had been in serious conversation the evening before, and not wanting to interrupt had waited outside long after he and Horace Singleton had traded mounts. He figured it might have had something to do with the Howards' claim that Todd was their grandson. In any case Todd would tell him when the time was right. Until then it was none of his business. His mind centered on the day's activities.

Later, when they were riding out to check for strays, Todd told Tom about the letters and what had transpired at the Howards. Tom responded enthusiastically to the news that Clay and Ellie were Todd's grandparents, then turned sober.

"Todd, I've never told you much about my background. My parents, my only living grandparent and my two sisters were killed by a band of Cayuse. My folks were homesteading near the lower landing of the Cascades. I was hunting and found them when I got back. Funny though, I've never really hated the Indians for what they did."

As they rode on silently in the dry morning heat, Todd was on the verge of expressing his condolences when Tom spoke again. "Did you know the Indians believe a coyote god created all of their tribes? They call him Speelyei. According to their legends he deliberately let himself be swallowed by a giant beaver who ate trees and men. Once inside the stomach of the beaver, who they call Wishpoosh, he killed it. Afterwards he cut off the head and threw it east. This became the Nez Perce. The arms he threw south. These turned into the Cayuse. The legs became the Klickitats, and from the belly came the Chinook. The pieces that were left he threw into Idaho. These became the various Snake tribes."

Looking at Todd, he asked a question that required no answer. "How can we judge these people by our standards? People born wild, who truly believe they are descendants of a mythical beast."

Tom then changed the subject. Shading his eyes and glancing up at the sun he said, "Looks like it's going to be a scorcher. Best we get our thoughts turned to the day's work."

Todd, realizing Tom wanted to avoid further talk about his family, replied. "No question about it. How long do you think it will take to finish up the branding?"

"A good two days, I reckon. But I don't know what we'll do with the cattle after that. In heat like this, we should be moving them into the woods and saving the pasture for fall graze."

"We don't have much choice, Tom. About all we can do for the time being is sit tight."

Tom, who was slightly ahead of Todd, suddenly reached out and grabbed the reins of Todd's horse.

"Hold on. I heard something."

Todd cocked his head. "Sounds like thunder." As he spoke, muffled booms rolled through the slanting foothills and spread down the valley.

"Listen again, Todd. There's not a cloud in the sky. That's more like gunfire."

Todd cupped both ears. "You may be right. Where do you think it's coming from?"

"I'd say from the north. Where Archie has his beef."

"Shall I go back and get the crew?"

"There's no time. If someone is hitting Ridley's place he'll need our help now. Shorty is gathering cows on the other side of that knoll. Let's find him."

Simultaneously they spurred their horses. Topping the ridge they spotted Shorty working three pair through a dense thicket of manzanita. Whistling shrilly, Tom caught his attention and motioned him over.

"What's up?" Shorty asked as he drew abreast of them, his horse blowing heavily from the steep climb.

"Shots over toward Archie's. We'll ride on ahead. Pick up as many men as we can spare, then catch up with us."

As they drew closer to Archie's ranch, Tom pulled up. "Soon as we get to that next hogback we'll have a look. But let's take a listen first." Tom got down and put one ear to the ground.

Springing quickly to his feet, he said excitedly, "We'd best get out of here and into that bunch of jack pine up above. There are a lot of cattle coming this way and they're moving fast!"

The two partners rode through the dense growth of small trees and tied their horses out of sight. Then they worked their way back and knelt behind a rotting log that provided shelter.

"God Almighty," exclaimed Tom, sucking in his breath. "Look at that."

In the dry wash they had just left, three riders were leading well over a hundred head of cattle. Flanking the herd were four outriders. These were followed by three horsemen riding drag. Touching Tom's arm lightly, Todd nodded toward several figures far to the rear of the group. This bunch had lassoed large clumps of heavy sage, which they were dragging over the ground to cover their trail.

"I see 'em. Pretty smart."

"Some of the cows have been branded and some haven't," Todd whispered hoarsely. "Those that have are carrying Ridley's Rocking A brand."

"Yeah, but where are Ridley's men?" Tom responded. "They should be right on the heels of these varmints."

Four riders topped the crest of the hill facing them. They were going full tilt and pulled up in a swirl of dust where the three who had been riding drag were waiting. All seven consulted briefly, then two left to follow the herd. The other five fanned out along both sides of the gully.

"Looks like Ridley's boys aren't too far behind at that," Tom observed.

Suddenly three more riders appeared over the brow of the hill and galloped by.

"So that's it," Todd commented grimly. "They're working in relays to slow up Archie's hands until they can get the cattle away." A moment later he stiffened. "Tom, quick. That last bunch of riders! See anyone you know?"

Uttering an obscenity, Tom replied. "Jack Bartels and Sid Bacon. Those two cutthroats are a long way from Portland. Well, what do you know," he added, pointing at a man in a light leather vest and fringed chaps behind the two seamen. "There's somebody you haven't met yet. The tall dog himself, Frank Allen. It's not often you see him doing his own dirty work."

Their attention was diverted from the three OSC men by the sound of shots from the rustlers who had remained behind. Looking toward the outlaws' back trail, they saw a group of horsemen scatter, then dismount and return fire. Among this group of new arrivals was one of Ridley's sons. Within seconds the air was again resounding with the popping sounds of gunfire and the acrid smell of black powder.

"What a spot," Tom cursed bitterly. "We're in the wrong position to be of any help."

Todd mulled the situation over, then rolled sideways and faced his friend.

"Tom, this can work to our advantage. They don't know we're here. After a while, they'll fall back again. I'm going to leave now and follow the herd. You wait until they pass, then tell Archie's boys what I'm up to."

Tom started to protest but Todd said, "No. This is something I want to do."

"Take care of yourself, then," replied Tom, knowing it would do no good to argue. "Don't take any chances. When you find out where they're going, circle back and join up with us."

Throughout the rest of the day, Todd stalked the stolen beef, taking special care not to be seen. He frequently lost visual contact with the cattle but was aware they were taking an easterly course. It was a good three hours since he had heard any shots. Obviously the rustlers had made good their escape. As he was slowly working his way around a pile of rubble left by the roots of a giant ponderosa pine that had been toppled by a combination of age, disease and the wind, a sharp command stopped him.

"Grab air, cowhand. Unless you want a bullet between the shoulder blades."

A chill crawled up the back of Todd's neck. He stiffened and raised his hands.

"Take your left hand and unbuckle your gunbelt. Then throw down your rifle."

Todd fumbled at the belt and dropped it. Then he removed his carbine and let it fall.

"Now," said the voice, "get off that horse. Slowly. Any sudden move and you're goin' to be deader'n a door nail."

When Todd lowered himself from the saddle he shifted just enough to see his opponent, who guffawed loudly as their eyes met.

"Well, looky here. If it ain't my pal from Portland, Todd Howard. I thought someone was skulkin' around, but I didn't know I'd be so lucky as to catch you. Come now, cat got your tongue? You remember your old friend Jack Bartels."

The speaker's face turned mean and his eyes flashed with hate. "I haven't forgotten you, Mr. fine and fancy Howard. Or your friend Tom Pickett."

"I haven't forgotten you either, Bartels. You're a big man behind that gun now, but you weren't so big at the Red Dog when Tom twisted your tail. By the way, how's your jaw?"

A hot rage swept over Bartels. His face flushed red and he screamed, "Move over to that pine and put your back to it. And don't try any tricks."

Todd did as he was told, wincing as Bartels savagely pulled his arms around the tree and lashed his wrists together.

After Todd was securely bound, Bartels faced his victim and chuckled gleefully. "This calls for a drink."

228

He disappeared into the woods and returned leading his horse. Opening a saddlebag he took out a pint of whiskey and walked back to face Todd. Pulling the cork out with his teeth, he took a long, hard pull. "One for me," he said, then taking another drink, he spat the contents directly into Todd's face. "And one for you."

His eyes burning from the cheap rye, Todd deliberately wiped his tongue over his lips. "I see you're still drinking rotgut. Good whiskey would be wasted in a stomach as sour as yours, and..."

Before he could finish, Bartels kneed him hard in the groin. Todd bent over in pain, gasping and wretching.

"Too bad you didn't enjoy it. It's the last one you'll ever get. When I finish with you, big shot, you'll be beggin' me to put a bullet in your brain."

Bartels stooped and built a fire. Then he sat and finished his bottle. After the fire died down, he took out his sheath knife and stuck its blade in the embers.

Looking at Todd with a malicious grin, he said, "This is a favorite Indian trick. There's nothin' they enjoy as much as skinnin' a white man alive. And they found that doin' it with hot steel makes it even more painful."

Jerking his head over his shoulder, he added, "There's a red anthill beyond that stump. After we've got all your hide off I'll stretch what's left of you over that. If you think gettin' skinned hurts, it's nothin' compared to what the jaws of those ants will do to your raw nerve ends." Rising to his feet, he took out a pocket knife and whittled four stout pegs about a foot long. Going over to the anthill, he pounded them into the ground with a nearby rock. "Before we stake you down, I'll stomp the ants to get 'em good and mad."

Bartels returned to the fire and withdrew the knife. Then he grasped Todd's hair in a beefy, calloused hand and viciously jerked Todd's head back against the tree. As he held the blade before his captive's face, he cackled maniacally. "Another inch and I could put your eyes out. The Indians like to blind their victims first. But not me: I want you to see who's doing it."

In a catlike movement Bartels whipped away. Going back to the fire, he again put the knife into the smoldering coals.

Glancing sideways at Todd he said, "You ain't much of a talker. Most men would be beggin' for mercy. But you'll start blabberin' the minute I start to work on you."

"It'll be a cold day in hell before I get down on my knees to you, Bartels. You're a gutless wonder. If you weren't so yellow-livered, you'd untie me and we'd have it out man-to-man."

With a roar, Bartels leaped to his feet and swung a ham-sized fist into Todd's face, catching him just below the cheekbone. Bleary with pain and dizzy from the shock of the blow, Todd gathered as much saliva in his mouth as he could and spit at Bartels.

Furious, Bartels returned to the campfire and withdrew the red hot blade. "I was goin' to make this short, but now I'm goin' to keep you alive all night long. First I'll start by cutting off your lips. Then I'll peel the skin off your cheeks and cut your face muscles. You'll want to scream, but won't be able to."

Todd could smell the rank breath of the madman in front of him. He closed his eyes and braced himself. Sweat soaked his brow and ran in rivulets down his back. He felt the heat of the knife before it pierced the base of his nose. The sickening odor of burning flesh flew up his nostrils, and a searing, blinding pain racked his entire body.

CHAPTER

26

A loud grunt from his captor caused Todd to open his eyes. Bartels was staring at him, a look of surprise frozen on his face. Blood ran from the corners of his mouth and dripped off his jaw. With a drawn-out sigh, he slumped against Todd and slid to the ground.

Todd stared down at the heap at his feet, his senses swimming. Then he looked up. In front of him, wearing Army-issue pants and a well-worn black flannel shirt, was a lone Indian whose jet black hair hung in a long queue over his right shoulder. An eagle feather dangled from an upper braid.

"Me Running Deer," grunted the Indian. "Warm Springs scout. Work for white men who want to find stolen cattle. Find your tracks. Think you bad white until you caught by this one," he said, contemptuously kicking the body of Bartels with the toe of an elkskin moccasin. "Was in mountains hunting when offered two cows to look for cattle." Pointing to his chest with his fingers extended, he continued. "Friendly Indian."

"Running Deer," Todd answered in a cracked voice. "I reckon my life's worth more to me than the two head you've been offered. I'll double that if you'll cut me loose."

The savage responded by severing Todd's bonds in one stroke. "Me watch. You brave man. No cry out."

Todd rubbed his wrists to get the circulation going and looked down at the remains of his tormentor. A large, bone-handled hunting knife was sticking out of Bartels' lower rib cage which Running Deer retrieved with a quick jerk, putting it back in its beaded and leather-fringed sheath. Still somewhat unsteady, Todd watched as the Indian dragged Bartels' corpse to the ant pile. "Him want ants eat you. Now ants eat him. In three, four days nothing left but bones, teeth and hair."

Shuddering at the sight of the excited ants swarming over the still, limp form, Todd turned away. He knew it would make no difference what they did with the body. If they buried it, the wild animals would dig it up. If they left it the birds and animals would feast on it and scatter the remains. The Indian's method of disposal was as good as any.

Squatting with his back to the ant heap, the Indian opened a leather bag which was attached to his belt. He withdrew several pieces of jerky. Holding these out to Todd he said, "Eat. Then we fix nose with plant medicine. After fix nose, follow herd."

Todd took the food that was offered and tried to swallow but his mouth was too dry. Not wanting to offend the Indian, he chewed until Running Deer finished his own meal and walked away to find the plant that would help heal Todd's wound. Todd then quickly pried the dried venison out of his mouth with his fingers and covered it with dirt in the hope the Indian wouldn't notice. What he really wanted was a drink of water, but as neither of them carried a canteen and there wasn't one on Bartels' horse, he would just have to wait.

The Indian returned with a mixture he had prepared and applied it to the cut below Todd's nose. "This help. Feel better soon." Miraculously, within a few minutes the throbbing pain began to subside.

"Running Deer," said Todd, "that's worth another steer." In answer the red man grunted happily, then went to the last few sparks of the campfire and covered them with dirt. Satisfied the fire was dead, Running Deer spoke again. "Moon tonight. We find herd, then watch."

Todd mounted, grateful for the chance to take the weight off his weak legs. His knees, still shaky from his ordeal, could not have held him up much longer.

An hour later they passed a spring-fed creek. Todd got down and drank greedily. As he started to remount, the Indian, whose sharp eyes had missed nothing, offered Todd more jerky. "Eat now," he advised.

They rode far into the night. Shortly after midnight the scout pulled up. "Smell dust. Cattle near. We stop, rest horses. You sleep, I watch."

Wearily Todd rolled up in his saddle blanket. He knew he should have offered to take a turn on night watch, but he was too tired. In seconds he was asleep.

At dawn he was awakened by a hand over his mouth. At first his mind refused to focus. Then he remembered where he was. Running Deer, seeing that he was fully alert, spoke softly. "Herd moving. We wait, then follow." Reaching into his pouch, he again removed some strips of dried meat, handing half to Todd.

All morning they tracked the rustlers through country criss-crossed with ravines and fissured draws.

At midday they came to a flat desert dotted with large mounds. The surface of these giant earth domes looked as if it had been painted: strips of vermilion mixed with shades of white, cream and sulphur yellow; muted greens highlighted bands of ochres and reds. The colors gave Todd the feeling that a giant rainbow had fallen and left its imprint on the land.

Several miles later they passed these varicolored hills and came to a hidden valley.

His eyes gleaming with triumph, the Warm Springs scout pointed downward. "There missing cattle."

It was true. Several hundred head were grazing contentedly on the bottom lands below. Distant shouts reached them as a dozen voices greeted the riders who were bringing in Ridley's stock.

"There must be at least thirty riders down there, Running Deer. We'd better go back and get help."

"Me know better way. Have cousin who ride with Ridley. Come."

Uncertain as to what the Indian was up to but trusting his judgement, Todd wheeled his mount and followed. Two ridges beyond the valley, the red man dismounted and built a small fire of green sage. As smoke curled up into the sky he took off his saddle, removed the blanket, and held it over the smoldering brush. After a few seconds he quickly pulled it away. He repeated the movement several times, then kicked the fire out. "Now we wait," he said, squatting patiently.

Ten minutes later he pointed west, where two puffs of smoke were rising into the air. "No have to ride. Help come in two days."

Amazed at this primitive yet effective method of communication, Todd shook his head in wonder.

"Now me sleep, you watch," said the Indian as he curled up on the ground.

At dawn of the second day, Todd was pulling on his boots when Running Deer's relative slipped noiselessly into camp. His shirt and pants were identical to Running Deer's. A string of trading beads, interspersed with massive bear claws, hung around his neck. On his head rested a shapeless, greasy hat with a torn brim that flapped as he moved. The two Indians held a prolonged conversation in their own tongue, after which Running Deer came over to Todd.

"Lone Bear say forty riders be here soon. Also four Indian scouts. One scout already sent to get Army."

His eyes gleaming in anticipation of the battle to come, he continued. "Lone Bear also say not wait for soldiers. Fight when cowmen come."

234

"I agree, Running Deer, but the decision is not mine alone. When everyone gets here we'll put it to a vote."

With a non-committal grunt the Indian left to give Todd's reply to his cousin.

Before noon the first group rode in. Tom was with them. He jumped off his horse and hurried to Todd's side.

"You're a sight for sore eyes. When I saw that body draped over an anthill a ways back, I thought for a minute it was you."

"It almost was, Tom. But thanks to Running Deer I came out of it in one. . ." Todd's explanation was interrupted by the arrival of a second group of riders. Slapping Tom affectionately on the arm he said, "I'll fill you in later. Right now we have a more important matter to take care of."

Archie Ridley and his hands came in with Tom. Horace Singleton and his men were next. Shortly after that the Columbia crew showed up, to be followed fifteen minutes later by Hal Murphy and his McKay Creek riders.

They wasted little time on greetings and quickly got down to business.

Ridley, still steamed up about the loss of his beef, wanted to move right away, but calmer heads prevailed. An agreement was reached to attack the rustlers at daybreak. The Indians were sent out to scout the opposition's camp, and guards were posted while Archie Ridley, Horace Singleton and Hal Murphy met with Todd and Tom to discuss strategy. Their plan was basic and simple. Before daylight the six Indians would take out the herd guard. At first light the cattlemen would move on the camp.

After the meeting broke up, Tom took Todd by the arm and pulled him aside. "Now I want to hear what happened and how you burned your nose."

When Todd had finished recounting the events of his capture, the cords in Tom's neck stood out in anger. "I should have killed Bartels in Portland," he said. Then in a flat voice added, "Like I'm going to kill Frank Allen."

CHAPTER

27

Archie Ridley had told the story at least a dozen times. And each time he added a new embellishment. Now he was sitting at the kitchen table in the Howard's cabin, a mug of steaming coffee held between his work-hardened hands, telling it to them.

Archie knew Clay would bring him up short if he added colorful details that did not actually happen. They had known each other too long for him to get away with that, so he did his best to tell it to them straight.

"Clay, it's too bad you missed all the excitement. We sent a rider to fetch you and your men, but you were over at the Deschutes with Elmer Johns, brandin' cattle. We were hot on the trail of the rustlers." Here he stopped, then started again. "Truth is, we were for a while, but the polecats outfoxed us. Then we ran into Tom Pickett. He and Todd Howard had swung in behind the thievin' varmints."

He stopped to sip the scalding coffee. Satisfied that he had their full attention, Ridley continued.

"Young Howard followed the rustlers while Pickett stayed behind to let us know we were bein' bamboozled by a rear guard whose purpose was to let the cattle get away. We thought we had lost Todd, but he crossed paths with a Warm Springs Injun who smoke-signaled where they were.

On the way to meet 'em, we found the body of one of the rustlers. He was. . ."

He stopped. Because of Ellie's presence he didn't want to go into the gory details. He would tell Clay another time when they were alone. Covering his pause with another slurp from his mug, Archie went on.

"He was dead. Killed by the Injun who joined up with Todd. We met Todd and this redskin on the other side of the Ochoco Range. Beyond the Painted Hills area. They had located all of the missing cattle in a big valley about halfway 'tween here and Canyonville. Guess the rustlers planned to move 'em to the minin' camps around John Day."

Knowing that Ridley was about to wander in his story, Clay Howard spoke up. "Ellie, get Archie some more hot coffee." When she had done this he said, "Now, Archie, what happened? And let's leave out all the guesses."

Nodding his understanding, Archie picked up where he left off.

"They had thirty-four men. We had over forty. One of our scouts reported back that the Army was due in the next day, but we decided not to wait. We went after 'em at the crack of dawn."

Archie pounded his fist emphatically on the table top, his pink cheeks flushing a shade brighter. "It worked like a whiz-bang. The Injuns took out the night guard without a sound. The rest of us left our horses and crawled in before light. The scoundrels didn't know what hit 'em 'til it was too late. In a half hour it was all over.

"Three that was gettin' out of their bedrolls went for their guns." His cherry-red lips twitched in the confines of his full beard while he recalled this incident in his mind. "That's the last thing they'll ever reach for. The rest were too sleepy or too scared to do much else but give up.

"Then Pickett sought out Frank Allen. Gave him back his six-gun and told him either to draw or be hung then and there from the tree he was standin' under. He even let Allen draw first, then put three shots in the skunk. That took the starch out of the rest of 'em."

Ridley paused at this point, his eyes roaming the room. Ellie guessed what he was looking for and suggested he might like a piece of dried apple pie to go with his coffee. "I reckon I could squeeze it in," Archie replied.

As she set the plate in front of him, Ellie asked anxiously, "Was anyone hurt?" She really wanted to know if Todd was all right.

When he replied, "Not a scratch on any of us," she gave a loud sigh of relief.

"Not any of us," Archie started again, "but I can't say the same for the nightriders. They got roughed up some. Most of the boys wanted to string 'em up on the spot, but Howard and Pickett wouldn't stand for it. Said they had surrendered peaceful-like and that we should turn 'em over to the military for trial when they arrived, which we did."

He stopped and chuckled. "Todd did agree to play a little trick on 'em though. We went through the motions like we was goin' to hang 'em. Even had ropes around the necks of the orneriest who were the ramrods. Suspectin' their time had come, they sang like birds. Seems the Oregon Steamship Company was behind the whole shebang. They planned to take over Wasco by driving all of the honest cattlemen out and taking control for themselves — just like they did on the Columbia River. By the time word of this gets out to the newspapers and the state legislature, the OSC won't dare show their faces in this part of the country again. And it won't help their cause on the Columbia River none, either."

Falling to the pie with relish, he hesitated with his mouth full only long enough to add, "We owe a debt of thanks to Todd Howard and Tom Pickett. If it weren't for them two, the OSC just might have succeeded."

Trying to appear casual, but anxious to hear the answer that would come, Clay asked, "Where is Todd now?"

"At his ranch I suppose. Funny thing, though," Ridley said, a puzzled look on his face. "He did mention that after

238

checkin' out his stock he was ridin' into town to visit his grand-parents. He's never mentioned them before. Guess they must be comin' in by stage to visit. Whoever they are, they've got mighty good reason to be proud of him."

"Yes, they have," said Clay, going to Ellie and hold-ing her closely. As she buried her face in his chest and wept silently, he added, "They have a good many reasons to be proud of him."

As Todd and Tom turned into the dusty road that led to their ranch, the distant rumble of thunder signaled the coming of a late afternoon storm. By the time they had reached the corral, a westerly wind was moaning through the tops of the towering fir trees.

Arnie Swenson, the camp cook, hurried toward them waving some mail that had arrived while they were gone. One letter was to them both. It was from Captain Geyer. The others were for Todd.

"Read what the Captain has to say, will you, Todd," Tom said, stretching out flat on his back, both hands behind his head. "I'm going to cloud-watch for awhile."

Geyer's message was written in boisterous good humor. He told them their venture on the Willamette River was going well and they now had three steamships making the Portland-Eugene City run: *Heroic Lucille* (the renamed *Lucille*); the *Todd Howard*, and the *Tom Pickett*. In fact, business had been so good he was making regular deposits to bank accounts he had opened in their names. They were both surprised to learn each of them had received well over $12,000.

The letter went on to say the captain, based on conver-sations he had heard on the *Heroic Lucille* and in the more exclusive bars in Portland, was convinced there was gold to be found in The Ochocos — just east of the Triple C ranch. This information, fueled by his own instincts, prompted him to grubstake a miner to seek it out. The venture was so speculative that he was willing to finance it alone if they were not interested. If they were, each could become a full partner for a thousand dollars.

Geyer concluded by wishing his two associates the best of luck. At the bottom of the page a scrawled P.S. had been added: "There was an item in last week's paper that Arnold Boden, an OSC director, had resigned and was telling all he knew about the company's underhanded activities. As a result the governor fired his secretary, who was also on the board, and has appointed a special committee to investigate Boden's charges."

Squatting down by Tom, Todd asked what he thought about the idea of investing with the captain in the grubstake.

"Sounds good to me. I have $12,000 I didn't know I had before, so I figure there's nothing to lose."

"I agree," said Todd, his eyes glinting with humor. "As long as we're successful cattlemen and shipping tycoons, we might as well be gold barons, too. And what the captain says about Boden should mean an end to our problems with the Oregon Steamship Company."

Seeing that Todd was eyeing the rest of the letters, Tom stretched and picked up his hat. "Guess I'll go check our future alfalfa field. You catch up on your mail."

"Thanks, Tom. I'll join you when I'm through."

There were two envelopes from his folks, three from Ann. They had been forwarded from Mrs. Blevins and had been written prior to the ones his grandparents had given him.

He read the Fields' letters first. They wrote about their train trip on the new transcontinental railroad and what the family had done in New York, as well as news of their neighbors and Mr. Fields' prospering investments.

Then he read the ones from Ann. After he had finished, he went to the wooden chest by his bed in the bunkhouse and got out the note from her that had arrived a few days ago. As he reread it, a wave of loneliness swept over him. He ached for the sense of happiness and feeling of well-being he always felt when he was with her.

In an instant his mind was made up. He would spend tomorrow night with his grandparents, then leave for Portland the following day. There he would send a telegraph message to Ann. It would say: "Not necessary to hire mule. Mr. Woo's spell working. Leaving for San Francisco on next packet. Will you marry me?"

Grinning happily, he went to tell Tom the good news.